A LITTLE BIRD TOLD ME

Vaden Chandler
A Little Bird Told Me

Published by BooxAi
ISBN: 978-965-577-989-9

A LITTLE BIRD TOLD ME

THREE MEN FACING THEIR OWN DEMONS

VADEN CHANDLER

CONTENTS

CHAPTER 1

The sun came streaming through the second-story of the ancient, prohibition-era granite building. His stone-cold, shark eyes peered open, and he knew today was the day. He heard the rustling up above the ceiling and laughed, showing his yellowed teeth. The rats are running around again, he thought sardonically. Not that it really mattered, he thought, considering it was just him and the damn rats anyway. It took him forever to get out of the bed, what with the creaks and groans of the ancient bed and the fact his juvenile arthritis always kicked him in the derriere in the morning. "Crap," he muttered under his breath as he finally got out of the old bed.

Turned on the radio, and it was the same old B.S. as always. Brooks and Dunn were talking about a neon moon for about the umpteenth time, and Billy Idol was dancing with himself on another station. After finally settling on a sports talk show where they were openly wondering if Peyton Manning would retire after another year in Denver, he sauntered over to the dreary bathroom for a shave. Today was the day he got even. He knew that, but he wanted to look nice. Today was the day he showed these people that they had railroaded him. Railroaded him good. He hummed to himself as the talking heads had switched and were droning on about Von Miller in the background. After getting the stubble off his face little by little in nice, precise rhythmic strokes, he ambled in his chubby, hairy frame clad in his boxers and selected his attire for the day.

Ah yes, he thought. *Attire is important, even on a day like this.* After donning a nice polo shirt and some stained blue jeans, he peered at his safe, which he kept in the kitchen for lack of space in the cramped apartment. Heck, he almost had the stupid thing memorized, and it was a big blasted safe. 16 forward, 6 backward, 8 forward, 8 backward, and 6 forward, and viola! He had it open for the umpteenth time, except this time he just might use what he had inside. The collection of five handguns glinted in the morning sun ominously, along with the collection of knives given to him by his grandfather a long, long time ago. He knew, though, he wasn't just looking this time. He fingered his Glock 19 and his Smith and Wesson M&P Shield and laughed at the irony. "Not supposed to have these," he grinned. "But I don't give a crap. Them black boys on the corner'll sell or do anything for a buck, trust me." Said to no one in particular, considering he lived alone. It was his "hit kit", just like BTK had in Kansas.

He examined the array of knives, in admiration of each one. Some of them were more exquisite than others, and some were intricately carved, museum-quality pieces. For his purposes, he only needed a simple one, one that was shiny enough for the intimidation part of his plans. It was something he had been thinking about for a long, long time, even though he was just in his early forties. Needless to say, he paid close attention to those AMBER Alerts that flashed across his cheap Walmart phone, but not because he was a good citizen. He enjoyed hearing about kids being victimized, and it was time for him to cause a kid to go through an AMBER Alert themselves. It was time for him to be the victimizer, not the victim.

He grabbed four of the knives and both handguns and sauntered over to the decrepit brown sofa in his living room, a journey of just a few steps. *Ah,* he thought. *Uncle George. How could I forget about Uncle George…*and with the guns and knives still clutched in his hands he sank off in a revelry.

The fondest memories he had of his uncle were out on the water in his old motorboat. The old thing used so much oil it was a freaking wonder he could even get it out on the water. The thing coughed and sputtered so badly, and it made Roger laugh at the memory. But it always made it out on the water just fine. And that, for Roger, was both a blessing and a curse, considering that his uncle was, well, his uncle. Things would always start out innocently enough, of course. George would cast out his line and get a nibble and reel in the fish, often a nice bass or trout. And he would take a nice shot of Jack Daniels every time he almost caught a fish. After about 5 or 6 of these fish, well, you get the idea. Uncle George started slurring his words, and he would always say, "remember, boy, what I told you?" Roger was just ten at the time, and all he did was just nod. Peering at his unshaven uncle, he had a weird reverence for him mixed in with an immense amount of fear. The drinking was just the start, and he always knew it, but there was no one he could talk to. Dad was in jail, and there was no telling where his mom was, dropping him for days, sometimes weeks at a time, at her brother's house. His uncle jabbed him playfully in the back. "Remember, Roger?" he asked. "I know," Roger said timidly. "What happens here stays here. It stays out on the boat and no one else needs to know about it." It was almost rote to him, and something he was used to, just like everything else that happened between him and his uncle.

And that's when the fun would start. Nothing bad to begin with, mind you. His drunken uncle's hand would linger a bit too long on his shoulders, and in mock admiration would say, "Wow, nice and strong, gonna be a man real soon." He would angle his grizzled hands around the back of his neck, and Roger would seem far away, just glancing at the sun shimmering off of the water slapping off the side of the ancient motorboat…. he supposed he had gotten used to it after a while, and he kind of felt like he was somewhere else while everything was happening. His uncle would do, well, whatever he wanted, and Roger would just stare timidly at the water, looking at the greenish concoction and wondering if it could swallow him whole. He knew what that escape hatch was when he was an adult, though. The shrinks called it grounding. "Focus on something else," they said. "Notice the texture on a table. Take a look at the clouds." Just simply pretend. Pretend you are someplace else and fly away.

And that's what he always did, sometimes staring when it was cloudy and peering at the shapes. "That one looks like a car," he would think timidly. "That one...well, that one is a horse....and that one is a ship, probably a cruise ship with lots of people on it, and they're smoking fine cigars, and dancing." Anything, just anything to take his mind off of whatever George was doing. He wasn't where he was, just like in the Secret Life of Walter Mitty. He was somewhere else entirely, and it was liberating.

As the alarm went off for the last time, he snapped out of his grotesque daydream before he got to the worst part. He disassociated himself a lot these days, and he didn't want to be called Roger in that way ever again. For the love of God, he thought, as he stretched his legs to try to get the stiffness out for the umpteenth blasted time. He nervously tapped the corners of his little Skoal can, pinched a few, and placed it between his cheek and gum. It was a force of habit that he did out of stress, and it was actually that provided little relief other than fulfilling his death wish. And of course, there were other things he did when he was stressed. He also fantasized, like he was doing now...

Memories, he thought with that sardonic smile. *Sweet memories, and they're so nice. So nice.* He thought in his revelry about the boy in the adjoining apartment, number 170. Watching him jump, and watching his lovely little legs stiffen as he tried to make a jump shot. Just ten years old, like he had been. He knew the kiddo would be going out for sports at one of the charter high schools somewhere in the Mile High City when he was older. *Blonde hair,* he thought. Lovely, just lovely, as the chill first ran down his spine and hit his nether regions. He knew he should take care of his feelings, but not right now. His eyes were void, reminiscent of sharks.

"Today, I get even," he said in the mirror with cold resolve. "Today, someone, someone's kid, will get hurt. But I don't care."

Staring in the mirror he saw nothing there, just a zombie, gray, wretched and decrepit, just like he was taking in an episode of the Walking Dead. Cold, so cold, just like rain pelting his face.

"Today," he repeated in a guttural, primal growl. "Today."

He walked out to the hallway with a purposeful resolve, just like

Eichmann or Rommel heading out to war in the trenches of Germany. Roger was a big history buff, no doubt about it, but today he would make history himself. He nonchalantly tapped his wallet – complete with a nice chain and a coin purse – and fingered the twenties inside. Before he headed out on his journey, he had one more stop to make. After heading down the stairs, keys in hand, he reached his parking spot and fired up his ancient GMC van (1987 Model). The damned thing coughed and sputtered but then predictably fired to life. Couldn't leave just yet, he told himself with a sardonic smile. He was headed to the Home Depot over on Sheridan first. He battled the traffic, cursing all the way, and when he made it to the store, he headed directly to the section he had in mind. Five minutes later, he went to the checkout counter with generous amounts of duct tape and chloroform. He was never one for idle chit-chat, and the tattooed and pierced cashier with the bluish hair didn't seem to care anyway, but he muttered, "Some paint stripping work I need to take care of," just loud enough so she could hear and to make it look good.

With his plastic bag in tow, he was off to the races once more and fired up that old van. He smiled widely, he was on his way. As the morning sun glinted off the cracked dash of his van, he had sudden pangs of guilt. It was an ugly specter, and he knew that very evening would be ugly for something. He didn't know exactly how, but he knew he would be the cause of it. So he snapped back into a revelry as he merged onto the morning freeway. He thought about being ten again. Laying on his back, looking at the stars, and feeling small and insignificant. He thought about seeing satellites and thinking they were stars, and seeing stars and thinking they were satellites. For once, however, he didn't think of his uncle. He was a void, just a kamikaze pilot on his grotesque mission. He was just a man pointing his ancient Chevy Van down I-70 and headed to the other parts of the state. *Hickenlooper's state,* he thought sardonically. *Just a liberal who is out-of-touch and will bankrupt this state, and someone who would be lenient on guys like me.* He let out a guttural laugh, and with that, it was time to put the politics to rest. Back to the locker room thinking, and that's all there was to it.

The chain around the waist of his khaki pants glimmered in the morning sun as his GMC van started to head down I-70. He mindlessly fingered the chain and pulled out the wallet attached to it from his pocket, and thrust it open. He took a brief glance at the fake I.D. at the top of his cards (have to keep your eyes on the road, mind you) and smiled in appreciation at the admirable work. *Just like "Welcome to the Jungle"*, he thought sardonically. *Those street hustlers will find you whatever you need to have.* His thoughts began to drift off yet again...

The first time it had happened with Uncle George was just a nondescript day, one that could have come right out of "Leave it to Beaver." George had a military pension, and besides drinking it up every month, he spent most of his time fishing. The first time his mom dropped him off at his house, he had only met the man a handful of times. He stuck his hand out and smiled. "We're gonna have a lot of fun, Roger." Little did Roger know. Little did he know, indeed.

It all started innocently enough on one of their daily fishing excursions. George was thoroughly soused, and the fish weren't biting. There was an awkward pause, and the mist of booze escaped from his nostrils. He put a finger up to Roger's mouth. "I like you, Roger," he said with sour breath. "I mean, I really like you." Roger peered up at him in bewilderment, especially considering he knew nothing of having a father figure.

"W-What do you mean," the little 9-year-old version of him asked him after what seemed an eternity of silence from Uncle George. "I mean, I like you, Roger," George replied. "You're not a nine-year-old brat. You're a man. You're gonna have feelings soon. Strong feelings. Urges."

Of course, George would never just come out and do it. No, he was too subtle for that...he would usually start with the roughhousing and the tickling games as the sun continued to glint off the water. The whole thing was so odd, Roger recalled. Very rarely did they ever catch any fish. It almost made him think his uncle's fishing trips had an ulterior motive...

The thundering, sinners-in-the-hands-of-an-angry God rantings of Bill Graham came into focus on the radio and snapped him out of his revelry. It was an older model, just like the van itself, and sometimes it kept searching for a frequency, and it might pick up a Bible Belt station in Kansas or Oklahoma. "God proved his love on the cross! When Christ hung, and bled, and died, it was God saying to the world, "I love you!" Graham thundered. Roger groaned and turned off the radio. *No time for Bible bangers right now*, he thought. Screw them.

He was 21 when the cancer was about to take his uncle away from him. Some would have called him an evil man, but it was okay, for Roger knew the truth. Roger was ever the obedient nephew, and no one but him and his uncle ever knew what went on during those fishing trips. Him, his uncle, his mother, and God - if he existed. When his mother learned that her brother George was dying of cancer, she'd had one of her rare bouts with sobriety. She came back from wherever she had been for a visit, and the first thing Roger noticed when she came to the door was this wild look in her eyes. He and his uncle were playing some kind of board game, and he couldn't remember which one, but his mother came in and made herself at home, getting a bottle of Pepsi out of the cooler. Not soon after that, she got real close to her brother and, in an ungodly hiss, exclaimed, "I know what you are," and proceeded to take her pistol out of its hiding spot in her purse and then literally blow his head off. She did the right thing and turned herself in, dying in the joint a few years later after the booze came for her liver. He hadn't even told the therapists about most of his family drama, though they tried with all of their might to pry it out of him. *Screw them too,* he thought as his ancient van motored down that I-70 freeway.

"Right is right, even if everyone is against it, and wrong is wrong, even if everyone is for it," Lloyd said to himself as he fingered his old military dog-tags from his time in the Marines. It was 5 A.M., and the stereotypical Daylight Donuts residue still clung to his slightly unshaven beard. He sat in his cruiser, still looking to get a respite from the day that was just beginning. *Oh well,* he thought, it was better than listening to that thing he called an ex-wife leaving him messages over his cell phone each morning. He groaned as he got up from the bucket seat and opened the door, and sauntered into the parking lot. *Getting too old for this*, he thought as he noticed his stiff joints. He was a small-town police chief, and he was the one and only until Sakura came in at 9. His chin was wrinkled in cynicism as he flipped on the light switches of the three-room police station - two offices with a break room along with an outdated bathroom. Ah, the bathroom, complete with the locked cabinet none of the underlings bothered to ask about, the latest Playboy or Hustler usually tucked inside for Lloyd's amusement. *Had to be a hard copy*, Lloyd thought, *can't be having porn on the police computers, now can we?*

As he made his way to the back office, he was whistling to himself a happy tune. He logged in to the computer and pressed the check-in program, entering his password and ID. It was something he required for all of his employees, and it wasn't something he was necessarily required to do. However, his time in the military had trained him to believe that uniformity was important. He had the news on as a nice background, and the MSNBC journalist was rattling on again about Trayvon Martin and Black Lives Matter. He sighed in disgust. *No one cares,* he thought. *No one cares. If you do the crime, you do the time.*

As he was getting up to get out of the nondescript office, the shadows changed in the opaque glare of the window. The light reflected, and he knew that someone was riding by on the sidewalk on their bike, just like the eerie glint of a shadow on a midnight sundial. He smiled scornfully, because he already knew who it was. How could he forget? He had a history with that kid.

It was a few years prior that he first encountered the kid, seemingly just aimlessly wandering around at the park and strolling on the edge of the freshly manicured lawns of their small town. As a police officer, he could lie, so that's exactly what he did after calling for backup. He and two other cruisers approached that kid as he turned down the main street. He and his employees stopped and that's when the kid finally noticed that he was being followed by them. He looked like he had probably somewhat of an exasperated look, but he said, "What's the problem?" very calmly. Even today, it gave Lloyd the creeps how calm he had uttered those three words.

"Well, Arthur, We've been getting some reports of you staring at windows," Lloyd had said. His employees just sat there agreeing with him and nodding their heads, just like those little gas-station bobble heads you would give to a toddler to keep him quiet. On the other hand, Arthur seemed confused about the conversation. "There are people who think you are being a peeping tom," Austin, Lloyd's second in command, explained. Art just stared at the floor with a frown on his face and still said nothing. "Why don't you get in the back of our police car and we will continue to talk about this?" Lloyd asked him, and Arthur went ahead and complied.

Of course, what they didn't know about the situation proved to be the most costly to their small-town reputation. As Lloyd, Austin, and Deputy Louie were about to reach a consensus that Arthur should be arrested, that is when Arthur's parents pulled up. The panic was palpable in the overweight Louie's voice as he said: "Oh my gosh! He must have a cell phone back there with him!" Lloyd and Austin simply nodded, gearing up for a heated confrontation with Arthur's older parents.

Arthur's parents were predictably upset, and it made Lloyd furious almost every time. He just *knew* the kid was up to something, but there was nothing he could do about it because the stupid parents showed up. He had no choice but to let the kid go, so that's precisely what he did. Hearing footsteps at the other end of the building snapped him out of his revelry. It looked like some of his lieutenants were getting ready for their morning shift.

Arthur had always been a fan of oldies. He didn't discriminate, either. Almost any song would do, including classic rock, rap music from MC Hammer or Vanilla Ice, even classic country hits also. There was something interesting about the varying styles of instrumentation, even in rock songs that he enjoyed, and he had listened to the songs so much he almost had them memorized. One of the things he particularly enjoyed doing was strapping on his headphones and riding his three-wheel bicycle down the main street. *Force of habit,* he thought, *and probably*

just simply an emotional catharsis. At five that morning, when it was still dark, that was precisely what he was doing. As he angled his bike past the police station on the main street that morning, he saw that Officer Lloyd was already on duty with his cruiser parked in the lot. He hurried on past, because he knew the man well. A brief sigh emitted from his face that September morning, but it was okay; he had "Bad Medicine" by Bon Jovi on his headphones.

He was sure that Lloyd had seen or heard him, and even riding by, he could feel the contempt even a hundred yards away. But that was okay too, because, much like Lloyd, he felt the same way. Indeed, He too remembered the mutual history they shared, just like the screaming child from a Van Gogh painting. Arthur had passed the liquor store on his way to his destination, and his eyed twitched as he considered the moment. He had gone in so many times before, but not this time. He knew more often than not it had to be that way. The street lights shined off his class ring, one in which he had ordered specifically from his online Bible college. That's why he knew he had to continue to fight the "Battle of the Booze" as he called it. It wasn't the "Battle of the Bulge", other than being his very own, very personal, battle, one that Lloyd could attest to as well.

When he considered how the contempt coming from Officer Lloyd was almost palpable like the mist after a dense rain, he also realized that he, unfortunately, had a hand in it as well. Of course, he hadn't asked to be this town's Boo Radley character, but he did not always turn to Holy Scripture like he should have. Sometimes he turned to vodka. He recalled one night in particular all too clearly, when the town was covered in a dense fog. That, coupled with the fact his eyes were watering from six straight hours of binge drinking Russian vodka, led to a dangerous combination. He remembered the tall glasses of it, coffee mugs, soft drinks, or whatever else. He could mix it with anything, and he did. Heck, he even drank it straight. Fresh off the "Dear John" phone call from his wife on that day in late 2012, he was looking to drain his sorrows in any way he could.

His eyes had peered deceptively at the class, and he downed in one swallow. "It will be different this time," he lied to himself. It wasn't, and the sleepwalking continued...suddenly he was awake, and more alive than he had ever been. After a few seconds, it all came into focus, and he saw the 1930's era solid wood of the interior of the downtown apartment complex come into view, just like a zombie suddenly losing the glazed eyes and becoming clear-eyed, with clarity of thought to match. He heard his wife on the other side of the door, and she was crying bitterly. "Let me in," he heard himself say adamantly. The only sound he heard was a muffled sob and then silence. She cleared her throat, and then she said: "Five seconds, and I'm calling the police! Five seconds, Art....five seconds!"

Lloyd was just settling in for the night when he got the signal from dispatch. He groaned. "That Jeffries kid again up to his old tricks," as he hurriedly threw on his uniform and his badge. The apartments were only caddy-corner from his house, and the moon had shone through the mist in an eerie, ominous glow. As he made his way to the apartments, he fingered the firearm in his holster and his taser. He stood at the doorway of the apartment. "On the count of three," he thought to himself. "One, two, three..." and he opened up the door to the main hallway of the outmoded building. His eyes met a palette of dancing shadows as he head Arthur shouting at the top of his lungs on the second floor of the stairwell. "Idiot," he thought contemptuously. "Arthur," he called out gently, belying his typically angry response. "Arthur, stop this!" he said with a bit more urgency, summoning up all the fake charm he could muster. "Arthur, I'm coming up the stairs."

"Come on up, you son of a -" but Arthur couldn't get all of the words out before the mucus and half-digested food came coursing out of his mouth, and he stumbled and fell upon the ancient wooden floor. Half-gagging, Arthur cursed on the floor, passing out for about thirty seconds or so. That was enough time for Lloyd, and when Arthur awoke, the police chief was promptly on top of him, trying with all of his might to cuff him. To say that Arthur was belligerent would be an understatement. "Stop resisting! Stop resisting!" Lloyd shouted in an authoritative turn. For a few minutes they squirmed on the floor, reminiscent of a macabre wrestling scene, and then Lloyd finally got the handcuffs on Arthur. "Good grief, you are stupid, boy."

"W-What?" Arthur said, his eyes glazing over. "I just wanted to talk to her!"

"Yeah, I get that, Art," Lloyd smirked. "Problem is she doesn't want to talk to you and there's a restraining order." With Arthur finally subdued, he was hustled off to the squad car. "Bakersfield 1 en route," Arthur heard the police chief say over the receiver before he passed out again. Alas, the brief trip to the sheriff's office would prove as eventful on that moonless night. The booking part? An entire different story for Arthur as he briefly uttered his guttural snores in the back of the squad car.

Growing up, Lloyd had discovered rather quickly that he was an Army brat. His father was a good man, but some would claim he was harsh. Even at the ripe old age of six, Lloyd was living proof of that, simply evidenced by the ominous welts on his backside. "Belt training," his drill sergeant father had always called it. The prototypical 70's family, Lloyd thought. His dad was the taskmaster and kept him in line, and his mother was... well...his mother was more like Edith Bunker. But as he fingered his dad's dog tags - he often alternated between his own and dad's - he remembered what his dad had said as a broken old man, a shadow of his prior formidable self: "Lloyd, I want you to have these," he said in the hospital bed, handing the dog tags to him with a degree of effort. "I know I was an a-hole to you, but it was all for your good." Stoic, Lloyd simply replied, "I know, Dad. I know." Boy, did he know. His dad was an a-hole to everyone. A loud shriek snapped the police chief out of his revelry. It was an old, thin building, just as everything else was in that dusty old town. Sound traveled pretty easily, and he knew right away that it was Arthur's scream. He groaned as he sauntered down the hallway to the jail cells. "..and that's another charge, Art!" he heard the young and rather tall upstart young Sheriff's Deputy say in an authoritarian fashion.

"What did he do, Casey?" Lloyd inquired as he poked his head in the cell, seeing the deputy standing pat and a pitiful Arthur still drifting in and out of consciousness. "Silly son of a...." Casey uttered. "He tried to slug me! Good thing I remembered to duck." Lloyd didn't even look over. "Well, Casey," he shrugged, "You'd better let the moron sleep it off. I'm gonna go to the E.R. and get myself checked out." Considering that Arthur had fought back, he knew that was the proper procedure. Especially considering he was chief. Of course, the injuries were only superficial and nothing worse than his basic training days, but the effects could be inflated, he thought with a smirk.

As his van was gaining a head of steam down that Colorado interstate, Roger was listening to Stevie Nicks belt out "Tell Me Lies". He briefly looked in his rear-view mirror at all of the cars darting back and forth down this mountain freeway. Nice middle-class people, he thought. Nice people with a house in Cherry Creek or Highland Village. Dogs, wives, kids going to playdates, the whole nine yards. Yes, they told him lies all right. And yes, they were very sweet ones. But only to the prosecution for sure. "Your honor," the young upstart in the blue suit a few sizes too big for him had started. "The defendant is a liar."

The inexperienced prosecutor's eyes darted around the room, searching for dramatic effect from the jurors but inadvertently being met with a death-stare from Roger. "He has built this facade of being a law-abiding citizen, but he isn't." Over at the defendant's table, Roger tried his best not to smirk. As he recalled, he'd half expected Jack Nicholson to dart out in his full, "A Few Good Men" attire and start bellowing out his testimony. Roger's eyes glinted in the morning, a Rocky Mountain sunrise, as he bitterly remembered that an acquittal wasn't meant to be in that case. "We the jury in the above and entitled action…" (this flashback always gave Roger a racing heart) "find the defendant guilty of the crime of enticing a minor in the third degree on a person under 14. The defendant is to be remanded back into Arapahoe County custody. We will convene for sentencing on December 1st." As they were placing him in handcuffs, he saw the prosecutor shaking hands with the judge, an elderly black man. "Job well done, son," the judge said to the young prosecutor and slapped his hands on his back. "Yeah," the young D.A.

assistant replied. "Hopefully we aren't so stuffed with Thanksgiving turkey that we let him off the hook with the sentence." And the judge laughed. And so did the prosecutor. Well, Roger thought as he reflected back on the trial, I'll be the one laughing after tonight. The year before his conviction was the last time he had enjoyed turkey of any kind.

It wasn't supposed to be this way, Lloyd thought. *I was supposed to be a hero.* Sitting in his cruiser on yet another nondescript day, Lloyd was bored, and that wasn't good. Thinking about his wife living with another man in a nearby town, he had an angry frown perched on his mouth. *Tears?* he thought. *Those are for wusses.* Screw her. He still had his uniform on, but the radio was off, signifying his off-duty status. "Time for some me time," he muttered to himself as he was on this old country road of his ancient family homestead. He peered at the faded white fenceposts with the ancient giant apple tree in the background. Had he not known the history of the place, he could have sworn it came out of a Norman Rockwell painting. The apples marking the ground had just about always been there, and he remembered picking them up when he was a kid and putting them on his head, pretending he was William Tell or something to that effect.

Fond memories for once, he thought sarcastically as he lined up some of the old beer cans by the road on the top of the fence. He had chased the hot-rodding teenagers away from here on more than one occasion. Probably could have handed out a bunch of MIP's or DUI's while he was at it, but they were from well-off families.....taking his first shot, he thought, "This one's for you, Dad," and pulled the trigger. Down the can went, some of the beer spilling out of its innards. Setting his sights on the next beer can, he said to himself, "This one's for you my dear Wifey," (he couldn't bring himself to say ex-wife) and pulled the trigger yet again. The silver bullet can fly off and hit the ground near the apples. Setting his sights on the third beer can, Lloyd thought about that butthole of a drill sergeant he had during basic training some 40-odd years ago. "This one's for you, Sergeant Armstrong," he growled as he squeezed the trigger. Then, with one beer can remaining, he thought about that Arthur kid again, and he thought about his family. He thought about how Art's father loved to collect things, and how his property was dotted all over the place, making the whole entire town look more like an eyesore rather than the idyllic Mayberry he wanted to create. With the resentment boiling up in him, he growled, "This one's for you, Art," as he took the last shot. The beer can went flying off, seemed to stay in the air forever, and then finally hit the drought-infested, dusty ground with the rest of its beer buddies. His break over, Lloyd smirked and sauntered in a regal fashion back to his patrol car. He had to get home now, and leave this back to the popular teenage hangout that it usually was. With alimony payments taking a huge chunk out of his paycheck and some grown kids that barely even talked to him, his only source of company was Banquet and DirecTV. Oh well, them's the breaks, but at least he had his badge. Because of that, the criminals feared him, and the regular, law-abiding citizens simply nodded at him in respect each time he passed by. Such is life. It can run parallel, and it also can take you into a head-on collision as well.

CHAPTER 2

The road got longer for Roger, and the buildings and landmarks got farther and farther apart. But it was okay, because Roger was listening to one of his favorite bands. "I am the man in the box," he sang along quietly. "Jesus Christ, deny your maker...see my eyes? Can you sew them shut? I'm the dog who gets beat..." His raspy voice trailed off. Indeed he was, he thought. That is a truthful statement for sure. He knew all too well what it was like to be a "man in the box." But as the highway continued to twist and turn, Roger faded into his revelry once again.

Silence. Dead silence. It was something that made Roger's eyes misty. It had been a dying art form for the last five years. It was a void, nothingness, and the strange irony in it all is that Roger couldn't sleep without the noise. Who would have thought that he would miss the screams of some mentally ill and delusional fellow convicts at 3 a.m.? But he did, and as he laid there in that bed that was hard as a rock in that fleabag weekly hotel, all he heard was the occasional car driving by. This was reminiscent of that night so many years ago, in that cold, grayish granite block that was a classic example of the archaic Prison Industrial

Complex. The silence here was like an old friend, but the silence there was only intermittent, broken by the occasional guttural scream from a few tiers down and that light. That blasted, constant, never-ending light. Another guttural scream. And another. And then the echoes grew closer and closer, creeping along the walls until the scream seemed to be right in the bunk with him. And then he suddenly realized that he was the one who screamed. He heard cursing in the next cell block. "All right, you cracker piece of…" the young punk yelled. "Keep it down!' Life would devolve into a predictable routine for the next three years, barring a few incidents.

Lloyd was bored, and even with his man of his high stature, he knew that wasn't a good thing. Not a good thing at all. Of course, he didn't know what he had to be bored about, he thought contemptuously. Considering that his whole life revolved around his job, even when he was off-duty. Some men enjoyed fishing, some liked collecting stamps, but he liked looking at his gear and practicing his field maneuvers. Today, he was at his dimly-lit home office, watching DUI training videos on YouTube. It wasn't anything he hadn't done for some time, especially when he was doing double-duty for a few years training new recruits in South Fork. The video was having the recruits get drunk, and on purpose, no less. Even alone, his eyes flinched with a hint of sarcasm. What a day, he thought, almost cracking up. Getting drunk and getting paid for it. And all on Uncle Sam's dime.

It was overcast outside, and the wind was whistling through the trees, reminding Lloyd of another day not so long ago. Lloyd must have been in his early twenties, somewhere in that range, and he was fresh out of the Marines with his friend Carl in one of those big old boats. Goodness, Carl could barely keep gas in it, especially considering that Jimmy Carter couldn't handle the oil crisis. They were laughing and cutting up, just like any good friends would do, and George Thorogood's "One Bourbon, One Scotch, One Beer" came on the radio, below Carl's pile of 8-track tapes. "Sounds good to me!" Carl bellowed obnoxiously while the sound was playing. "Let's go party, Lloyd! Loosen up!" Even back then, Lloyd was a bit of a stickler geek, but he just grinned. At that hide-out on the outskirts of town was the first time Lloyd imbibed, and he indeed did have a bourbon, a scotch, and a beer. He hadn't talked to Carl for years. They'd lost touch like friends often did. Last he heard, he was upstate in the mountains, and he worked as a prison chaplain. Ironic. Ironic the paths they had taken. Oh well, it was better than thinking about that witch he had had for a wife.

~

Roger's eyes flinched as the Puerto Rican gangster sitting across from him sneered at him with his prototypical gold-capped teeth. "You're not one of those Chesters, are you?" he asked. Play dumb, Roger thought. Play dumb. He hesitated. Bad decision. "What's a Chester?" Roger asked. "You took too long, S A," the thug responded. "Oughta shank you right here. Maybe I will." Roger just kept his head down, belying the flood of emotions he felt. "What's your name?" the gangster asked. "Roger."

"Oh well, that isn't your name anymore, a-hole. Your name is now Chico. You don't like it, that's too bad," the Puerto Rican said in a half-grunt, half-laugh. In one fell swoop, the Puerto Rican got up from the table and motioned to Roger. "Let me show you what happens to Chesters, Chico," he snarled in a low guttural tone, and arched his head toward an older man with a long flowing and graying beard on the other end of the room. With a loud whistle, Mr. Puerto Rican caught the old man's attention, and the bearded man's eyes shot up. "Hey S A!" Puerto Rico screamed, and the rest seemed to be in slow motion. He rose up, running to the other end of the room, kind of like a morbid John Elway evading a sack. The guards saw it too, but they only half-heartedly ran up to stop it. Mr. Puerto Rican had them beat by almost a mile, and in the bearded guy's case, that mile was stained an unholy red. In an effort to resist, the older bearded man also got up in one fell swoop, and Roger half-expected the man to resist, but he saw the white in the man's eyes. Besides their coldness, he saw a hint of submission, reminiscent of a scared little chihuahua or toy poodle, and Roger knew that the man understood what was coming.

In that split-second, something in the hands of Mr. Puerto Rican glinted in the dull light of that prison chow hall, and even Roger knew that it was a shank just simply from his earlier habit of watching all of those prison documentaries on Court TV. In yet another split-second, Roger peered at the face of the bearded man. Eerily, it reminded him of a little toy soldier, very stone-faced, either like matchstick men or one of those British guards he had seen on the movie screen when he was there with his latest prey. The terrorist Puerto Rican thug made it to the man, and his homemade weapon sliced him from one side of his protruding gut to another. Oddly, the old bearded pervert didn't make any sound whatsoever. In the aftermath, with blood coming out everywhere, the bearded man grunted and then clutched what was left of his stomach as the guards led him out of the chow hall on a stretcher. Roger didn't see much of that old bearded man after that. Did he croak? Had he met his maker? Hard to say, but either way, it was a shame. Probably would have made a good cellie. Goodness knows, they probably could have swapped a few stories.

Arthur stared straight ahead, lost in a revelry of his own making. There was no question that he found his demons in his own solitude. He half-laughed, half-grimaced as he looked at his ingredient options. *No,* he thought ridiculously, he wasn't some mad scientist or creepy chemist like his weird neighbors down the block with their open-secret of a meth lab. No, instead, he was peering at an older bottle of chocolate milk with a looming expiration date, and on the counter next to it he saw his secret stash of Russian-brand vodka, with just enough left to create another off-the-wall concoction. As he grasped the vodka in one hand, he took the chocolate milk with another hand and poured the vodka inside it. His laughter spewed out, with alcoholic breath thick enough to wilt a rose. He even had a name for his new-fangled concoction: Count Chocola (not the kind for kids, mind you!). He grimaced in mock anticipation as he held the first sip from the travel mug to his lips. He hesitated, twirling it around so he could get the full effect. "Here goes nothing," he said, talking to himself. Surprisingly, this hangover-bait concoction actually went down his palette quite easily. It had just the right mix, kind of reminding him of one of those sweet-and-sour candies at the Dollar General downtown. Hangover bait for sure, he thought. After a few minutes, with the buzz thoroughly setting in, he looked around the crowded, messy room for his father's TV remote. *Good thing he's away on one of his car buying trips,* he thought. *Heaven forbid he sees me this way again, ha!* He finally found the remote buried under mounds of papers by his chair, with the characteristic soot from his mechanic dad making it blend in with the dark oak ottoman. Ignoring it, he started flipping through the channels. He cruised through them so fast it was almost like he was like Jeff Gordon out on the race track. Soon, he settled on something, and it was a very familiar scene with the familiar chants of "Jerry! Jerry!" *Ah yes,* he thought, *the Jerry Springer Show.* What a microcosm of my life.

He peered, his eyes big and prying, at the people arguing about boyfriends, ex-lovers, and whatnot, and about the time the gloves came off is when his concoction finally hit him. As the guests on TV began their fights, he began to feel dizzy, and that was putting it mildly. The Springer guests were crowding all over each other as he staggered to what was left of the cluttered kitchen sink in a vain attempt to splash his face. The coldness felt foreign to him, like an ungodly and unwanted baptism, as if he was drowning under the ice of nearby Rutherford Pond. He belched, and it wasn't a dry one either. It was a watery, snot-filled belch, and he knew what was likely to come next. He would mess up an already cluttered sink, because he was going over Niagara falls in a barrel, but he wasn't in the barrel. He was part of the falls. But in the next split-second, nothing came out. *It's a miracle!* He thought bitterly, and then- wonder of wonders!-he proceeded to stumble down the stairs, into his basement bedroom, and pass out in a booze-filled stupor and oblivion.

～

"You know they put a K O S out on that old bearded dude, right?" the equally old and grizzled cellie said from the top bunk. Roger flinched, belying his intense discomfort, and pretended to be smart. "Well yeah, uh..." his voice trailed off. "But what's that?" The cellmate coughed and replied in a raspy voice. "It means kill on sight." Roger stayed in abject silence for a full 30 seconds, and then the only word uttered from his mouth was, "Oh."

A few minutes passed, and other than a few hacking coughs echoing throughout the cell block, there was nothing but silence. Roger sunk into a revelry, and he was letting it go, but then the whisper of his grizzled cellie pierced through the air. "I know what you are, asshole," he said.

"What?" Roger replied.

"I know what you are."

"What do you mean?"

"Don't play dumb with me, kiddo."

"I know."

Roger put up his best tough exterior, and in what was supposed to be a tough voice that only came out as a hoarse allergic one, he said, "All right, asshole, what am I, since you seem to know so much?"

"You're one of those. You're just the same as he was."

"Yeah? So?" Roger was trying to seem uncaring, but inside he was terrified. Summoning up some false bravado, Roger said, "How do you know I'm not hiding a shank right here and getting ready to cut you right now?" The grizzled out cellie just laughed. "Well, how do you know I'm not?" he rasped. Without so much as a word, the old man then proceeded to hoist himself up into his top bunk, and soon, he was snoring audibly just like nothing had happened. For Roger, sleep didn't come as easily. He recalled yet again that when he was just in grade school and he kept hiding under the tables, all they did was pass the buck; they referred him to that shrink who said that he should focus on something on the wall if he was nervous and that would help him stay in his seat. Well, the shrink did make an impression because he absolutely was doing that now, lying in his bottom bunk and looking at the cracks in the ancient prison near the ceiling. It was surreal, and he felt like it was someone else, not him. I'm at home, he thought. I've got my headphones on listening to James

Hetfield, but all he's doing is telling me to sleep with one of my eyes open. One. Eye. Open. So that's what Roger did. He continued to tell himself just to keep to himself. He knew all too well the old refrain that "snitches get stitches."

~

Art had his headphones on once again. What's it going to be this time, he thought, as he rattled through his YouTube playlist on his cellphone. "Enter Sandman," he said to no one in particular. "I'll go with that one." Ah, the "Monsters of Rock" video. He had watched it many times, and it always did something to him, something he couldn't explain. I don't know, he thought, maybe it's those endorphins going through my head? He laughed as he walked down the street. Boy, oh boy, I do sound like Sheldon from the Big Bang Theory. As he walked down the street, a bit of a breeze was blowing during that early morning. He began walking laps around the city park as James Hetfield started bellowing out the part where they were going to Never Never Land. He wasn't sure which part of the song he liked better, that part or the one where the boy was chanting his night time prayers and trying to sleep. But sleep, well, sleep was always hard to come by. But the booze helped...even though his Bible was on his desk and he was a recent Bible college graduate, the booze still helped him get the shut-eye he needed.

"Lloyd, we need to talk," the voice on the other line said. Lloyd cringed. "What do you want, Becky?" he replied. "Don't be calling me Becky anymore!" she snapped, her voice dripping with contempt. "I've called the movers. I'm moving out." Lloyd cleared his throat. "You bothered me while I'm on duty to tell me that?" Becky paused. "Yes, I did. Get over it. You're not my knight in shining armor anymore, you're not my protector, you're not anything. You're just a damned hypocrite!" She was seething, and he knew it. "Well, honey, do what you have to do..." She cut him off. "Don't call me honey anymore, either!" and then the line went dead. And that's how Lloyd's marriage ended. The big-shot small

town police man was about to become a statistic, another divorced man
in a sea of divorced men. Oh well, his dispatcher girlfriend was much
better in the sack anyway. "Time to go back on duty," he grunted as the
remains of his fast food diet were flung into the trash can just outside his
cruiser. "Baker 1, coming back on duty," he said to his receiver. "Affirmative, Baker 1," was the answer. The sun was high overhead, and the
rest of the day was blissfully routine. No traffic accidents, no domestic
disputes, nothing of that sort, and he was thankful for that. He simply
patrolled most of the time, and he tried to avoid daydreaming, but he was
drawn to it like a moth to a flame. He thought about his time in the
Marines, mostly.

Roger was lucky. Although his first day in the pen was eventful, the next
day, and the day after that, and the day after that, slowed down to a
predictable routine. "Keep your head down, keep your head down, keep
your head down..." That was Roger's mantra for those first couple of
days, and that's what he did. He didn't see anything, but boy, the things
he saw. There were kids not much older than 18, and they were stacked!
(not quite his type, but still...) He wasn't sure why they let him go into
the yard, but they had, and the first day he was there, he must have
looked at the nondescript guard for an eternity before he asked him the
question: "Sir, I want to PC up," Roger quietly asked. "I'll see what I can
do," the guard said, but that was the last he had heard about anything
regarding PC'ing up. Thus, he was in the yard, and no one was mixing.
Literally, no one was mixing. The whites were staying with the whites.
The blacks were staying with the blacks. The Mexicans, Cubans, Puerto
Ricans, Guatemalans, and other Hispanics were staying with their own.
Interspersed within the yard were those with odd tattoo insignias, hear-
kening back to a less civilized time like Aztec warriors gearing up for
battle to defend Tenochtitlan. Mexico City? It didn't exist yet! The only
thing that existed were these warriors, these disgusting warriors with
eyes that glared straight ahead, and right below them Roger couldn't help
but notice a small, seemingly insignificant teardrop. Some had an

outline, and some were filled in, but as a newbie, that's all he knew. "Keep your head down, keep it down, be low, mind your own business. Who cares about their tattoos?"

It continued to be his assertion, his "polly want a cracker", just like a caged bird singing. Things were quiet, and it seemed to continue unabated for as long as he knew. One day was the same as another day until things changed, and Roger had to know that they always change.

∾

"You know, I'm just fascinated with serial killers."

It wasn't the first thing he expected to come out of the mouth of one of his fellow recruits, so Lloyd couldn't help but be surprised. It was 1975, and he was a fresh-faced punk out of high school (Eagles flying high!), and he knew he just had to follow in his father's and grandfather's footsteps. He still had all of his hair too! So no, when his bunkmate uttered those words, he had to say he wasn't expecting it.

"Uh, well, okay," he said, trying to process what this freckly-faced bunkmate, who looked to be no older than 14, was saying. "Probably too late to ship us to Vietnam," the weirdo bunkmate said. "That's a shame. That's truly a shame." Uttering it to himself now, because Lloyd simply rolled over and tried to sleep. "I really wanted to take part in chasing some of those dipwads down the jungle, if you know what I mean." Lloyd turned back over and began acting older than his years, more like his 48-year-old father or his 75-year-old grandfather. "Oh brother," he rasped to the bunkmate, as his allergies from the dust of the forced hike of basic training were kicking up. "You're not taking this seriously, are you?" That oddball bunkmate of his just laughed. "Maybe I am, Maybe I'm not, you Captain America dipshit! I guess time will tell." And indeed it would. Time would indeed tell.

∾

"Okay, time to wake up, sleeping beauty!' came a roaring voice, and Roger's eyes darted open with a start. It was his grizzled old cellie, and he was staring at him directly in the face. He took his decrepit finger and grotesquely caressed Roger's scalp. "A bit of a sweat, eh?" he sneered. "Just what were you dreaming about there, hot stuff? I have a sneaking suspicion you aren't in here for knocking off the neighborhood liquor store." Now that he had gained his composure, Roger just glared right back at him. "It's. none. of. YOUR. DAMN. BUSINESS!" Roger exclaimed, his voice rising in intensity like a two-year-old and not someone pushing forty. "Whoa! Slow down there, horsey!" the cellie laughed. "Getting a little bit too big for your britches, now, aren't ya? I need your status, and I always get my way. Get used to it." Roger tried to pretend like he was nonplussed. "Well, you aren't getting mine." The old cellie lit a makeshift cigarette with a smuggled match and took a few drags. "Oh, trust me, I will." A serious tone. A deadly tone. "If I just sit here staring at you all night long, I will. You have an R before your serial number, don't you?" Roger knew that an R meant someone had been sentenced of a sex crime. He did, but he wasn't about to let this a-hole know about it. "Well, douchebag," Roger replied, "how do I know you don't?" The cellie laughed. "Oh, trust me, you don't. But I know you do. You prance around here, in your effeminate movements, looking just like the fairy you are. You have an 'R'. I just know it. Better watch your back. Better keep after that guard, because if I find out you have an 'R', I'm your landlord, kiddo, and you're late with the rent!" And with that, the bearded old cellie laid back down on his top bunk and was snoring no less than five minutes later.

CHAPTER 3

The fluorescent-sounding chirping of the birds was among the branches just outside his basement window, and it pricked on Art's head as his eyes peered open. The guilt collapsed upon him, but that taken by itself would have been okay. His eyes were watery, but not from depression. It was from the pounding, hangover-induced migraine he had instead, and that was immensely worse than those feelings of self-condemnation. *What was that Bible verse? He thought. Oh right....I'm having my conscience "seared with a hot iron..." 1 Timothy 4:2.* Goodness knows, he'd memorized so many Bible verses in bible college that he could hardly keep track of them all. Ambling out of bed, he agonizingly threw the covers and the blanket off. It was the one that mom had crocheted for him a few years back when she was still lucid, and he smiled in spite of himself.

"Art," she had said, "this blanket tells you that I'll always be here for you, no matter what." That's why he always took care to make sure it always stayed on the bed, and that particular time was no different. The air was thick, assaulting his nostrils as always, but that was okay, considering it had always been nothing more than a musty old basement. Hanging his legs and his Colorado Rockies boxer shorts over the bed, he perched his hand on the mattress to study himself. Up we go, and up he went, albeit with a bit of stumbling.

I'm ready to face the day, he thought with a sarcastic smile. *I'm a bit dizzy and crazy, but I'll get by, just like that Grateful Dead song.* It crossed his mind to laugh, but it would be too painful. He lurched out the door, kicking the messy papers and leftover food out of the way, and miraculously made it to the stairs. Grabbing the railing to continue to steady himself, he made it to the top of the staircase, ready to greet the new day, albeit about five hours too late. It was ten, and he heard that familiar nasal voice of Drew Carey from the TV in the living room.

"I still liked Bob Barker better, Dad," he remarked to the older version of himself sitting in his ancient brown chair.

"Oh well," Dad said quietly, without looking at him. Arthur cleared out a space on the couch, which likely hadn't been cleaned since Mom had been sent to the nursing home.

Dad cleared his throat as Drew's announcer bellowed, "A new car!"

"Are you going to go see her today?"

Arthur paused, thinking about answering, but Dad beat him to it.

"She's been asking about you…" his voice trailed off.

The silence would have been as dead and settled as the perishing, crusty old flies settled all over the furniture, as well as on the carpet and stacks of old tattered papers…all of it in the middle of Drew Carey's dorky smile saying, "Show them what they've won!"

"Well…" Art said. "Do you think that she knows…"

Dad cut him off.

"That's not really the point," he said quietly into the air, as the dust in their abode seemed to dart to and fro before finally settling on the lamp-shades. They sat in silence as Drew Carey's silly mug kept giving away prizes on the boob tube. *He definitely is moving up in the world,* Art thought. *He's no longer on that boob tube yelling and hollering about how "Cleveland Rocks" or having to deal with Mimi Bobeck. The more things changed, the more they remained the same. And the more that people wished they would stay the same as well,* Art mused bitterly. Either way, Carey wasn't sitting in some shanty somewhere in a back room in the middle of nowhere blaring Metallica's Welcome Home Sanitarium song.

The TV cut to a commercial, one of those deals where they were trying to sell the Swiffer or something, and something in the tone took him back to a few years prior. He was standing outside the diner, and an old familiar tune came over the loudspeaker. He must have been in his late twenties, and it was after he had gone through another failed teaching assignment. It was that old familiar melody of that sixties one-hit wonder Procol Harum, and they sang about skipping the light fandango, and that's when he saw the gargantuan high school activities bus. He'd been off in la-la land the last couple of years, but even he knew what was going on when he saw that escort. Ah, he thought, the small-town Bakersfield ritual is alive and well, still. That damned football team still couldn't play their way out of a paper bag, but they sure did have spirit! The police even flashed and blared their sirens for them! Better than running from the law, right? It was truly a locale that was dripping with small-town pride, but not for him, and that's why it wasn't a particularly good memory. And that's why after Art finally left the house that day, he ultimately decided against going to see his mother.

Much like the song "Glory Days" by Bruce Springsteen, Lloyd loved to reflect on his time in the Marines. It was so much better than the grind and mind-numbing drivel of being a small-town police chief. Even though he was in his nondescript office (no family photos at all, mind you) and he was supposed to be doing paperwork, he sunk back into that comforting revelry once again.

It started with the trumpeters playing "Reveille" and then everyone except the unenthused Lloyd started rustling. He just turned over until he heard..."Annie, get your gun, buddy!" the voice of his bunkmate came out in an ungodly screech, jarring him awake. 'Wait....w- what?' Lloyd stammered, his droopy eyelids fluttering open from his slumber. "We've got to go out to the fields now, Lloyd," his overly enthusiastic freckly teammate continued. *The fields*, Lloyd thought. That was his fellow recruits' name for the firing range. Time for target practice, and on an empty stomach at that.

"Yeah, Clarence," one of their neighbors jeered at Lloyd's bunkmate. Clarence's demeanor changed in a heartbeat, and he whirled around at the other guy, an African-American who could have given Kareem Abdul-Jabbar a run for his money. "Don't call me Clarence..." the bunk-mate rasped. "I go by Slim." Mr. Jabbar just laughed it off, but Lloyd could tell by his eyes he didn't want any disciplinary trouble. He did inherit his father and grandfather's nice ability to read people, and he was proud of it. And with that, the drill sergeant had them fall in, and off to the shooting range they went.

Lloyd peered at the set-up as they marched, and his eyes briefly twitched, belying that he had experience in the first place. Even though his father and grandfather had taught him briefly in his childhood, he still smiled apprehensively. He'd seen his share of firearms, but experience shooting? Not that much. From the time that he was five years old, it was almost a given that he was going to join some branch of the military, almost a rite of passage, if you will. Each recruit had his own firing station, which was pre-loaded with all of the equipment and ammunition that he could ever hope to have in a lifetime. They had told each recruit his corresponding number, and since he already knew the drill, he fell into his station in full obedience, just like his father and grandfather had done before him.

"Fall in!" the drill sergeant, a middle-aged man of color, bellowed. He walked copiously among the lined-up recruits, his graying head studying them, and then for whatever reason, he stopped at Lloyd's station. "What is your serial number, recruit!" the drill sergeant bellowed.

"R forty-seven forty-seven seven seventy-six," Lloyd hollered back after a moment's hesitation, remembering it because the numbers repeated and the seventy-six was the year of the signing of the Declaration of Independence. "Too slow, recruit!" the drill sergeant belted out in reply. "And are you a man, or are you a maggot! You always call me sir!"

Lloyd knew the drill even though his brain was still foggy from the lack of sleep. "Sir, yes, sir!" he replied, and the drill sergeant went on to harass the next man in line. The morning sun revealed the almost-microscopic glint in Lloyd's eye, and he couldn't help but grin a little snarky smile. Good thing Mr. Drill Sergeant didn't see that, to say the least, he thought. He didn't know what was worse, the drill sergeant here or the one he had back home. Oh well, seconds later, everyone, including Slim and his obnoxious bunkmate, had all gotten into the marching formation and began heading out to the range. It was Lloyd's time to shine for sure.

Roger was staring at the clock, but he wasn't really sure why. The con in front of him, with probably a bit of a smirk and a drawl, said, "Long line at the commissary, eh, Chester?" Taunting him, trying to get him to break, but Roger slowly closed his eyes just like a clock, and suddenly he was back in the fishing boat with his uncle. "Time for us to do some fishing, squirt," his Uncle George had said, and for whatever reason Roger hadn't taken offense. It was one of the rare times that his mom had been home for a while and not running off with truck drivers. "Hey George!" she hollered out in a loud squeal, "Just have him back by night fall, yah hear?" She was slurring out her words, and Roger flinched at it, just as he was doing now in this seemingly eternal commissary line. Should he scream at her? He just kept his mouth shut. His uncle...well, at least his uncle would give him a break. Sort of. Roger came out of his revelry after the behemoth commissary clerk, reminiscent of an old biker chick, said irreverently, "Name, please?" Roger studied her and hesitated just a bit. "Name, please!" the burnt-out corrections employee repeated. "Roger."

"Nope," she said. "No funds have been added. Check back next week." What a shock. Oh well, at least it provided a repast from the steady drumbeat they called routine behind these walls. Uneventfully, he went back to his cell. "No funds for you, eh, Chester?" the guy rubbed it in. Roger said nothing, and back to the cell he went.

His bearded cellie continued to glare at him. "How'd commissary go?" he sneered down his nose at him. Roger just grunted, but the bully cellie didn't even skip a beat. "By the way, I'm still waiting for that paperwork. The walls have ears. The walls have ears," he rasped, and off to sleep he went, snoring again not more than five minutes later. And all of a sudden, Roger had the Rolling Stones playing in his head in a surreal fashion, and he almost morbidly wanted to sing along to himself: "If you start me up, start me up...you'd make a grown man cry..." Better get in some practice, Roger thought, and even though the cellie was sawing logs, he looked away from his cellie and stared at the wall. *No showing weakness here for him. Uh-uh. No, not happening.*

The men were marching out to the firing range now, and Lloyd was getting ready. Little beads of sweat were forming on his neck and forehead. "Those trees..." the obnoxious trigger-happy bunkmate whispered. "They're so beautiful...."

"Oh brother," Lloyd whispered back, loud enough for him to hear but not loud enough for the drill sergeant to catch wind of it and reprimand them. Slim apparently heard it too, but he just grunted his disapproval. Lloyd couldn't help himself. "You're in the army, dipwad, not the park ranger department. Spare me." And Mr. Obnoxious peered at the ground, saying no more.

At the firing range, Lloyd quickly picked up a skill that would serve him well for the rest of his life. He was a bit off today, and it didn't take long for the drill sergeant to take notice. "Oh, what a shock!" he bellowed sarcastically as Lloyd fired the rifle but kept missing the target. "Mr. Military family man can't hit his marks!" Lloyd didn't say a word, not responding at all. His jaw clenched, zeroing in on the target about fifty yards away, and he had a split-second epiphany. He didn't see the bullseye any longer, and he didn't hear the drivel from the drill sergeant breathing down his neck. No, the drill sergeant was fifty yards away, and with his next shot, it was right on the money.

"Well, well, there is a God!" the black drill sergeant screamed at him.

"Let's sign this boy up for the Kentucky Derby. He's a thorough-bred!" Lloyd didn't care for that comment either, but his blank expression did not betray his irritation. All he knew was that they had been on that firing range for three hours, and he hit every mark after that. Presto. Right on the money.

But suddenly, Lloyd was much older and grayer, and he was right back in his small police chief office. He now had not one, not two, but three drill sergeants that he had dealt with. Becky, ah, his soon-to-be-ex-wife, Becky. Sergeant Armstrong. His father, ten years departed, but still looming over him. He had a long day of drab small-town police work ahead of him, but that makeshift firing range kept calling his name. It was going to be a slow office day with boring office work, and Lloyd already knew it, so he had the radio on at the country station to pass the time. At some point during the afternoon, his shift was coming to an end, and Jim Reeves' "Four Walls" came on, and his eyes peered at the radio. He couldn't help but laugh at the irony. When his shift was up, back to the "firing range" he went.

The glare from the lunchtime sun was perched ahead high above the trees, and after about six blocks of walking to Main Street, Arthur had changed his mind, despite the fact that the muscle mass in his legs was cramping up. He would go see his mother, indeed.

The combination nursing home and the hospital was one of the largest buildings in Emory County, and it was also one of the largest employers as well. Art's eyes flinched in the overpowering sun as the whitewashed brick structure came into view. He took one step at a time, knowing that he would have to take care to avoid his ex, who was still working somewhere in the large complex. He pressed the button on the side door, and it rang him in, just like it always did, and soon enough, he was in mom's room. It was mom and Elizabeth - Aunt Lizzie, everyone in the family called her - and it all looked fairly normal and nondescript. Mom was just staring straight ahead at the bulletin board and Aunt Lizzie was looking at a Reader's Digest, magnifying glass in hand.

"Oh, it's you," Lizzie said, looking up from her dog-eared copy of that well-known periodical. "Been a while."

"Yeah," Art said, still looking at the floor. Even though he made an imposing presence, Lizzie still had to squint at him. Those eyes peeked out at him, and they were indicative of an old soul, reminiscent of a holy woman from some Indian backwater.

"Can't tell," she said, "but she seems to be babbling a bit..." her voice trailed off. For Mom's part, she was looking at Art with rapt attention, and it wasn't long before he heard it himself.

"They're coming, they're coming," she muttered faintly, and her eyes seemed tired. No, not tired, just missing. The cards of fate could be cruel, and sometimes it was the luck of the draw that a woman that was only in her mid-seventies was already afflicted with Alzheimer's and his aunt was almost a hundred and still sharp as a tack.

Lizzie peered at Mom, who was staring blankly ahead and just muttering away.

"I had to strain my ears to hear that, you know," Lizzie said, "but what does she mean by that?"

"The Bearcat," Art said without skipping a beat.

Lizzie's ancient eyebrows arched. "Bearcat?"

"Oh right," Art replied. "That's what Dad always calls that police scanner."

Her eyebrows arched up yet again. "The police scanner?"

"Yeah, Liz. She's probably just repeating what she's heard on that god-awful scanner," Art grumbled.

"Oh."

"Oh" was right, indeed. He had lost track of how many family photos where that little nondescript machine had been in the background. How many times had he been wearing a Halloween mask and cutting up for the camera and that little black-and-silver box had been just peering up at them silently, just sitting there in the background unassumingly? Countless times. There was silence in the room as his mom stared off into the air and Aunt Liz had her magnifying glass out, looking at some type of lasagna recipe she would never get to try in that periodical. Revelry time for Art once more, and even though everyone was older, he still recalled when everything was different, including when that silly police scanner acted differently. He must have been ten the first time he heard the unusual noises emanating from it. Ah yes, voices. All kinds of voices.

"What is that?" his ten-year-old inquisitive mouth asked. "Why are people talking on that thing?"

"Oh, that scanner?" His mother replied cheerily. "Oh, don't you worry about that, Artie. When we bought that at the lumber mill, they told us it was going to pick up people's cell phones!" And she laughed. And so did Art, both at that time and now in the memory, because even to the present day, she was the only one that could call him Artie without him feeling resentful over it. He loved his mother a hell of a lot more than that god-forsaker police scanner, that was for sure. But that was the way it was for the next twenty years or so until cell phones got more advanced. However, dad still wouldn't throw out the scanner anyway. He liked listening to the police, and he wanted to make sure they weren't messing with his cars. Ugh. Art liked to think about the soap operas he'd heard on that thing instead from those cell phones, so that's what he did right now, seeing no other use for it.

"Why are you seeing her?" the high-pitched voice said over the box.

"I just am," the other raspy voice said.

"What about us?" the feminine voice replied.

"Well, I don't know. What about us?"

"Don't you care about us?"

"Hey, Art!" and he was snapped out of his recollections by the nurse's aide. "Would you like a bit from your mom's lunch plate? She probably won't eat it anyway."

"Yeah, I suppose I'll take some," Art replied. It was a nondescript ham-and-cheese sandwich, but it was still a change of routine for him. The kitchen of this small-town hospital had won several awards over the years, but as he was chewing that sandwich, it felt tasteless, as his taste buds were momentarily glazed over. It was just as well; it wasn't his food anyway, and he would probably get a bite from the cafe downtown, and the entree would taste wonderful. He knew he wasn't allowed to enjoy this sandwich, and he diverted his thoughts to that god-awful scanner yet again. Ah, a nice distraction, to say the least.

Suddenly, he was no longer in his mid-thirties and the town iconoclast. He was twelve, and he was sitting in his designated spot, an easy chair that had seen better days and reading the latest Hardy Boys mystery book he had picked up from the school library. He would read and read and read. Sometimes in his earlier years, he would even get so engrossed in a book that he would sit out the recess period. He was reading about how Frank and Joe were spying on an interloper at the lake when it went off again. Ah, the Bearcat, and even back then, his pre-adolescent eyes flinched up in resentment. "Baker 1," the gravelly voice of the then-police chief came out over the wires. "Plates clear on a 1991 Pontiac Grand Prix...." and Art didn't recall the rest of what the cop had said, because he spaced out, just staring incessantly at the police scanner. He just about had that phrase "plates clear on a..." memorized, especially considering that it would go off like a funeral announcement even at two in the morning, waking him up out of a dead sleep, even though mom and dad had very much had it tuned out years ago, sleeping right through it. The day finally came when he had enough, and his eyes perched up with an angry glare at the Bearcat for the last time. Mom was at her postal cleaning job and dad was away on business, so it was the perfect time. Going to the backyard, his eyes glanced around at some of the best candidates. The shovel and the grass? He supposed he could bury the blasted thing in the ground. The pool? Hadn't been used in years, but it still had water in it, so that was a good candidate. What about the dumpster in the alleyway? Another good candidate for getting rid of this irritating electronic private eye. Yes, looked like there were plenty of alternatives for getting rid of it, and he would just have to come up with an excuse to his parents why he had to throw it away. Decisions, decisions. I'll have to sleep on it, Art thought. Even though his dad was getting up there in age, he would still have to come up with an excuse why it was no longer there.

Lloyd ran his fingers through his graying temples and receding hairline. What a headache, he thought, dealing with another fender-bender in the Toot N' Totum parking lot and having to wait twenty minutes for an interpreter because one of the accident victims only spoke Spanish. Oh, how he wished he could go back to his time in the Marines. He tried not to smirk. "Always be good to everyone you meet, L," his mother had said forty-odd years ago when she wasn't getting smacked around by his old man. "God made them just as much as you and I." He did, but inwardly he groaned when he realized that the driver of the car was probably one of them damned illegals. "Can't trust them Mexicans," his father said. "They would steal your shoes right off your feet." Oh brother. Thank God, back to his makeshift firing range, he thought. Oh well, at least it wasn't some bloody car accident on the side of the road, and his old man had been gone for years now. He found more cans on the ground as the gentle breeze tickled his hair and his three-day growth of a beard. He didn't need too much wind because it would defeat the purpose. Setting them up on the posts, he walked back and got into his firing stance. His finger trembled on the trigger, and he knew just exactly why. Forgot my blood pressure meds, he thought. Hope to the Good Lord up above I don't have a stroke out here. Oh well, no bother, at least I'm a better shot than that silly Slim ever was, wherever he is now.

He finally steadied his fingers, took aim, and fired. One Coors Light can off the post and bleeding out from a bullet wound. He took a minute to steady himself before locking in on the next target. The birds circled overhead and there was hardly a cloud in the sky. Tranquil. That's the best word to describe it. Nothing else was tranquil, but this was. He took aim once again, and soon the irony of a Dr. Slim can be breathing its last on the ground. His eyes flinched as he was the Gunslinger character in Stephen King. Such a post-apocalyptic world, but the world wasn't fiction. It was his world, his real life. He left the cans on the ground and got back into his police chief cruiser. He hesitated very briefly, but spoke into the receiver. "Baker 1 back on," and away he went.

~

"I'm still waiting for your papers," the familiar cold, decrepit and raspy voice said in the all-too-familiar gray walls of the concrete block overlooking the bunk bed. His eyes flinched, but he pretended he was asleep even though it didn't seem to be working. "Still waiting," the voice said with more resolve. "Still waiting." With a start, Roger jerked awake. Disoriented, he looked about the room. Still gray, and still the rampant concrete block with all the cracks therein. That voice? Just a dream. His bullying cellie was still sleeping, sawing logs even. Suddenly he had Procol Harum in his head, saying that his face was just ghostly, but now the whiter shade of pale. And so it would ever be that he knew. Even reflecting on the memory many years later, he wanted to say it was surreal, but that truly didn't give life to that very moment he was in, those first couple days of his incarceration. Oh well, he had slept uneventfully for the rest of the morning, and when he awoke, his cellie in that cold, gray slab said nothing and did nothing, other than staring at him while he was inches away from him on the john with slitty eyes, the kind you would find on a rat or other common rodent. Nothing was said, no words were exchanged, that is, until the time for the chow hall at lunch time. The guards herded everyone in with chains at their waists, and the chow hall was the same nondescript room as the cells.

Roger just picked at his food, glaring at the overly obese, heavily tattooed lunchroom attendant who had handed him his food. His eating behavior belied the fact that he was known for the huge dinners he would consume on the outside. Whenever he was with one of his many girl-friends (he had to keep up appearances, couldn't let them know he was just dating them to get to their son, now could he?), he would have a feast worthy of a medieval king coming back from the Crusades. Mounds of shrimp, gallons of tea or soda, and steak reached as far as the eye could see. Heck, he even tried his hand at the 72-ounce steak challenge at one of the local restaurants in town, but he couldn't remember which one, though. What little hair was left on his head stood up, and he felt the eyes on him. Across the room, he saw his cellie. He saw the weird mystery meat on the man's tray, the carton of milk, and the odd-colored applesauce reminiscent of some macabre school lunchroom, and he saw that he hadn't even touched any of it. Even though it was a long walk away, he saw the white in his eye, and his green eye color. And the daggers, he saw the daggers emanating from him. "If I swallow some-thing evil, put your fingers down my throat," Roger whispered. "If I shiver, please get me a blanket...." Sleep with one eye open, that's what he had to do, and his heart pumped like an incandescent candle, flickering and fuming within his chest. He was going to die. He just knew it. But if he did survive, he was going to get even. He was the victim, not the family or the boy they had asked him to babysit. "

Excuse me?" The little, timid voice out of the roar of guttural voices in the cafeteria pulled him out of his hallucinations. It was a twenty-something kid at the end of the long table, with a clean-shaven face and eyes reminiscent of Pee Wee Herman.

Roger drew in an apprehensive breath.

"What?" he replied to the baby-faced fellow inmate.

"What's the matter?" he asked.

"What do you mean?"

"What's the matter?" he repeated, with a bit more insistence.

"Well, what do you think? I'm in here…"

"Yeah, we're all in here...have you ever considered reading a good book?"

Roger was getting irritated, and he raised his voice a few decibels.

"Have you ever considered shutting the fu-"

But the words didn't come out before he was slapped upside the head, and he momentarily had double vision and became dizzy.

"Leave him alone," the next inmate across from the table growled. "That's my boy if you know what I mean…"

"Yeah," Pee Wee said. "Just read a book, dipwad."

Gathering his bearings now.

"What does that mean?" Roger asked calmly.

"Just read a book," Pee Wee repeated. "Simple as that."

Yeah, Roger thought. Simple as that. And he ate the rest of his meal in sulking silence.

∾

Arthur was playing the "Morning Has Broken" song by Cat Stevens or Yusuf Islam or whatever his name was, coincidentally quite early in the morning. As he was singing away very lowly so as not to disturb his dad's snoring in the chair, he was still pondering what to do about the police scanner, and the stupid thing was still going off like always. Apparently, the highway patrol had somebody stopped at the ten-mile corner for the umpteenth time. Such a speed trap, he thought. Got me a couple of times, too. That's for sure. The special education doctors had classified him as having "autistic-like" behavior when he was a young boy, and his autistic mind was sick and tired of that damned thing.

It was stuck in the corner, and so it wasn't like he could pretend to spill some ice water or tea on it. As the morning wore on, he continued to ponder it, and dad went about his routine, leaving for his janitorial job at the post office around ten. Art knew he wouldn't be back until the late afternoon because of visiting mom. What to do with that ridiculous piece of garbage called the scanner? What to do, what to do....he stared at it as he had many times before, frowning and lamenting how it always woke him up at three in the morning constantly, like he was some kind of infant and not some twenty or thirty-something who had failed to fully launch. Now was his chance, but he had to come up with a good cover story. I'll submerge it, he thought. I'll dunk it in the pool a few times. That should do the trick, but I can't just leave it in there. Or could he? Dad hadn't talked about the silly thing in years, ever since the dementia had gotten the better of Mom. It seemed that the Bearcat had faded off into obscurity. And he wasn't just tired of hearing the thing. Considering that his mind was pushing forty now, he was tired of even *looking* at the stupid thing as well. Why not have his cake and eat it too? He walked deliberately over to the Bearcat as bright afternoon sun squinted through the blinds and the curtains on the large picture window. The thing had seen better days, but it was still chirping along just like a trooper. Most of the time, it was just sitting there minding its own business, but every now and then it would spring to life, just like those bodies that the mortician had paid too much attention to. Okay, so he had made his mind up that he was going to throw the scanner away completely, but what would his story be? Obviously, he would have to say that it went out, but then he would have to admit that he even noticed it in the first place. Good grief, he thought again. How many childhood photographs have there been where this stupid little piece of electronic art has been a part of the background scenery, and no one even acknowledged it or gave it a second thought at all. It used to be a big part of the family conversation, but by his teenage years it was completely ignored. Trying to figure out what to do with this dumb thing was a bigger paradox than he thought, and his heart raced even though he was just approaching his mid-thirties. His eyes arched up in epiphany. Wait a minute, he thought. What about a temper fit? I could just say I got mad at the computer crashing again and took it out on the Bearcat! Perfect! He lumbered around the house with a resolve usually only reserved for when he was writing, looking around. His eyes peered around the room, and he was looking for one thing in particular. The hammer. Where was that hammer? The house, like everything else, had seen better days. He began rifling through drawers looking for it, and he knew it was only a matter of time before he found it.

"Where is it? Where is it?" Art muttered to himself. "For the love of God, where is it!" And he kept thinking that instead of taking the Lord's name in vain, he ought to start humming Johnny Cash's "He'll Understand and Say Well Done" or just look at some Bible verses instead. He had a brain fart, and he knew it. Suddenly his eyes perked up. *The garage! It's got to be in the garage! It obviously wasn't just lying around because the house had been in disrepair for years now.* He didn't go in there very often, but as he did, the memories flooded back, just like one of those nut jobs that wanted to go over a barrel in Niagara Falls in upstate New York. Ah, the Mustang. It was probably his dad's most prized possession in his whole entire collection of cars, and he had a lot of them. Cherry red with racing stripes across the top and the trunk and hood, the car had seen better days since sitting here collecting dust. Not that he should be getting distracted from the task at hand, so his eyes peered around the decrepit garage, which was in much worse shape than the Mustang, which was in mint condition other than the dirt. Some old tables in one corner, a cabinet over there, but no hammer in sight.

Then, something shiny caught his eye on the trunk of the old Mustang. Apparently, the key was still in the trunk, and dad kept just about everything in that trunk it seemed. Maybe the hammer was in there. Art went to check and viola! Sure enough, among the rifle, old newspapers, and the remnants of Art's old stamp collection, there was that ever-elusive hammer. As he picked up that marvel of home construction aficionados everywhere, feeling the power of it in his hands, he peered at the old rifle as well. He yet again breathed a quick sigh of relief that his old man had never been able to get it to fire. *Thank you, God,* he prayed. *I've got way too many demons for us to have a working firearm in the house.*

Either way, he closed the trunk and it was back to the task at hand. Making his way to where the scanner was always sitting, he knew he was ready. He held the hammer at his side like a Roman centurion, and he stared down the scanner, now directly in front of him, by the couch and perched just behind the lamp on the nightstand behind dad's chair. There was nothing in the way now. Determined, he raised the hammer up, and he brought it down with a crushing blow. He didn't hit the Bearcat scanner though. In the middle of his arch and stance, his arms stopped, and he was flailing around in the corner because it almost threw him off balance.

"Oh, brother!" he snapped, gritting his pearly whites to where they were in full view.

"Come on, Art!" His heart sped up. "What is wrong with you?"

This time! he thought, and he raised his hammer in full resolve, and he was getting ready to bring it down, not turning back.

Suddenly the scanner sprang to life. "Baker 1 coming back on duty," came Lloyd's voice. "Affirmative Baker 1," came the reply.

Trembling, Art lowered the hammer back to his side. He couldn't do it. He just couldn't. He would just ignore the Bearcat. He went and put the hammer back in the Mustang like it had never even happened at all.

~

Lloyd heard the "Affirmative Baker 1" reply from the dispatcher, and it had zero effect. Other than the fact that it wasn't the normal dispatcher. It was actually some part-time dispatcher. Where was the regular dispatcher? Well, ironically, she was right there in the bed that he was sitting on the edge of. Not to mention that, but she had a thousand-watt smile aimed directly at him, even though his wrinkles and receding hair-line showed off the fifty-plus years of a man who had spent too much time in law enforcement. Again, Dispatcher Eliza was twenty years his junior, but she was not only laying there, but looking at him with adoration, with the kind of eyes of a woman placing her man on the pedestal even though his once jet-black hair now had plenty of white mixed in. She wasn't perfect, but considering she still idolized him, he would take her in a heartbeat over that god-awful soon-to-be ex-wife called Becky.

"Why don't you call in sick today, Lloyd?" Eliza purred.

Lloyd grinned in spite of himself. This woman was so much more than just a dispatcher, for she knew how to stroke his ego more in just one sentence than his so-called wife had done in at least the past ten years of their marriage.

"You know I can't do that, Liza," he replied.

"Never hurts to try," she said with a sly smile.

"Gotta keep the chatter about us at bay, you know, Liz," he said. "It's already a bit too obvious as it is."

"I know. Fun, fun, fun."

And with her free-spirited remark, he was ready to start the day and become one of his town's Finest.

The day was pretty much routine, and he was thankful for that. There was a driving while intoxicated arrest he had to perform, a couple of speeding tickets, and the typical routine of the beat of a small-town police chief. Oh, and he had to give a lecture to some teenagers hot-rodding their Mustang in the afternoon, but he had to let them off with a warning because they had some well-known last names. Throughout the day, he kept thinking that he wanted to get back to her. He wanted to get back to her safely. Not his wife, but his mistress. At the end of the day, he was able to do exactly that. But the first thing he had to do was take his police cruiser back to his house, which was sitting just across from the city park. Don't want the townspeople talking any more than they already are, now do we? He thought dryly. The keys to his house were jingling in his pocket, but there was no point in going in. It was empty, and nothing was there for anyone to see. Heck, Becky had even taken the dog and cat, so he simply got them out to search for his vehicle keys. It was an older Ford model, with an extended cab, a 2000 model. He was the chief, and he could afford better, but he had a fondness for the truck. He and that truck were just two old guys going fishing, going to his made-up firing range, or just going to see his girlfriend. And after he cranked it up and backed out of his driveway, that's exactly what he did, motoring his Ford F-250 to the neighboring town to go see Liza.

He cringed as he met a couple of people he knew going the other way down the highway because yet again they would talk, but he still waved. He was in a good mood. He was always in a good mood when he went over there. He wasn't just a burned-out little police chief when he was with her. He made her feel like a teenager, and not some fifty-something, and that's why he was humming along to that Hysteria song by Def Leppard on the radio. Of course, he was sure that his soon-to-be ex Becky was listening to "You Oughta Know" by Alanis Morissette, but oh well. He didn't care for his estranged wife, but he did enjoy that song when he was just a rookie cop with the station.

He pulled into the driveway of his gal's house, and his eyes flinched slightly in disappointment. She was not at home. He could tell because the driveway was usually more crowded, but oh well, he might as well go inside and relax a bit, considering that he had his own set of keys anyway. He unlocked the door and walked inside to see Liza's familiar digs. It looked the same as it always did, with the sink nice and empty and everything in its place. A couple Hobby Lobby paintings graced the wall, and there was her latest cookbook sitting on the kitchen table, and along with that, there was a note:

"Lloyd, dad had one of his asthma episodes, so I drove over there to see him. Be back later. There's tea in the fridge. XOXOXO, Liza."

He couldn't help but have a chuckle escape from his lips at that last part. Funny how they were more of a married couple than who he was really married to. Just waiting until it's all final, he thought. Come on, Becky, let's get this over with. For the love of God, let's get this over with.

He sat down on the easy chair, complete with that bunched-up section that fit him so well, and sipped on the tea for a while. After the cup was downed, he put it in the sink and went ahead and rinsed it, something he hadn't done in years for Becky. Then, he was bored yet again. Time to go out to my firing range, he thought. So he jumped in his truck and headed that way. He had one more stop to make before he made it to that range, though. He stopped by the little, decrepit combination five-and-dime and convenience store and bought two twelve-packs of Dr. Slim, dumping out one pack of them to use for his purpose, because he knew that Liza's teenage kids would take care of the other pack. He made it out to his field and his fence posts, and the sun was still high overhead and getting ready to go down in a few more hours. He set the first empty Dr. Slim on the post, and he was getting to take aim...

"Baker 1, do you copy?" he heard on his walkie-talkie way back on the dash of his truck. He cringed. "What now?" he said aloud but not in the dispatcher's earshot. He half-sauntered, half-jogged back to the walkie-talkie on the dash of his old truck, and he heaved a sigh as he picked it up. "Baker 1 over."

"Baker 1," the other dispatcher's voice said over the receiver gravely. "I think you need to get back to the station right away."

Lloyd groaned in spite of himself.

"What is it now?" he said brusquely.

"Well, I don't think I had better say it over the airwaves like this, nor should I use the codes, Baker 1. Just get here as soon as you can."

And as a little baby raven started circling ahead of those fence posts he called his refuge, he sighed yet again. "I'm on my way."

Roger kept driving, and he thought about that first time he had been permitted into the exercise yard. It had been a few weeks since his sentence, and everyone was cordoned off like grade-schoolers on a play-ground. His eyes quivered as he made an immediate observation. There was a whole sea of people in that yard, but all of the colors were just bunched up together like an ink blot on a psychiatrist's test. Blacks were not talking to whites, and whites were not talking to Hispanics. Roger just stood there for what seemed like an eternity, not even daring to move a muscle and not sure what to make of it. Finally, someone approached him, and his eyes flinched, getting ready to be jumped. It was a guy that was fairly short in stature, probably no more than 5'7, with a toothy grin. An eternity seemed to pass in that split-second, but Roger failed to get comfortable just because of the man's slight build. He knew from experience how quick these short guys could be. In that split-second, a bird flew through his line of view, and Roger seriously thought it would have been so much better if he had been a bird-watcher rather than a pervert. It was also in that split-second that the man's arm seemed to shoot up. Before Roger could react, the fellow convict said, "Hey man, what's going on?"

Roger stuttered. "I -uh, -uh, um, I..." An unexpected turn of events for sure.

"We got card games for y'all," the man said as he angled his head toward the end of the yard. "...and we've got a couple of chess games at the tables next to it. That group over there."

"Oh, well, I..."

"You know, that group," the guy said, and his eye went down in a large wink.

"Well," Roger began to lie. "I'm not one of those..."

The short guy cut him off.

"If you say so," he said with a smirk. "Come get yourself a game or else."

He ambled over to that playing table, and all the white men were engrossed and barely paying him any mind whatsoever. He settled on a table in the middle of that dusty old prison yard with a group that was angled over an old Uno box that, just like the yard, had seen much better days. Jagged and faded, Roger could barely tell it was an Uno game and he hadn't played one in years. In spite of himself, he sat down, and it wasn't long before he had a fellow player. He didn't recall much about the game itself, as the man sitting across from him didn't say much. He did recall a guy a couple of rows over playing the same game and suddenly getting up out of his seat, cursing and yelling, "Skip card? That's not a skip card!" and the other guy getting up in his face, "It is too!" and abruptly he decked him square in the jaw. Right on cue, the guards came and broke it up. Roger almost got up, and his silent partner suddenly spoke. "Don't worry about it. Happens all the time." The other thing Roger remembered during that first card-playing session was the birds flying through that yard. All the while, his grizzled old cellie was across the way glaring at him, so the birds provided a nice distraction. Still trying to harass me for my papers, even out here in the yard, Roger thought. One of the victims at the impact phase statement of his trial had told him that he hoped they would bury him under the prison, and that sure was ironic that it was preferable to him versus getting the living tar kicked out of him from a bullying cellie. Oh well, look at the birds, look at the birds, because there were plenty of them. The ugliest ones were the sparrows, with their nondescript black feathers and their quick darting to and fro. He half expected them to swoop down and snatch up one of the mice inmates, a morsel for a nice jailhouse snack. Interspersed with those were the tiny hummingbirds, finding solace from the sun in that dim prison yard. Stranger still, thought Roger, were the white birds he saw here and there. They flew gracefully, almost in slow motion even, but Roger couldn't tell what they were. Doves? He wasn't sure. It was just as well, though, because Roger hated anything beautiful, and he wanted to kill them. That's when the contempt and rage started. It wasn't when he was arrested. It wasn't when he was formally charged and couldn't bond out at all. It wasn't when he was tried and convicted, and the hot-shot young D.A. got patted on the back. It wasn't when he was finally sent up the river. It was then. Life wasn't beautiful and how dare he see it. It was time. It was time for him to devise a plan and make someone else realize how ugly the world truly was.

CHAPTER 4

L loyd grimaced, and he made no effort to hide it. "What is it now?" he asked in that all-too-familiar police office. It was night, but the place was lit up like a Christmas tree. "I hate to bother you, sir, but I think there is something you should know," Sakura uttered.

"What?" he snapped, agitated that this was taking away from his mistress' time. As he instantaneously noticed Sakura's Tweety-bird coffee cup, he saw that her ever-present cream was nowhere to be seen. She was drinking it black, and she never did that. More serious now. "What is it, Sakura?"

She looked him dead in the eye.

"Sir, they found a body out at German Shepherd Lake. They think it could possibly be foul play."

"Really…" his voice trailed off. This would be his first murder investigation in years.

"Well, tell them that I'm on my way," he said, and he headed out the door and to his cruiser. "Baker 1 en route to German Shepherd Lake," he said over the receiver, and he started to make the lengthy drive to the lake that was located at the edge of the county. Baker 1 had never been Lloyd's first choice for the first-responder handle for his department; he actually wanted to go with "SP 1" when he had been hired as chief years ago, but the town council had nixed it. He had fought long and hard for it, and it had been his brainstorm alone. Not Sakura's, not the town council, but Lloyd's. His logic had been that SP 1 would stand for "super police" and as he squinted through the late afternoon sun and at the road smugly, he still thought that it sounded so much better than "Bakersfield 1" and absolutely better than "Baker 1" for that matter, which sounded more like they were kitchen workers and not police officers. Oh well.

The cool, peaceful lake had always been popular with rangers, hikers, fishermen, you name it. There had even been talks about turning it into a national park off an on over the years. The lake overlooked an old cabin, dating back to the 1920s when it was still nameless. The fishermen back in that day would just crack a smile and say they were going to "that lake", probably taking some moonshine with them while they were at it.

The cabin was where the caretaker had lived, and he had raised German Shepherds, so when he died, he stipulated in his will that he wanted the still-nameless lake to be called German Shepherd Lake, and that's what it had been called ever since. The long drive out to the lake flew by, and as Lloyd pulled up to the scene of the lake, he saw several of his deputies and a lot of other blue guys that he didn't recognize at first. Getting out of his cruiser, he peered at that boyish-looking Casey approaching him. "Baker 1, I've arrived at German Shepherd Lake," he said into the receiver, and he got out of the cruiser and met his protege's gaze straight on. "Casey, what do we got?" he asked him. "Female, partially nude, looks to be mid-30s, a lot of lacerations on her neck, so probably strangulation."

"Local?"

"No, could be from the neighboring town in Oklahoma. Possibly, she looks to be Native American. You know, they have a big population of them up there."

"Yeah."

"Well, anyhow," Casey replied. "We've got the feds up here, they can tell you more about it."

Lloyd spat on the ground as a reply. "I know. I'm sure they will fill me in."

The scene was cleared, and the deceased was finally transported to the morgue. And Lloyd doggedly sat in his cruiser filling out the police report. It was finally one when he trudged back to his house overlooking the city park, back to his warm bed and the loving and willing mistress that awaited him. After looking at that woman's body, he knew she was possibly a hooker, probably killed by a trucker or something, but it got him going, and even though he was drowsy, he didn't need a Cialis this time.

"Looks like they found a body out at that German Shepherd Lake," Arthur's dad said without glancing up from his newspaper. "Wonder why that Bearcat didn't pick it up..." and his voice trailed off.

"Seriously, Dad?" Arthur grimaced, not even trying to hide the sarcasm. He was now having regrets that he hadn't gone ahead and disposed of the damned thing like he had originally planned.

"Don't you have somewhere to be?"

Dad cleared his throat.

"Yeah, Mom, you know, but gotta keep up with the gossip...."

"Well, Dad, they probably didn't announce it over the scanner because they wanted to avoid the damned lookie-loos like you," and he stifled a laugh in spite of himself.

Without saying a word, dad put on his ancient blue mechanic jacket and headed back to the nursing home, leaving him to his old devices again. He sneered yet again at that Bearcat, and he knew he was about to lose that "Battle of the Booze" again. He had some Jim Beam hidden under his bed, and he fetched it, and in no time flat, he had poured himself a drink, mixing it with tea, the only thing available! Sitting his drink on the end table, he went over to the cluttered desktop computer in the room by the kitchen and pulled up YouTube, firing up Motley Crue's "Girls, Girls, Girls." He blasted it as long as he could and yelled belligerently, "Might as well have a party right here at my house!"

He could just picture a lady dancing at the pole and the drinks just flowing, and he raised his makeshift drink to his lips just as Vince Neil reached the bridge in the song. At that instant, the music began to skip from the ancient Windows desktop. Frowning, he sat the drink down, and saw that it was buffering, and it was going agonizingly slow.

"Oh, for the love of God!" Arthur exclaimed. "Does nothing go right for me?"

He sat down in the front of the ancient desktop, and he messed around on it some, and then yet again the song began playing, so he ambled back to the easy chair, and the song was pumping out the beat yet again and running hot. He was ready. He raised the glass to his lips, but yet again, nothing. The silence was there once more, and not even a peep from the birds in the overgrown backyard could be heard. He swore as the song was buffering once more. Where there's a will, there's a way, he thought, and he obstinately went back and tried playing the song again. Motley Crue was yet again playing up a storm, and he dropped back into his easy chair and raised his devilish concoction to his lips, just an instant from chugging it and becoming totally dog-faced. The song cut off yet again, and instead of his drink going down his palate and making him three sheets to the wind, it was all over his shirt.

"Damn," he snarled. "Stupid old computer! Let's throw it in the lake!"

With that, he shut off YouTube completely and went downstairs, looking at himself in the mirror while still holding his now-empty glass, with no alcohol in it that he could enjoy. He peered at the curly hair and his stocky frame, complete with his khaki pants and the loafers that he was wearing on his feet at the bottom of the full-length mirror. Seething, he half wanted to throw the drinking glass against the mirror and crack it, but he checked himself.

"Forget it!" he screamed at himself in the mirror. "Not meant to be this time," he uttered. "I suppose I'll go see mom. Why in god's name would she want to see her pathetic, divorced and jobless son pushing 40, I don't know, but I guess I might as well…"

He placed the glass in the sink almost robotically, and no one would be the wiser, washing out the glass like he should do with the rage from his quivering hands. "Let's go see mom, let's go see mom…" and that was his mantra for the rest of the walk from his house to the nursing home.

Mom still had an empty, blank expression, and she was staring straight ahead at the news on the overhead tv, but her dementia-addled brain was not comprehending any of it. Aunt Lizzie was nowhere to be found, but she was probably playing cards in the activities room. Oh well, Dad seemed more chipper than normal.

"She's been asking about you," he exclaimed enthusiastically but quietly.

"Oh," Art simply replied. "Well, let me try to talk to her," and he met mom's empty gaze straight on. They were eyes that had seen a lot in their seventy-plus years, empty but full of compassion, understanding, and tenderness.

"Mom! Can you hear me? Are you doing okay?" For a moment, the lightbulb in her eyes seemed to come on, but it was gone as quickly as it came, just like a shadowy entity coming out of a dense fog. Suddenly he regretted not taking his drink of Jim Beam just like he regretted not dismantling that aggravating Bearcat. The blank expression of his mother morphed into words, and it wasn't just mere babbling this time. She somewhat coherently stammered it out.

"Not. this. time. no. not. this time," she uttered, and he looked at Dad quizzically. Though he didn't respond, his look acknowledged it. *What did it mean?* He glanced at the entrance and right then and there decided he had better bounce it off of Aunt Liz. "I'm going to ask Aunt Lizzie about this, Dad. Be right back." He nodded his acknowledgment. Lizzie was indeed playing Canasta in that sun room, and those rapt centenarian eyes peered at him again. "Hi there, Art!" she exclaimed, pausing from her game and her playing partner.

As if reading his mind, she asked, "Are you wondering about Mom?" Art nodded. Lizzie looked at her playing partner. "Give me a second, Florence," and then she turned to Art.

"Yeah, she ate really well and watched TV for the most part," she reported.

"That's good, Liz," he replied. Now on to the most pressing question. "Did you hear her saying anything interesting, like just now, she was saying something like 'Not this time' or something like that?" Lizzie's mystified glance met his. "Yeah, I've been hearing that for the better part of the day now, couldn't tell you what it means, though." Art cleared his throat. "No, me neither. That's why I was asking you."

Oh well, no bother, and he bid Aunt Liz adieu and walked back to Mom's room. His brow furrowed in disappointment. Mom was dying, and he couldn't help but recall how she reacted when it was her own mother who was dying when he was a teen. It depressed Mom, and it made her irritable. Now, the circle of life had shifted, and it was Art's turn to watch her die. *How to handle it? Where was the Southern Comfort from the liquor store when you needed it? It's not the answer.* He thought as he took a respite in the bird room of the nursing home. It's just going to make things worse. He knew Mom would never approve of it if she was well, and he knew that Dad would quietly disapprove, but his "Battle With The Booze" raged on.

CHAPTER 5

The following weeks were a study drum beat of the usual mediocrity for Police Chief Lloyd. He was a man seasoned in criminology, and that's what he had gone to school for right after he got out of the service. But the wait for receiving word on the Jane Doe at German Shepherd Lake had gone agonizingly slow. He did his part by scouring the missing persons reports in both Colorado and Oklahoma, but to no avail. Whoever this Jane Doe was, no one was busting down his door trying to help him identify her. Then, three weeks to the day after she had been found, he finally got the phone call he had been waiting for.

"Chief Bridges?" the voice on the other line inquired.

"Yes," Lloyd replied. "But please, just call me Lloyd."

"Well, okay, Chief Lloyd," and it was then that he cleared his throat because he realized that he was talking to a fed.

"This is Detective Gomes, and I just wanted to tell you that the lab has finally found a match on your Jane Doe from German Shepherd Lake."

Lloyd quietly pumped his fist in the air. "What is her name?"

"Well, sir, we ran her fingerprints into the national database and it came back with one Antonia Ramirez. She was all the way from Florida, Lloyd. Could have been she was picnicking out there or traveling through or something. We've got our guys doing some swabs of the DNA in the surrounding parts and up in her body to see if any suspects come up."

Lloyd leered smugly at the wall. Or it could have been that she was a whore or some sort of drifter like he had originally suspected, but he let that comment go. *Her last violation.* He had an obvious next question, but Lloyd went with it anyway.

"Are you guys swabbing her fingernails?"

Detective Gomes laughed at the question, and even though it was probably just to clear the air, Lloyd felt like he was being mocked.

"Yeah, we're doing DNA to see if anything comes back."

"Okay, appreciate that, Gomes, and I've alerted social media like you suggested, but no responses yet."

"Good for you, Lloyd," the detective replied, and Lloyd felt like he was a dog getting a treat for doing a trick. "We'll be in touch soon on whether we get a hit on the DNA."

With that, the phone call was completed, and Lloyd clicked off his official police cell phone. The first thing he did was cross himself, even though he hadn't been an active Catholic since he was a young boy. The second thing he did was swear under his breath. "It's my lake, you son of a bitch."

There had been a lot of local chatter and gossip when he had made the initial social media post a few weeks prior, but like all other small towns do, it had died down and people had gone back to their day-to-day lives. As if right on cue, though, Lloyd saw the glint of Schwinn metal and he knew that yet again, it was Art's tricycle passing by on the sidewalk.

Cameras. Roger was finally starting to notice the cameras in that prison. They were everywhere, even in the hallway looking into his cell, and they were watching him, monitoring everything he did, even when he was taking a dump on the little combination toilet and sink. His grizzled old cellie had momentarily stopped bugging him for his papers at the moment, but he wasn't worried about that. His plan for after he got out of the prison was coming into focus little by little, developing, just like an infant turning into a toddler and then clumsily taking their first steps and saying their first words. Cameras. He knew that for this plan of revenge to work, he would have to find a place that didn't have cameras.

A few hours later, it wasn't just the cameras that were bothering him. It was those communal showers, and he felt the eyes fixed upon him. They were all herded in like cattle, including his bullying old cellie, Pee Wee, and everyone else. He kept looking up, but he couldn't catch anyone in the act. That is, except for his cellie, who was scowling at him yet again. The cold sweat came upon him even though the water caressed him like an indiscriminate lover. *I jinxed it,* he thought. Now he's going to start harassing me again. Sure enough, once the guards marched everyone back to their cells, he did start up again.

He was using the john once more, and the cellie was in his bunk staring down at him in mock admiration, and the convict's eyebrows arched up again.

"Papers, kiddo?" he uttered derisively in a mock school marm way.

Roger didn't try to hide his disdain for the hateful cellie.

"Like I said the other day," he began. "It's none of your damn business where my papers are!"

"You know, Roger," the cellie replied, "I've seen you at the commissary line, and I'm sure you've seen me. I've got family on the outside, but it sure looks like you don't, Chester boy. What's to stop me from calling my old lady or my mama and having her search for you on the internet?"

"Nothing," Roger grunted.

"I can't hear you..."

Roger was about to repeat "nothing" again, but that's when he saw the shank that was protruding from his left hand. He couldn't hide it forever, and now was the time for Roger to react. In one fell swoop, he got up from the john even though his pants were still around his ankles and took a swing at his cellie. His accuracy was dead-on, and the homemade shank fell out of his hands and clattered to the concrete floor with a morbid, twangy song, sort of like a guitar being played by Hank

Williams Sr. Momentarily dazed, the cellie took a rebuttal swing at him, but he missed. Roger again connected with a powerful blow, and suddenly both men tumbled off the bunk in that tiny cell.

By nothing short of a miracle, they landed on the floor without banging their head on anything, and they continued wrestling and decking each other for what seemed like an eternity. Finally, Roger gained the upper hand, and he was on top of the cellie and he was pounding him in the face with one fist and choking him with his other hand around his large gangster neck. The incident only lasted for a few moments, but the cold sweat collected on Roger's face as he gritted his teeth in an unprovoked rage, and suddenly he wasn't seeing his cellie. He was seeing his future victim, perhaps in a baseball cap, with a crooked smile or a tooth missing altogether, and he was just pummeling and choking the life out of him. He was getting even, just like he was with his cellie.

The man's eyelids fluttered, and it was only then that Roger let up very casually, letting the cellie collect his bearings even though he could have killed him if he wanted. Something told him to do it, and it wasn't long before he figured out why. Both men retreated to their respective end of the room, and the decrepit cellie began quivering and retching into the toilet-sink combo. Roger peered at him inquisitively, and all the while, he kept waiting for the guards that would never show up. It was taking forever for the cellie to collect his bearings, but it also was taking Roger a long time to collect his constitution as well. It was for a different reason, though. Suddenly, Roger was feeling things he had never felt before, and he knew that he was a lost cause. His heart was pounding like a jackhammer, but it was not out of fight or flight. It was out of orgasmic ecstasy, and it was then that the rest of his plan for revenge came into focus. It was then that he realized that it would all be worth it.

He knew it would only be a matter of time before he would be caught, but he didn't care. He had enjoyed choking the life out of his cellie, and now he knew that he would need to do it again. It was only a matter of time. The final retching of his cellie snapped him out of his musings, and the man looked at him and rasped, "Hold on, cowboy....I want to show you something," and the older inmate started rummaging through his papers in his top bunk. He held up his intake papers, and there it was for all to see. There was a large "R" emblazoned in yellow highlighter right by his name.

"What?" Roger gasped. "You're kidding me? All this time.....?"

His cellie cut him off mid-sentence. "Yeah, I'm one too. Takes one to know one, I guess."

Roger's eyes didn't leave the demeanor of his ancient cellie. "But why would you...?" The man cut him off again.

"Gotta play the role, cowboy," he said in that strained voice. "Everyone in this cell block knows that I am one, but they don't mess with me because they think I'm reformed."

Natural light was peering through the dusty blinds as his old man was once again watching Drew Carey on the boob tube.

"Lizzie was glad to see you, and I know that Mom was glad, too....even though it's hard to tell," Dad said quietly as Mr. Carey was chatting up one of the service members from a nearby Los Angeles military base. *Oh, to get lost in the world of Hollywood for a while. Oh, indeed,* Art thought. Suddenly, the silence was deafening, and things were getting awkward, very awkward. His old man's quiet demeanor cut through the air yet again.

"She's still asking about you, Art."

Short, sweet, and to the point, as always.

Arthur played it off.

"Oh, really?"

"Yes," his old man said without removing his gaze from Drew Carey's Price is Right antics. "Really...."

Guiding his words very carefully now because Arthur knew he was delving into the unpleasant.

"I know, Dad. I know. But it's the same problem..."

"What, Art? It's not fair....? Of course not, but life isn't fair. You know that."

Such a quiet man, but boy, did he ever have a way of getting at the heart of a conservation when he wanted to. Arthur stared at the local car dealership commercials so he didn't have to look at his father.

"Well, it's still kind of hard...."

His old man cut him off. "Yeah, what do you think it is for me? After all, I'm married to the gal," and he chuckled a bit in spite of himself.

"I know, I know, dad, I'll have to think about it...."

"You know she was so proud of you going to Bible college even though we never went to church. She still would want you to do her funeral when the time comes...." Such a piercing comment in that awkward, mucky air. Art knew it was time to be a bit diplomatic.

"I know, Dad. I've got to make time to go see her for sure."

Before he went quiet again, his last words were, "All right. Don't just say it, though. Do it."

And he was right. Yet again, he was right. As Art left the house again that morning, he knew that the man, in the middle of all of his Blue Collar sweat and blood, was absolutely right. He just wasn't sure how to go about it. But walking always cleared his head, so that's yet again what he did today, what with the walking path on the park in the middle of the Bakersfield, Colorado town square.

As the birds flew high and mighty above the trees in the park, he made several laps among the paths. He was about to resolve himself that yes, he should visit his mother, when he saw his old friend Richard coming out of his antique apartment building directly across from the park, him and his purebred Siberian husky. Goodness knows, what with the low cost of living in Bakersfield, the dog probably set him back more than the cost of the monthly rent. He had the dog on one side of him and his toddler, Richard Jr., on his other side, but when he saw Art, his ears perked up.

"Hey bud!" his middle-aged bearded friend hollered across the street. "How's it going?"

Arthur tried to at least feign a smile.

"I guess it's going okay, Richard...."

To his credit, Richard picked up on it immediately, not even breaking a sweat.

"That bad, eh?"

Art just nodded.

Richard just met his gaze.

"Why so glum, chum?" he said, playing it off.

"Oh, the same ol', same ol'," Arthur replied, just looking down at the gutters where the sidewalk met the street.

"Oh well, why don't you come in for a minute?" the bearded Richard said without skipping a beat. "Just as well shoot the bull and talk about it..." and with that he called out to his husky, and they all headed toward the apartment that he shared with his wife and three kids. "C'mon, buddy!" Art beckoned to Richard's dog and his ears perked up and he jumped upon Richard's sofa, which had seen better days. After the slobbering, licking and laughing fest that ensued, Art noticed the new photo sitting conspicuously on the wall, reminiscent of a wild west shootout.

"Oh, that's a neat photo, Richard," Art remarked. "Where'd you all get that done?"

"Up in the mountains," Richard replied. "Took me and Kelly and the kiddos up there. You know, one of those touristy places."

Art cleared his throat.

"Yeah, you're one lucky guy, no doubt about it."

Richard met his gaze dead-on.

"Luck ain't got nothing to do with it, kiddo."

"Really, Richard?" Art retorted back. "How so?"

Richard took a swig of his glass of Coke.

"Well, it really isn't rocket science, Art. The only reason I got that younger bride you went to school with and all my kids clowning around in one of these novelty Western photos is because I got back on the horse."

Arthur furrowed his brow.

"The horse?"

"Yeah," Richard replied, yet again without skipping a beat. "I didn't quit after I got that Dear John letter like you did. I gave love another shot. Is that what you are down in the dumps about?"

Arthur couldn't help but chuckle a little.

"Yeah, that's kind of what it is. That and Mom not being well. You must be a mind-reader, Richard."

"I can't help you with your mom being ill," Richard replied in between sips of his coke. "That's just the circle of life. But there really isn't anything wrong with trying to get yourself another gal. Go for it."

Arthur just looked straight ahead, but the light bulb absolutely went off in his head, and all he could say was, "thanks, Richard."

"No problem, man. Now, before I forget my manners, would you like a Coke?" "Yeah, why not?"

"Hey, Junior! You mind grabbing our friend Art here a Coke from the icebox?" "Okay, daddy," Junior replied and toddled off to the tiny kitchen, and all the while, ironically, "Why Not Me" by the Judds was playing on Richard's boom box radio.

The cellie kept staring at him over the next couple of days, in the rec yard, the chow hall, the commissary, wherever they went. But Roger noticed the difference. The dark void of contempt was no longer in his eyes, the coldness of a predator was replaced. With what, he wasn't sure, but the emotion in the cellie's eyes was different. It was three days after their last exchange that the cellie finally approached him yet again.

"I guess we're friends now, Cowboy," the cellie said matter-of-factly and stuck his hand out after lighting a mashed-up version of smuggled prison tobacco contraband. "Name's Charlie, but everyone calls me Monk because I'm quiet as a monk. I've got your back now, Cowboy. I've got your back."

It was true that Roger still had to segregate; he didn't dare associate at the black table, nor did he dream of messing with the white supremacists or those involved in the Mexican mafia, but he discovered that he had his own group now, and his own set of kinship, with his own playing table. There was still contempt, there was still anger, but it was fewer and farther between. The guards still looked at him sideways, but the guards looked at everyone sideways. And he was soon to discover that Monk wasn't that bad of a guy to have around at all. They literally talked about everything, it seemed. Roger had to laugh when he was at the Domino table with some of the other sex fiends, though: Everybody might hate segregation on the outside, but boy, these walls are about as racist as you can get. Monk never joined in on the gaming tables, and that didn't surprise Roger. Didn't surprise him at all. It might have surprised him when he first met him and didn't even know his name, but it didn't now.

Monk knew just as much as everyone else that the Dominoes table was a place where fights erupted at the drop of a hat, and Roger saw it with his own eyes. Monk even described it to him one day, and to Roger, he was almost psychic:

"Watch what probably happens at the Dominoes table today, Cowboy, and you'll see why I'm perfectly happy just to watch," Monk said. So Roger did, and he quickly got quite an education. Sure enough, it didn't take long, as Roger saw one Dominoes table that consisted of two Puerto Rican inmates with about three dozen gang tattoos between the two of them.

"You're blocking me?" the indignant Puerto Rican inmate yelled in reference to the move that his fellow Dominoes player had foisted upon him. In one fell swoop, the hot-tempered Puerto Rican rose from his seat, flipped the table, and growled, "Get ready, S.A.!" The two men started exchanging blows and the whole section erupted in a cascade of fists, cursing, spitting, and screaming for what seemed like an eternity. "What?" Roger and Monk's ears finally perked up as they heard the guards finally responding to the commotion. "What's going on here?" the guards shouted as they approached the cell block. "Prison fight, Cell Block F!" the guards hollered as they entered the room. Soon enough, both of the combatants were being drenched in Slim spray, with the aggressor having the tell-tale sign of a taser needle sticking out of his arm.

"You're probably not going to see them for two weeks or more because of this altercation, Cowboy," Monk whispered to Roger.

Roger's eyes perked up.

"Really?" he replied.

"Really."

And Monk was absolutely right. Day after day, they went out to the yard, mostly keeping to themselves, and those two were nowhere to be seen. That didn't stop others from saying cross words to each other or staring at each other sideways, but it did quell the riots for a while. As the days, weeks, and months went by, it seemed that Monk took Roger under his wing, and as he reflected on these days as he drove down that highway to his final reckoning, he couldn't help but be appreciative. But now, he didn't care about Monk, he didn't care about life, he didn't care about anything at all. He didn't care about the young life that he was going to destroy, and for that, there were no tears from his myopic shark eyes. Ironically, he heard the faint sounds of "Let's Go All The Way" from the 80's band Sly Fox on the van's ancient radio.

Richard's little mini-me bounded back from that tiny apartment kitchen and handed Art a soda. "Thanks, buddy," Art said, and Richard Jr. smiled shyly and toddled off to his bedroom with the dog hot on his trail in the cramped apartment. Richard Sr. peered at Art with an intense and understanding look.

"I want you to take a long and hard look at that youngest child of mine," the elder Richard said. "He wouldn't even be here if I had given up. And look at me! I'm not the world's biggest catch for a hubby either. But I went ahead and gave love another shot, and that's what you need to do."

Art paused for a moment, trying to think of a cynical comeback. He had sworn off dating or marrying ever again forever. His eyes were watering up, and he wasn't sure where it was coming from....was it allergies? Either way, Richard didn't skip a beat.

"Come on, buddy!" he laughed. "Don't be turning on the water works with me!"

"Nah, Richard," Art replied, staring at the floor. "Just allergies."

Richard laughed again.

"Oh brother, tell me another line!"

Arthur cleared his throat.

"I don't know, man. I don't know."

Again, Richard didn't skip a beat.

"Two words, Art. Two words: online dating. If you can't date someone around here, take a look online."

Art's eyes perked up. "Really?"

"Yeah! You already do that writing online. You can date online too!"

"Yeah, I do…" and Art's voice trailed off, the hesitation and trepidation evident.

"Just think about what I've said," Richard replied, undaunted. "Nothing ventured, nothing gained, right?" and Art had to smile at that because it was one of mom's favorite phrases when she had been well.

"Yeah, I guess you're right. See you later, Richard."

"All right, bro, take care of yourself."

"You too."

"Oh, you know I will, what with Kelly and these kids and the dog to keep me busy, I ain't got no choice," he capped it off with another easy-going laugh.

And with that, Art left the park apartment yet again, buoyed by a brief rush of endorphins from his friend's pep-talk, but unfortunately, it didn't last that long. The bad guy started resurfacing again, and it was almost like he was whispering in Art's ear.

As he made his walk down the avenue, putting one foot in front of the other, the entity's cold and clammy hand smothered him, clouding his emotions and intellect with brain fog.

"Don't even try it," the draconian entity hissed in his ear. "You aren't good enough. You're too weird."

Those water works came back, in spite of the fact that Richard's words had been inspiring. And so he took a detour. Instead of going immediately back to his dad and mom's house, he went to the liquor store, buying some top-notch Jim Beam. And he came back into the doorway of his parent's home, his childhood dwelling, with that omniscient brown bag of liquor in tow. All the while, the robins kept circling around in the trees in the front yard, mocking him with their singsong voices indicative of their lives of perfection.

He couldn't figure out the drivel that was his life, and he couldn't figure out why nothing worked out for him, but he knew this bottle would. That's what the voice lied to him and said what it did, but it was a comforting lie nonetheless. Deep down, in the canyons and the pits, this creature within this abyss kept telling him this falsehood, and he knew it to be so. He knew it to be a falsehood, but the lie was more comforting than the cold, hard truth. He was an alcoholic. He was unemployed. He was divorced. He lived in his parent's basement. He had a failed marriage and two failed careers. Yes, he was a writer, but what good would that do? As those carefree birds continued to play and circle ahead, he knew that was the reason why he preferred the lie. And as he continued to walk, he couldn't help but have Jim Reeves' "Four Walls" running through his head once again.

Making it home, the house was empty as usual, which was good. His eyes glinted at that obvious truth. Of course, it would be empty. He snorted as he dug around in the kitchen for something clean to use as a glass and finally settled on the prototypical red solo cup, reminiscent of all of those huge family get-togethers when he was a kid.

He poured the Jim Beam in that cup nice and straight. "Because I'm not a wuss, mind you!" he said, talking to himself. Even though he had the solo cup about three-quarters full, he went and ahead and downed the drink in one swallow, no sweat, and he was already starting to feel the buzz, yes, almost immediately.

"This buzz is good enough," he said to himself deviously. "This will work." Again, an obvious lie, but better than the truth. And he proved that it was nothing more than a bald-faced lie no more than five minutes later when he poured himself another drink. It went down easier this time. It always did, and the buzz grew. That always happened too. After about the third and fourth drink, the stirring of his words started to come, and then the fifth and sixth, the room began to spin yet again. The seventh drink he was about done with Mr. Jim Beam, and then the eighth was the pièce de ré·sis·tance, and then he was devoid of memory completely.

~

Lloyd was in a court room for the umpteenth time, but this time it wasn't as a witness in a law enforcement capacity. He listened to the Hispanic attorney in the oversized suit that was representing his soon-to-be-ex, the woman who had borne him his children, listened to him vent over issues at the office, and was now seeking to destroy him after he got slightly depressed and she decided to go into law enforcement herself.

"Your honor," the lawyer in the cheap three-dollar Goodwill-inspired suit said, "my client is still requesting alimony until the divorce is final, even though she has her own career in public service now. She needs it for dealing with all of the trauma and pain and suffering of being married to this man for over two decades." Lloyd couldn't help but roll his eyes at that one, and thankfully no one saw him do it.

"Motion granted," the judge said without looking up. "Court is adjourned until November 10th."

With a jagged frown on his unshaven face, Lloyd headed for the door of the timeworn courthouse. Forget Becky. He didn't even look in her direction. He was driven with a primordial urge back to the arms of his mistress, and thank God Eliza was off today from the County Dispatch. Off he went in his cruiser, not even taking the time to stop at the convenience store for a cup of obligatory iced tea. He was off-duty and in Eliza's arms in twenty minutes flat.

He loved that she still looked at him with warmth and affection, even though he was in his fifties and had the paunch and the receding hairline to prove it. "Isn't it time for us to go out? You know, stepping out? Like that Joe Jackson song?" Eliza loved her version of the oldies.

Lloyd cleared his throat even though he was relaxing in bed.

"Well....." his voice trailed off.

Eliza's loving-but-firm voice pierced the air, an atmosphere normally reserved for lovers. "It's an open secret now, you know."

He was thinking about giving in. "I know," he agreed, with the slightest hint of trepidation. "But how about the next town over?"

"I'll settle for that," she said lightheartedly.

Lloyd nodded and went ahead and motioned to get out of the bed. "Okay, let's go." Clad only in his boxers, he started putting on some slacks, along with his button-down shirt and a good belt to hold it all together. His gal was in the next room when his phone went off, and he groaned. Oh, for the love of God, let it be a spam call. It wasn't. It was Deputy Louie. Good night, now what? What about his hot date....?

"Yeah," he said as he answered the cell phone.

"Sir," Deputy Louie said, "I know you're off-duty, but we need you again."

Lloyd sighed in exasperation. "Oh, for the love of God...What now? Why can't you guys handle anything on your own?"

Louie fired back almost immediately. "With all due respect, sir, cut the crap. Everyone in town knows where you're at, my friend. I hate to say it, but you're needed here."

Now was not a time for having words, and Lloyd knew that.

"Really?"

"Really, sir. It's German Shepherd Lake again, chief."

Lloyd's eyes suddenly came into sharp focus.

"German Shepherd Lake? Again? Now what?"

There was a slight pause on the other end of his cell phone.

"Another body, sir."

Lloyd put the cell down but didn't hang it up. It was a Samsung Galaxy Note 4, so it was brand-spanking new. He momentarily stared into space in the air, listening to Eliza humming along in the next room as she was changing, completely oblivious.

"I see. Give me about fifteen minutes."

As he hurried into the next room where Eliza was almost done changing, her gaze met his. *Disappointment.* She was either a mind-reader or she had overheard the phone call.

"Liza, I'm sorry...."

"I know," she said. "I know. Police stuff again, even when off-duty....C'mon Lloyd, I'm a dispatcher, I know this stuff...so it's German Shepherd Lake?"

"It is."

"Is it....." There was no longer disappointment in her voice but dread.

"Yep, I'm afraid so."

As he headed out to the lake when he was supposed to be off-duty, he was just grateful that this one was more understanding and didn't belittle him like Becky did. *The joys of being a law enforcement spouse,* he thought.

~

Suddenly, in the midst of his watery eyes and blurred vision, all Arthur saw, all around him, was the color green. Green here, green there, green everywhere as his eyes peered open through the darkness. Where was this green and where did it come from? Was he suddenly living among Martians, what with this completely off-the-wall hue? His eyes were watering and blurring so bad he couldn't tell, but it seemed to be a solid component of some sort. He had to get his bearings; he knew that, and somewhere off in the distance of that uncharted territory, he heard a rooster crowing. That couldn't be good, but it wasn't normal, no. It wasn't something he normally heard. He continued to keep his head laid down because he didn't have the gravitas or the muscle strength to lift it up. He stayed in that position in that unknown, forlorn place for eons, as the Earth revolved around the sun more times than he could count, and the birds gave rise to thousands of generations, with the plentiful variation of color making a lovely and ungodly kaleidoscope, threatening to manifest itself in his stomach and out through his mouth.

Finally, something in him snapped, and like a shy kindergartener, he raised his head. The blur made him dizzy, and he nearly put his head down again. The room gradually came into focus, and it was a cramped space, reminding him of one of those small bathrooms in those monstrous RVs that all the local rich people kept bragging about. There was a small wall with an opening, and he was in some sort of greenish tub. That was what he knew for sure. With an ominous migraine in the bowels of his temple, he peered outside of the opening. The precipitous booze-induced throbbing in his head and the flooding within his eyes went down long enough for him to realize that he was in some kind of church, for there was a row of pews on the upper deck, probably for a choir, and then, at the bottom of the steps, there was a pulpit and then more reddish-colored steps leading to the small auditorium filled with those pews.

He would be panicking if it weren't for the excruciating head trauma he felt. Confusion. That was the word. He was lost. He was a lost vessel, an immense Spanish Galleon that drifted way off course, and the swash-buckling captain was blind. He slowly made his way out of the baptismal tub, where many people had been before, and made professions of Christian faith. He was a blasphemer, and his eyes were watery yet again, not from the intoxication but from his own shame. He was being crucified upside-down, but there was no one to persecute him, for he was perse-cuting himself. He managed to get down both of the steps, and he stood forever at the front of the pews, with the sound of silence and the crickets chirping outside making violence in his skull.

Suddenly, the unexpected crowing of that distant rooster jarred him, and he knew he had gotten inside this church somehow. As his cognition began to come back, snapping out of his zombie state, he began to recog-nize the church, realizing he had been there before. It was the local Church of Christ, and he had attended for a few funerals a time or two. He had to see how he had gotten inside, and he slowly crept out of the auditorium to the hallway leading to the main doors.

Locked and tight as a drum at that.

Suddenly, the hangover pain was taking a back seat to his feelings of bewilderment. Undaunted, he continued down the darkened hallway, complete with white walls with paintings of crosses, Christ, and angels meeting the purple flooring, and made his way past the bathroom to some of the side doors at the very edge of this place of worship. Viola! One of the doors was open with a small, almost unperceivable crack, and even though it almost killed his face, he heaved a sigh of relief.

He hadn't vandalized the church. The door had apparently been ajar and he had gone in while sleepwalking, best as he could gather. Before trying that back door further, Arthur was drawn to the next little piece of artwork hanging next to it. The painting was only about the size of a lunch tray, but it had a depiction of Christ looking into the air, with the unmistakable image of a dove soaring just overhead.

Even coming down from his inebriated state, Art knew the accompa-nying verse well: "This is my son, whom I love, and whom I am well-pleased." He had studied that verse in Matthew during many a late evening, even writing a few term papers on it. Was God pleased in his Son? Sure, why not. Pleased in him? Not so much, especially considering he had just caught himself breaking and entering into a church without even remembering it.

Bit by bit, Art inched open that door, half expecting to see a menagerie of police officers out in front greeting him and making him blind with their flashlights.

But it was nothing. Silence. A vacant parking lot, in a vacant neighborhood, in his sleepy hometown, with not even the street lights to greet him in that darkness. He closed the door and painfully walked the appallingly long trek back home. All he knew in that blurry and slurring fog was that he had slapped God in the face and he had still been forgiven, so maybe Richard was right. Maybe he should get back on that horse after all.

CHAPTER 6

"Do you need some help, buddy?" the mid-day sun was just sitting in the sky, and the cars kept zooming by on that busy highway that Roger was headed down, well on his way to his macabre destination. He was taking his own sweet time, and he sized up the situation and his would-be Good Samaritan. If only he knew. He was a bit plump, with a thick mustache, a grizzled chin, with a fishing hat, driving a late-model Dodge truck. "No, I'm fine, just stopped to take a breather and collect my thoughts." The man didn't skip a beat. "Oh yeah, I hear ya. Well, have a good day," and he pulled away. Roger thought again of his corrections days, and they beckoned to him, welcoming, his daydreaming just like that of an ancient tree growing through the cracks of an immense concrete sidewalk, but at least the tree knew his place, and the tree was comfortable. It wasn't stuck in between two worlds like Roger was. So, he still thought of those days, and he strangely wanted them back.

"Please don't hurt me," said Pee Wee in the now-familiar little squeal that emanated from his lips. Roger had just caught him red-handed, as he had spotted Pee Wee's hand was on his milk carton, getting ready to swipe it. "Please don't hurt me."

The barren landscape of Roger's retina didn't turn away from his puny fellow sex offender. "I won't hurt you," he said, and Pee Wee heaved a visible sigh of relief. "But, you damn well better not do it again. I don't care whose boyfriend you are…"

Pee Wee meekly went back to his place in the yard, and Roger learned something new. Fear. Fear could get him what he wanted. That and power. All of a sudden, for the first time in his life, he wasn't that tree stuck in concrete, and he wasn't that little boy stuck on the boat with his drunken and depraved uncle. Instead of an old beat-up Rambler, he was now a Mustang 5.0 that all of the high school kids were drooling over. Even Monk noticed the difference. "What's up with you, man?" he asked after he saw the uncanny glint in Roger's eyes.

He smirked in spite of himself. "Nothing, Monk," he lied through his teeth, and with Monk's unassuming demeanor, he just let it go. That was one positive thing about the whole entire thing that Roger quickly learned. If he played the actor, the strong hand, or the athlete instead of coming across as the victim, he would get people to leave him alone must faster. He realized during that exchange that no one wants to hear a sob story. While he had Monk cornered, he went ahead and asked him some pointed questions, though.

"Hey, Monk," he started. "Just what is it that brings you here, in this prison, you know, if you don't mind my asking?"

Monk paused for what seemed like forever, and Roger started to think that he had angered him. Finally, he slowly responded.

"Well, cowboy, the reason I'm here is because I went too far with someone's kid. I was supposed to be their babysitter, but I ruined that and I was a monster instead. I believe they call it indecent liberties with a child. What about you? Why are you here as a chester?" Roger's eyes raised in surprise, and he was fairly certain that Monk caught it. Really? And Monk had been bullying him….it really should have been the other way around….

"I was trying to arrange a meeting with someone I thought was a 13-year-old boy. Turns out he was an FBI agent instead. Oh yeah, and they figured out after the fact that I was looking at terrible pictures."

Monk stared at the floor. "Looks like we both deserve to be here."

Roger met his gaze directly, the arrogance of a million convicts backing him up. "Speak for yourself, buddy. I don't deserve to be here."

Monk didn't look flush at that statement, nor did he look angry. He didn't appear to have a reaction at all.

"Well, part of rehabbing, Cowboy, is that you admit what got you here in the first place…"

"I'll never admit to anything, Monk!"

"I know, I know, you don't like being told what to do. I get that. I get that we are victims, too…." his voice trailed off and it appeared that he was looking right through him. "Who was it, Cowboy? What is it your father? Grandfather? Maybe an uncle?" That cut to the quick, and he noticed that Roger flinched. "For me, it was a family friend." For a split-second, Roger peered at this grizzled old man, with his unshaven, graying beard still the highlight of his features. He was a man who Roger had grown to respect ever since he had stood up to him, but at that very moment, he wanted to take a swing at him yet again.

"An uncle," Roger said in a nearly imperceptible mutter.

"What?"

"An uncle!" Roger repeated, his voice breaking.

"Ah," Monk replied. "A pretty common story." Then he changed the subject. "How long do you have?"

Roger cleared his throat. He wasn't thrilled about sharing details, but for Monk, he did it anyway. "The judge gave me 2-10."

"You're luckier than me, Cowboy. I fought mine, and I ended up getting 25 to life."

Roger met his gaze head-on, and it was a look of dried and resigned acceptance. "I don't know why you aren't trying to get even, Monk. I don't know why you aren't giving these guards a living hell."

"What's the point, Cowboy?"

Roger paused ever-so-briefly to collect his thoughts. "For revenge. For evening the score. For a lot of things. To clear up the hate."

Monk seemed nonplussed. "Yeah, a lot of good that would do me. I *do* have a few privileges, you know. Why assault the guards and then get thrown into solitary?"

"Well, you didn't mind trying to assault me, did you, Monk?"

Again, Monk was nonplussed.

"That's different, my friend. You have to do that every once in a while, so they stay off of you."

Roger didn't have a comeback to speak of. "Oh."

Monk continued. "I might get out one of these days, but either way, Cowboy, I'm going to be looked down upon for the rest of my life. I'm kind of like a spider. I've got redeeming qualities, but everybody's afraid of me."

Roger nodded, and Monk kept going.

"I'm gonna try to be a law-abiding citizen if I do ever get out, but it may not happen. I might die here. You're very lucky, Cowboy. If that had been a real 13-year-old, you'd be right here with me, and you would deserve it."

Roger gulped.

"You have a chance to get out, Cowboy. Don't blow it. The next time, you probably won't be so lucky. Don't say I didn't warn you."

Roger laughed nervously.

"I know, I know, Monk. But I don't care. I just hate everything."

Monk didn't let up. "That's a sad way to live, Cowboy. A very sad way to live."

Roger lay in his bunk a few hours later, listening to Monk snoring away, and the tears started to cascade unabated. So much wisdom from a fellow convict. What was he, some Indian guru posing as a jail inmate? But just like the flies that kept landing on his bedding in the dry air, he knew he was damaged goods, and he knew these insects held higher esteem to some than he did. It made no difference to him, and the wheels of his plan continued to turn regardless. He was going to make people pay.

Lloyd arrived at the crime scene just in time to see Detective Gomes conferring with the other state guys, just like a crossing guard directing traffic. Before he knew it, an involuntary groan escaped from his lips, and he was just glad that he had come without the radio on. Gomes was looking like his usual suave, dapper self, and so Lloyd sucked it up and stood there, holding out his hand.

"Gomes, what do we have?" he asked him after they had exchanged greetings.

"This time it's a black female," he began as if this was a common occurrence in Emory County. "No ID on her, but we are doing all of the standard stuff. We've already cleared off the scene, swabbed off the body, and checked her out for any signs of sexual assault or recent intercourse."

He glared at Lloyd momentarily, and he couldn't help but notice that brief look of superiority that Gomes had. "Does she look like anyone that you recognize?" he asked Chief Lloyd.

Lloyd ignored the smirk from his newfound associate. "No, can't say she does, but let me know what the lab boys tell us in a few weeks."

After a couple of hours, Lloyd went home to Eliza and played the waiting game yet again. Sure enough, after a few weeks, they called, saying that they didn't have any results, and that was that. It remained an open investigation, but that wasn't the end of it. The bodies kept piling up that summer at German Shepherd Lake until, one day, it was even someone local. It wasn't until that hiker, that fourth body, had shown up at that lake that Lloyd started getting those notes in his personal post office box.

As he looked in the mirror and the final dregs of his booze migraine nightmare were gone, he said, "he's right, you know." Arthur was finally on the mend, and he had a new resolve, finally coming into agreement with his friend Richard. "Time to make a profile," he told himself in the mirror, and that's exactly what he did upstairs.

After he created a profile, it didn't take long for him to get a hit. She was a lovely lady in her late 50s, and her name was Marilyn, and he noticed that she kept browsing his profile over the next week. Throughout all of it, he kept seeing the miniature hummingbirds right outside the sliding glass backdoor playing at the birdbath. Dad had gotten

Mom one year for Christmas, long before she had gotten sick, and it brought a smile to his face.

Maybe Richard was right. *Maybe he was*, he repeated inwardly, and maybe it was time for the circle of life to begin yet again. When he was still married, he would get up for an early-morning ride on his three-wheel bike, regardless of the leers and glares that would come his way. He would sometimes ride down the main road on the edge of town just across from the fairgrounds, and he would watch the sun just peeking out among the canyons and the alternating shades of red, orange, and yellow that it defiantly presented.

It was always a brand-new day, with the Earth rotating on its axis yet again. And as those new days passed by and he got to know this wonderful creation named Marilyn, the more he liked her. The viewing of her pictures and the reactions he had to her posts started to morph into long phone conservations, and it didn't take long for Arthur. He was in love yet again. It was only a few months of courtship over the cell phone before they had their first date, and he showed her around this small town that he called home.

He knew it would be a hard-sell, simply because it was just a one-stoplight town and she was a big-city gal, but on that first date, he tried to make it as special as possible. He knew that sometimes the simple things were best, so they drove out in Marilyn's small Chevy to German Shepherd Lake, and they stayed there for a long time, just talking, sharing, and getting to know each other. The lake had some decent picnic tables, and so they would take their roast beef sandwiches, ham sandwiches, chips, cheetos, and other food items and snack on them as well.

Art felt like a kid all over again as they watched the sun crashing into the swarthy water, and he and Marilyn kept looking for rocks to throw out on the water and see if they would skip. Art was only able to do it a few times, but Marilyn proved to be a regular pro at it. The laughter flowed right along with the soda and the snacks, and the best part of it was that Art was starting to think about his future yet again, and all because of his buddy Richard. Now he knew soon enough that a man could have a three-course meal in front of him in the grandeur of the

Waldorf-Astoria, but it would mean nothing if he had no one to share it with.

As he saw her off later that evening, she winked and said, "I had a lovely time. Let's do it again soon."

They had agreed to meet at the city park, and as he walked back, his heart kept skipping a beat. The high school where he was on the marquee in the entryway for the class of 1999 was on the adjoining avenue, and the sidewalk was about the same length as their football field. He bounded down that path in no time flat because the love endorphins kept churning away in his brain. When he reached the end of that sidewalk, well, that was another story. That sidewalk was as old as the high school itself, which had been dedicated back in the 1950s. Even though he was now in his 30s, Art's autistic hippocampus knew every crack in that sidewalk by heart because he had walked that sidewalk countless times, even during his adult years. Stories of kids driving up in their nice middle-class cars, other kids in rich sports cars, and the vehicles where some simply had no choice but to save up for all emanated from those cracks. Tales of "Dear John" letters, promise rings, fall flings, jocks, and nerds clowning around just to fit in all came from those cracks.

Blame it on allergies, but the effervescent glint in his eyes was returning. The Jim Beam, the Jack Daniels, the pot, the depression, and all of the other dark stuff people had a tendency to do emanated from those sidewalk cracks, too, Arthur realized, and that he knew all too well. Being stuck in special ed for his whole K12 experience taught him that he would never amount to anything, and sure enough, here he was, pushing forty and still nothing to show for it. But oh well, at least he had a girlfriend now.

～

Time wore on for Roger, and he and Monk never spoke of his future plans again. His hate and anger solidified as he went through the predictable routine of prison life. The roach colony in the decrepit house in the recesses of his mind grew and grew, and everyone kept getting older; him, Monk, and the other inmates, and then one day, some odd people in robes started visiting the wing of the prison that he and Monk were in. Roger literally gagged when those people first came around, and it hadn't gotten much better since. But for some reason his buddy Monk loved them. For Roger, they were just more of the status quo, and it just solidified his break from reality, his conviction that someone's beautiful child, someone's whole world, was going to disappear once he got out of there.

But those devout men kept visiting, and with each episode, Roger peered at them anxiously as if they were extraterrestrials encountering his own alien world and imposing upon his predictable routine. These walls were not their own, and how dare they infringe upon them. They were trespassers, with their red robes a total eyesore, and Roger knew what would happen to trespassers on the outside. Monk began adopting their style and habits repeatedly after each visit, and suddenly he was watching his friend, his only friend, becoming something unusual and unknown to him.

Roger cleared his throat to stop his heart from racing, but he couldn't stop the resentment from coming, and he thought he could see the mist rising from his decrepit face as he looked in the mirror each morning. He should have stabbed Uncle George. He should have stabbed his worthless mother. He should have stabbed everyone in his life.

He wanted to stab Monk too, but even now, his heart wasn't in it. Instead, one day he finally got up the courage to ask just who the men were. Monk blinked ever so briefly, then he had a weird grin on his face, "They're Buddhists," he proclaimed. "The Zen type." Roger stared at his old friend in bewilderment, totally bereft of speech. His mouth was agape, and Monk brazenly reached his hand out and pushed on Roger's chin to close it.

"It's all my fault, you know," he continued. "I'm the one who did that to that kid. That's what these guys have been telling me. I put myself through this hell and no one else. It doesn't matter if it happened to me or not. It doesn't matter if it happens to you. We are the captains of our own destiny. We are the captains of our own ship."

Although it was a knee-jerk reaction, Roger rolled his eyes. "Is your sermon over with yet?" He asked snarkily. Monk's eyes pierced through the discord of his old friend. "Not hardly, buddy. Not hardly."

He cleared his throat before he continued. "My goal now is to reach people with the freedom of the Zen, my friend. One of their main goals is that you are supposed to renounce all types of sexual desire for the rest of your natural life."

Roger did a shocked double-take. "What? Are you kidding me?"

Monk calmly met his surprised gaze and almost looked right through him. "No, Cowboy, I'm not kidding. Sexual desire is what got me in this boat." Call it an impulsive reaction, but with that errant comment, Roger reached out and started choking the daylights out of his old friend.

For what seemed like an eternity, his hand was smashing into Monk's vocal cords until some unseen force made him remove his hand. For once, the guards were completely oblivious as Monk began to attempt to regain his composure, large retching and coughing fit ensuing. Finally, Monk returned to normal, but the bright-red bruises on his neck were evident. "What was that?" he rasped finally.

Roger hesitated, glaring at him. "There is no higher power, you fool." Monk shook his head. He glared at Roger forever, and both men could see the whites in each other's eyes. They both were at a stand-off and peering into each other's soul, but Roger could not tell if hate or love was coming out of his injured cellie's pupils. Finally, Monk broke the ice. "I-I-" he stammered. "I forgive you." Roger was at a loss for words, so he let the moment pass, retreating to his corner of the cell and trying to get into a boring Western novel. Monk laid down on his bunk, and but for his snoring, he remained silent for the next couple hours.

Roger put the book down and tried to sleep, but soon the snoring from Monk picked up and stopped suddenly. Even though they were housed in an interior cell, he knew that it was still the daylight hours, but that didn't stop him from trying to pass the time with some sleep. Lord knows he needs to de-stress somehow after attacking his friend. But his pierced the air yet again, in the faintest of whispers, "I forgive you...I forgive you, Cowboy."

Roger decided it was time to stop the charade, and his firm, a skeptical voice piped up. "You can forgive me all you want, Monk, but why?

I don't want it." Monk was wide awake now and picked it up like he had never left off. "I'm doing it for me, Cowboy. I'm doing it for me. I hope someday you will think about what I've said. Anger is cancer, Cowboy. I see that now. I see it now. About sixty-five years too late, but I do have to see it now."

He made a mock tip of his invisible hat and continued. "I'm reminded, my Cowboy friend. I'm definitely reminded. My anger can give me great power, but if I let it, it can destroy me." With that, the dust settled in that bland white correctional room for the rest of the day, what with Monk having his epiphany and Roger just becoming increasingly sullen, quiet and befuddled.

~

"Are we having fun yet?" the note in the envelope read. Lloyd had just barely returned from his early morning coffee trip and relieving himself to the porn mags in his office to check his post office box when he saw the post card with the abnormal cursive handwriting. Curiously, he opened it up to reveal more of the peculiar writing on the inside.

"Seems to be to me that there is sure a big to-do out at that German Shepherd Lake. The mockingbirds tell me that people are just dying to get there! No, Lloyd, I'm not done yet...put this in that fancy taxpayer pit you call a police vehicle, you ass!" Somebody was killing people out at his lake and now they had the nerve to brag to him about it? Lloyd's blood pressure kicked up a notch, his face now totally beet red.

"I'm going to find you," he muttered. "Mark my words. I will find you!" With that, Chief Lloyd put on his prototypical aviator sunglasses and went on patrol for the rest of the morning. Yet again, it was the typical day of a small-town police chief, and besides a fender-bender between two old ladies at the local Catholic bingo hall, nothing really of interest went on. Lloyd put the obvious hate mail out of his mind, writing it off as some gossipy kid playing a dark prank on him.

He thought about running it by Deputy Louie, but what was the point? They all had things to do and mindless paperwork to catch up on. He started focusing on what he was going to do with Eliza when he finally had some time off. That is until the next letter appeared in his mail box a few weeks later. There was no return-address listed, and his name was listed in print form from a black pen. After he hastily opened the otherwise nondescript envelope, the first thing he noticed was that simplistic, folded notebook paper. After unfolding it, he read the following:

"Roses are Blue,

Violets are Red,

You, sir, have both a wife and a girlfriend,

but while you're busy getting head,

everybody at that lake is dead."

For a brief second, his heart skipped a beat, but he immediately went back into police officer mode. He knew that the rumor wagon was going crazy about those bodies at the lake, so could this yet again be a prank from a sick teenage jokester, maybe from one of those goth kids he had been seeing while he was on patrol? So many questions, but ultimately, to the evidence locker at the station, this note went. It was lunch before he even thought of the note again, and he elected to go to Subway with Deputy Louie to take his mind off of it.

"Sir, you know that we have a new sheriff's deputy, right?" Louie said while munching on his BLT.

Lloyd laughed. "As always, I guess I'm the last to know anything around here…"

"Yeah," Louie replied. "He's been on the force for about a week now, just graduated from the academy. This is a bit of second career for him. We're mostly going to have him doing security work at the high schools throughout the county. Name is Clarence, about your age, sir."

Lloyd's eyebrows arched up and his intuition was going about a mile a minute.

"Is he kind of a short guy, with a lot of freckles, and he doesn't really like his first name?"

Deputy Louie did a double-take. "Yeah, chief, he sure is….how did you know?"

"Just a guess. I think I had a brief encounter with the guy when I was much younger, just starting out in the Marines. Small world, I guess. Well, tell him I said hi, and we'll have to catch up sometime."

Louie laughed. "Will do, chief. Will do."

No need to tell the deputy about the weird mail he was getting lately, Lloyd thought, and the rest of the lunch hour passed by with the usual idle police chit-chat. As far as Clarence went - did he still go by Slim? - Lloyd really had no opinion, and it wasn't long before his mind refocused on other things.

No, it didn't take him long to notice that an older version of the Slim he knew from the chance encounter on the bus in his 70s Marines days was indeed doing some work here and there at the high school, as noted by his Sheriff vehicle being in the parking spot just beyond that long sidewalk. He drove by a few times that month before he finally decided it was time to stop and say hi, and that was the day that he saw him in the parking lot, walking nonchalantly to his Sheriff's cruiser. After getting out of his own cruiser, he walked toward him and stuck his hand out. "Hey, Officer Clarence? Do you remember me? It's been a long time."

He had a large melancholy fake grin on his face, and he responded with, "Yeah, I think I do, and I still go by Slim, my friend....Lloyd? From the Marines? This is kind of second career for me, just got out of the academy..."

For once, Lloyd had a real grin on his face, and he said, "Sure thing, Clarence, I mean, Slim....sorry! And congrats!" His newly-minted law enforcement buddy just laughed it off, even though his demeanor still seemed shady. It was probably nothing, though, he reasoned, and his heart actually swelled up with pride as he continued on his patrol later. It was the same old boring stuff, but he had Mussorgsky's "The Great Gate of Kiev" playing in his head from his classical music phase just after he had gotten out of the Marines as he was thinking about his newly-minted co-worker. Maybe he was finally getting the hang of this law enforcement stuff after nearly three decades.

～

"So, has it crossed your mind what you are going to do when you get out of here?" Monk asked. Roger's lips perked up in an automatic smirk. "Guess I haven't thought that far yet." The years had flown by, and the age had shown on their faces, what with the wrinkles on Monk's face and Roger's receding hairline. Monk was now a full-fledged Buddhist, going to zazen as often as the guards would allow and meditating in his cell nearly every day. "Well, whatever you do, whatever your endeavors might be, do it wholeheartedly..." Roger tried to hear his friend out without any resentment, but the anger won out. "What is that?" he replied. "Another one of your cult deals, or what?" Monk remained calm even though he could tell Roger was getting ready to slug him again. Why the guards hadn't switched his cellie, Roger didn't know.

"No, Cowboy," Monk replied. "That is the essence of my being, the interdependence between you and I, the recognition that the sun, moon and the stars are giving us life at every moment, and the...."

But Monk was cut off from his dialogue because he had to duck his head, avoiding the greasy fist from his friend. He barely even flinched, remaining calm as steel. "This is my rite, Cowboy. Just like the ant hill, this is my essence of being..." he repeated. Roger looked at Monk like he had lost his mind, and he had reached his breaking point after year after year of his cellie's new-found piety.

Roger was fed up. He had a shank in his pocket, and his fist trembled as he grazed the parched fabric of the prison uniform and intensely sharp weapon. Perhaps it was time he put his homemade weapon to good use. It was now or never, but instead, Roger started pounding on the cell door. Pounding, pounding, pounding, until finally, he caught the attention of one of the guards, a butch lesbian who was nearing retirement and had seen better days. "Yes?" the female guard replied.

"Get me out of here!' Roger shouted. "I can't stand this guy anymore!" All the while, Monk was just staring ahead in a trance-like state, looking like a zombie, but a compassionate one, directly upon his old friend. "I'll see what I can do," the butch lesbian said like they did countless times, and as she was starting to turn around, Roger held up the shank, making her demeanor change. "Tier three, we have a dangerous inmate, I need to have backup!" she yelled into her receiver, and Monk sat on his bunk as they extracted Roger and took him to the hole, which is what he had wanted all along.

As he stared down those dividing lines of the highway heading to his ghastly revenge, little did he know that was the last he would see of Monk and he never knew what became of him, nor did he care. He ended up getting a new cellie after he finally got out of the hole, and one who was more similar to his personal views at that. His new cellie didn't speak that much, but they did have one memorable conversation. He was a black man who had been sent up the river because he was taking advantage of his 13-year-old daughter while his wife was battling cancer, so there was that bond. Come to find out, Roger's new cellie also agreed with him getting even. "How are you going to do it, Georgie?" the cellie asked him one evening after chow. Roger flinched at the nickname because of that damned uncle of his, and he still couldn't understand why no one in there couldn't just call him by his given name. He was just a number to the guards and just a nickname to the fellow convicts.

The best way to deal with it was to ignore it, so that's what he did. "Got a couple of ideas, man. Got a couple of ideas." The cellie kept staring down the female prison guard as she walked by. "Well, tell me, Georgie, I'm all ears," and he laughed at that remark. "Might give me some ideas too…"

Roger flinched but then smirked immediately after. "Oh, maybe random violence, I don't know. Just go shoot someone in front of their kid, something like that."

The cellie laughed hoarsely. "Oh, that's good. That's a good start, Georgie. A good start."

Roger knew that his plan was like that of a good horror novel; it was probably going to undergo a multitude of edits before he finally settled on it. He knew that whatever retribution he came up with, it was going to be organized and well-thought-out, but he couldn't say he was sure how it was going to play out. Still, he was glad he had himself a cellie who wasn't trying to fill his head with all of this nonsensical forgiveness talk, for Roger knew that forgiveness was just for suckers. The only problem that Roger had with his new cellie was that he wasn't always there. One time in the chow hall, that cellie was just minding his own business, and all of a sudden, some of that weird grape-colored, watery kool-aid they were constantly served suddenly hit the cellie square in the face.

Just an instant later, there was a gleam from the overhead lights emanating from the cellie's pocket, and that was when Roger knew that the cellie was hiding a shank. The rival inmate, a Hispanic gang-member covered in tattoos, was laughing and calling the cellie a chomo, but in the next split-second, the cellie got up, dove across the table, and began plunging his shank into the culprit gang member's neck. Roger knew he wouldn't see the cellie for several weeks at the very least after this offense, but still, he started crying, and as the salty liquid began dribbling down his cheeks he felt the inspiration of the moment. "Allergies," he said in his own defense to some of the shocked fellow gang members of the inmate who tried and failed to egg his cellmate on. True to form, the guards quickly broke it up and led the two men away, most likely into the solitary hole.

The inspiration, he thought. *Ah, the inspiration!* Here was a man who wasn't taking no for an answer, and he knew he would learn so much from that one action, and he knew he was a black spider. He was a black widow spider emerging from an egg sac, and at that instant his head was swimming with so many possibilities that he thought he just might pass out. It was all of a month and a day before the cellie finally came back into the general population with Roger. They both laughed it off.

Roger grinned, showing off his ugly teeth stained by the hideous beef and broccoli the inmates had eaten the night before. "What took you so long to come back, buddy?"

"I was a little bit tied up," the cellie replied dryly.

Roger again flashed a rare smile. "No shit, Sherlock," he drawled in a mock Southern tone.

The cellie took on a serious tone then.

"Let me tell you something, Roger…don't let anyone ever screw you around. We don't have victims. We are the victims!"

There was an emphasis on the word "we".

As the birds were circling overhead on Roger's demonic road trip to ensure a youngster's eternal perdition, he knew that yet again, his adulation for his cellie wasn't going to last very long. Just a few days after that, the bellowing of an obese and obtuse prison guard shocked him out of his revelry in the chow hall, but luckily for him, it wasn't directed at him but that cellie.

"Inmate 213K, back to your cell!" the guard roared at the cellie after he had thrown some of that slop they called beef stroganoff in the guard's direction. "Did I stutter, inmate? Back to your cell!" In response, all Roger's new cellie did was simply stand up, and for a brief second, it did look like he was going to comply. However, in one fell swoop, his hands were suddenly grasping the fat guard's neck. Roger felt like cheering, and he finally did once the other inmates began to do so themselves. Not five seconds later, though, some of the other guards rushed up and almost tasered the cellie half to death. Roger still thought it was wonderful. That is until his cellie came back yet again after his stay in the infirmary.

When the guards escorted him back to the cell that he and Roger shared, the first red flag was in the next five minutes that he and the man were alone. He didn't say a word. Not a peep. Roger just kept staring at the cellie, and soon he turned around because he had to use the john right by him in that cramped cell. The solid blue of his iris was still present, as was his pupil. Luckily for him, it hadn't been damaged by any of the other psychotic inmates during his stay in administrative segregation. But it was bereft, and it looked heavy for some reason. A couple of hours in, and Roger quickly realized that besides the ungodly silence, his whole body looked heavy, and soon enough, he would realize too late that was a precursor, a red flag.

His cellie had seemed to take a vow of silence over the next couple of days, literally looking like he had aged a quarter-century. He knew those walls could do it to anyone, and if he stayed there any length of time, they would do it to him. He looked at those absent eyes of his cellie when he was trying to appear to be reading his book, and it brought more questions than answers. Roger did not know what his cellie had seen when he was in ad seg, and as luck would have it, it ultimately wouldn't be meant for him to know at all.

～

"We've got to stop meeting like this." Lloyd's eyes glinted in the early morning sun as the Earth had turned on its axis yet again. The birds were flying high, turning cartwheels in the air, and the fish were totally care-free and oblivious at that German Shepherd Lake. But not him. Sergeant Gomes skipped the greeting and had a serious frown on his face, and Lloyd could have sworn he could smell the Hispanic fed's cologne from a mile away. "Yeah, Lloyd, this is becoming a common occurrence. Good thing Uncle Sam takes care of my gas money. It's personal now. This time the gal looks Hispanic like me." Gomes motioned with his hand. "The crime scene is under that tree. Go take a look…." Lloyd did as he was told, and he kept the sarcastic comments to himself, staying professional to boot. After he saw the remains, his heart immediately sank, and momentarily he was gasping for air. Gomes caught on rather quickly.

"What is it, chief?" he asked. Lloyd cleared his throat.

"I know her, Gomes. I know her personally. She's had a job bagging groceries at our local food mart for like forever. She's even bagged mine several times."

Gomes stared at the water of German Shepherd, lost in his thoughts. "Oh."

"We've had several interactions with her over the years, Gomes because she's had a bit of a mild drinking problem. She's kind of a town retard…."

Gomes cut him off. "Excuse me?" he retorted. "What did you say?"

Lloyd still wasn't getting it. "She's a town retard…."

"Yeah, chief, that's what I thought you said. What's your problem, man? This woman is deceased, and you're calling her by a slur? Really?"

Lloyd didn't skip a beat. "Yeah? So what?"

Gomes was no longer staring at the water or the crime scene tape but staring him down. "I'll you what, chief…" the last part, his voice raised sarcastically, in a mocking tone. "I have a son with down syndrome, buddy, and coincidentally, he's worked at a grocery store off and on. You should take that back, buddy."

"Oh," was Lloyd's only response.

"What the hell is wrong with you?"

And that is when Lloyd got irritated at Sergeant Gomes.

"What?" he retorted. "Seriously, Sergeant Gomes, with all due respect to your son, this is my jurisdiction, and I'll call people what I damn well please!"

Gomes spat on the ground. "Oh, brother, Chief Lloyd. I saw right through you the minute I saw you."

Lloyd's expression stayed void, but it belied his true feelings. Even though he was a quarter Italian on his mother's side, he knew he shouldn't fire back with a boisterous response. The words stung, and he really didn't have a retort. Looking at the partially nude body of his grocery store worker, the only thing he said was, "Well, I guess let me know what all evidence your technicians can collect from her."

"Will do," Gomes snapped with contempt. "Will do, chief."

"SP coming back on, returning from German Shepherd," he said into his receiver later as he was back in his police cruiser and on the ride back to the station. He continued to be in law enforcement mode, but his duties were merely robotic, his eyes a blank expression, and he couldn't help but notice a flock of birds roosting in the forlorn elm tree on the side of the road. What to do about this, he thought. How should he approach this? How should he approach the fact that Sergeant Gomes thought all along that he was less than a true police officer, even with his years of experience? He would have to sleep on it.

"Art, your total is going to be $20.51. Art?" his eyes flinched. "Oh right," he replied and pulled his debit card out of his wallet. His head was still in the clouds. The black cauldron that was his life, complete with a wrinkled gypsy witch stirring slime into it, was no more.

For the first time in a long time, he had a decent, god-fearing woman in his life. He knew that this waitress taking his ticket wasn't all that thrilled with him, and she would probably make a snarky comment later, but he also knew that the good Lord would find a way for him, just like he did for the Andy Dufresne character in the escape scene in that Shawshank Redemption movie.

"Sorry, brain fart," he muttered to the waitress and then departed through the main door of the restaurant. He hopped on his bike and away he went. But he didn't make it more than five blocks before he saw him, complete with the official insignia denoting that of the county sheriff's office and the unrecognizable diminutive figure getting out of it. He was a shorter man with freckles.

"Arthur?" This is Sergeant Clarence from the sheriff's department," the man said. Arthur stuck out his hand and it just remained there awkwardly due to the fact that the man in blue didn't take it.

"Call me Sergeant Slim, though," he said with scorn after refusing to shake Art's hand. "Did I just catch you trying to run over that lady as she got out of the beauty shop?" It was a lie, and both men knew it. Art didn't take the bait.

"Excuse me, Slim, but I really don't know what lady you are talking about...."

The ire rose in Slim's eyes, and he cut him off, changing the subject. "You know, Art, there have been a lot of bodies out at that German Shepherd Lake. Would you happen to know anything about that? The word around town is that you've been talking about going out there, with that new girlfriend of yours...anyhow, buddy, that's what the little birds are saying because I don't know you from apple butter, but I already know that you talk too much, just like a retard," he concluded with a mocking and menacing smirk, "pleased to meet you, and I will be watching..." he then put his hands up to his eyes in a circular motion and walked away from a now-trembling Arthur on his three-wheel bike. Slim stood at the end of the block as Art finally got the gumption to pedal away, and as he passed the grassy knoll where the flock of birds was trying to catch food, they flew away, oblivious to the irony of it all. He and Chief Lloyd were going to get that boy that he knew for sure.

"Don't worry, Slim, I'll go ahead and take care of the tip," Lloyd said to Clarence as he laid down the five on the table. "Good to catch up with you and glad to see that life's been treating you well since our Marine days." Slim laughed. "Yeah, it was good to go to the academy and get out of that grain silo, that's for sure. Fulfilled a lifelong dream."

Slim's tone in that main street diner got more serious then. "Hey chief, before we go, what do you know about that Arthur kid? You know, could he be a suspect in those murders out at the lake?" Lloyd's eyebrows flinched. "Yeah," he replied, "to be honest, I've thought about it..." Slim was overzealous.

"Well, Chief Lloyd, he's been telling people that's he been out to the lake anyways. Seems like he has a new girlfriend."

"Well, let's hope to god that the dumbass treats this one better than the last gal he had," Lloyd said, stifling a laugh. "Seriously though, Slim, I know he's been out to the lake if you know what I mean."

"Do you think he could be a -"

Lloyd read his mind. "Yeah, yeah, I do, but I've got to run it by that fed guy, name's Gomes. I already got cross-ways with him yesterday as it was. Anyways, good talking to you and glad to have you on board."

The two men departed and Lloyd decided that it was time to give Gomes a call as soon as he made it back to the station.

To his credit, Gomes answered his cell on the second ring. "Hey Gomes, Chief Lloyd here. First of all, let me apologize for my slip of the tongue yesterday. I wanted to run something by you. Have you heard of another local we have, a kid by the name of Arthur?"

Gomes cleared his throat on the other end of the line. "No, can't say that I have. Go on...."

"Well, we've had interactions with that kid several times. He has a history of domestic violence, violating restraining orders with his ex-wife, and things like that. He likes to ride around on his bike, one of those adult tricycles, and I guess he's been seen out at the lake. He's been bragging to people that he has a new girlfriend from Texas and all and telling them he's been out there skipping rocks, having a picnic and whatnot."

"Okay, he could be a possibility," Gomes replied. "What does he drive?"

Lloyd paused. "Well, he doesn't have a car, necessarily..."

Gomes sighed, and Lloyd even heard it on the other end of the line.

"All right, chief, slow down, back up here. If he doesn't have a car, then how it is, pray tell, that he would hypothetically be this bastard we're trying to track down? How? His girlfriend's car? His dad's car? Does he have any parents that are still alive? What? How is he doing this?"

The rancor was palpable to Lloyd, but he let it go. "Well, I don't think his dad lets him drive his cars anymore. He used to, but not anymore. The girlfriend's car is a possibility, but of course, he's said she's from Texas, so she's out of town…"

Gomes couldn't help himself. "Oh, brother, chief…"

"I know, I know, Gomes, but his dad's a used car salesman too, works out of his home. How do you know he's not borrowing a car…"

"Could be," Gomes replied. "Could be. Sounds like a stretch to me, but could be. All right, Lloyd, I've got to go. Talk to you later."

After the conversation, Lloyd went about his usual small-town police chief routine, going on patrol and making all of the usual traffic stops of teenagers showing or driving too fast, but he couldn't get Art out of his head. It didn't help that he saw him on his bike and walking several times. No, he hadn't seen him behind the wheel of one of his Dad's cars, but he didn't have to tell Gomes that. He had to call his Fed acquaintance yet again and force his hand, so that's exactly what he did the very next day.

"Gomes?" Lloyd began during the second cell phone call. "I'll just cut to the chase here. I want to bring that boy in for questioning."

Gomes paused. "Well, have you discovered something new on him, or what?"

"No, not really," Lloyd replied. "Just a gut feeling…"

"Well, you need more than just gut feelings, and you need more than just seeing him once at the lake with his gal. Seriously, do you have anything else?"

"Well, I have reasonable suspicion…"

Gomes snorted, and the chief could tell he was stifling a smug laugh. "Well, unless you've actually seen him on the lake on the very day a body was discovered, you need a lot more than that. Seriously, chief, you can't bring a guy in just because you don't like him. This isn't Mayberry. How long have you been a cop?"

"Oh, brother, Gomes. This is my jurisdiction. I'm bringing him in…"

"Not if I have anything to say about it. You do that, and you'll have to answer to me, buddy. This is my case now."

Lloyd was getting mad now. "Like hell, it isn't!"

"Calm down, chief. Seriously, you need more to bring him in than this…think about it."

"All right, I'll keep my eye on him, but I won't bring him in," Lloyd lied.

"Good," Gomes replied. "Good to see that you are talking some sense now." And that was the end of the second cell phone conversation Chief Lloyd had with Sergeant Gomes.

Lloyd put the mobile phone back in his pocket and went and surveyed himself in the mirror in the nondescript police station bathroom. "This is my case, Gomes," he growled at his reflection. "I'm the one who is going to crack it."

Needless to say, when Chief Lloyd went out to the country to his makeshift firing range and took aim at those beer cans yet again, Sergeant Gomes was a new target for his ire.

Chapter 7

Roger was back on the road again, and totally out of his macabre revelry once more. He was now in a town similar to Denver, but only with a hundred thousand people, and he stopped at a Starbucks to take a break from his damnation journey. After ordering a sandwich and a white chocolate mocha from the pierced, purple-haired barista, he sat on the patio, just staring at the birds flocking to and fro in the trees in the midst of the mid-day rush.

The city was in the midst of their fair share of urban decay, but they were doing the best they could. *Starbucks, I suppose, is an example of capitalism at its finest,* Roger thought bitterly, *and I guess I am an example of communism or totalitarianism.* But for now, he was shutting his mind off and just enjoying his mocha and sandwiches.

Either way, Roger couldn't help but notice the decrepit gentleman on the sidewalk near the noll. He looked to be about middle-aged, with a scraggly unshaven beard, and long, brownish hair. He could have been a dead-ringer for Charles Manson in his younger days. His eyes were drawn to the cardboard sign that he was carrying as he made his way to the street, dodging cars as he hurried to the intersection of that busy city. *Ah,* Roger thought. *He's a panhandler. He's not quite as bad off as I am, but pretty close.* It was then that something told Roger to go get that man something from Starbucks. So without another further adieu, Roger briefly departed that veranda and went back inside to the counter and ordered another white chocolate mocha and a sandwich, the exact duplicate of the order he had. He made his way to the intersection where the man was standing, handing the order to him. "Here, sir," Roger said. "I got you a Starbucks treat."

The homeless man looked at him for a brief second and lit a Swisher Sweet, an old stogie that would have made Fidel Castro proud, and then had a wild look in his green eyes that yet again was a dead ringer for Manson's mug shot. "Thanks, and bless you," he rasped, and as Roger was turning to walk away, he started speaking yet again.

"I know who you are…my father was a Pentecostal preacher, and my mother believed in reincarnation. I just want to tell you, sir, that I know you are headed on the road to perdition, but there's still time, sir. There's still time…."

The man was baring his soul, and in the process had exposed Roger's innermost being as well, but as he was standing in the gutter of that intersection, he was bereft, and his only reply was, "Well, I don't know what you mean, but enjoy your sandwich…"

Without skipping a beat, the drifter said, "You know what I mean, man. You know. You all know. Yes, thanks for the food, but you know. For you to change your ways, that would be the pleasure to end all pleasures."

"Yeah, some German guy said that," Roger muttered as he headed back to the terrace. He ultimately settled for enjoying his sandwich and enjoying the fact that the Millennial baristas were totally ignorant to what he truly was. To them, he was just another customer, simple as that. The bum continued to panhandle, oblivious to the fact that he had said anything to him at all. *Was it just a brief moment of clarity for him?* Roger wondered. And as he sat there on that veranda finishing up the remnants of his meal, he stared off in the distance at his van. He thought about the cache of weapons in that nondescript vehicle, a supply that would make any revolutionary proud. He gazed at the homeless guy who continued to stand at the intersection, and then he looked back at his van in the nearby Walmart parking lot in the middle of all of the family shoppers.

"You know," he said to himself, "he's right. I could turn back. There's still time...." but then he immediately thought yet again about the array he had in his van. A smile creased across his lips as he thought about what he was going to do to his captive, and the fact that they were going to be afraid and in terror made other members on his body began to respond as well. He had to get even, homeless guy is damned, and he knew his name really wasn't Roger. It was Kurten. It was Lawrence Singleton. It was Ted Bundy. It was BTK. It was the Zodiac, and it was Gary Ridgway all rolled into one.

His resolve continued, and he was now the Red Baron streaking out on the evil German sky. He had to keep going. His mission was retribution, and he knew that those that were going through their day-to-day lives, discussing their sports teams with the gaudy colors of overseas soccer or the flashy logos of the NFL on ESPN, talking about politics over beers at a backward bar in the steakhouse, or having their backyard barbeques where they entertained other white picket fence owners were going to realize who he was. He was going to be famous, made that way by some twenty-something crime aficionado, some YouTube personality. The pleasure of all pleasures for him was to destroy a life the way his had been destroyed. With that, his eyes blinked and he was back to that prison industrial complex and the last time he ever saw his final cellmate...

Lloyd spat on the ground as he yet again thought of Sergeant Gomes. As a small-town police chief, usually the biggest issue he encountered was teenagers hot-rodding or simply just dealing with weirdos such as that Art kid. There had been an influx of illegals in the town about a decade prior, and they had brought the drugs with them. *Lord knows,* Lloyd thought, *I had to lobby half to death to be able to get Sammy, and then Sammy Jr., the drug dogs on the force, but I was able to do it.*

Speaking of Art...Lloyd's head jerked up as he saw that familiar glint in the window of his office, telling him that yet again the kid was riding by on that dumbass bike of his ad nauseum. He hated the kid just like he hated his soon-to-be-ex-wife, and just thinking about that annoying 30-something brat and that crazy dad of his made him mad.

He went to the security closet and fished out his keys to the safe, looking for those Hustlers yet again. He needed to get off, and Larry Flynt would be so proud. Although he was normally conservative, thank god that his mistress was liberal and not some churchie like his ex-wife. It brought some brief satisfaction, but again he had to put them back in their hiding place and go back to being Chief Lloyd, law-and-order guy and pillar of the community.

He knew that only the strongest would survive, and he knew that his mistress was his only refuge, his very reason for toiling in this moronic small-town police chief job. *Just a few more years of this monotony and torture*, he mused. *Just a few more years, and I will be in a mountain cabin somewhere with her, and we'll have some mini-me running around and I'll be the child-rearing father all over again, but this time I can collect my police pension. I'll be out of my own personal dystopia. Just give it time.*

His cell phone vibrated with a cheerful jingle, breaking him out of his revelry. Lo and behold, it was his favorite person, he thought sarcastically. The sergeant was calling yet again.

"Yeah?" he uttered as he held the cellphone up to his ear. "This is Sergeant Gomes," came the response. "Chief Lloyd, we have another problem out at that lake. There's been another homicide, so get out here as soon as you can."

Thankfully, even though his head was spinning with just what could possibly be the issue at the lake this time…*another body? For the love of God, no!*…the drive out to the lake for Chief Lloyd was largely uneventful. As he parked his squad car, he crossed himself across his heart and chest even though he hadn't been to Mass in well over three decades. Then he stepped outside to confer with Sergeant Gomes, who was right there, prototypically barking orders and yet waiting for him at the same time. He held out his hand, but Gomes didn't take it, probably because he was still bitter about his snarky comment. Chief Lloyd ignored it. "Gomes, what's going on now?"

The Fed simply stared at the weeds immersed within the lake. "Well, unfortunately, it's another body, Chief." He angled his head over to one side. "Here, let me direct you to the crime scene..."

Lloyd glanced in the direction that Gomes was pointing, and he immediately had a brief lip compression that quickly made a morbid evolution into all-out quivering. He knew those tell-tale tan hiking boots anywhere, and it was only a second later that the wind from that day's cold-front picked up, briefly blowing the tarp partially off the corpse. The red of that baseball cap was also present, and suddenly he knew who the victim was...

"Chief? Chief?" Gomes snapped, and Lloyd was back in reality with a jolt. The sergeant's piercing eyes met his, and Lloyd couldn't help but flinch. "You know this one too, don't you?"

Lloyd stepped back, momentarily dazed. "I-I....I do."

Gomes cleared his throat. "Go on, chief. Go on."

"I would know that ball cap anywhere," Lloyd replied with halted breath. "He was an avid Niners fan, and it used to drive me crazy. Worked at the local forest service here, was an avid bird scientist, or something like that."

Gomes frowned but continued to glance at the tarp covering the body.

"You mean he was an ornithologist?"

"Yeah, Gomes," Lloyd replied. "One of those, for sure."

The state sergeant met his gaze yet again.

"Married?"

"Well, no, not really....he was one of those queers...."

Gomes visibly flinched and didn't skip a beat.

"Oh brother, here we go again, chief," and the last part of his voice was raised in a mocking ire. "He was homosexual or gay! Boy, you are bigoted. Keep these comments to yourself or I'm going to have to file a complaint, chief...."

Chief Lloyd ignored it.

"Okay, yeah, he was homosexual."

Gomes' demeanor softened somewhat.

"Boyfriends? Husbands?"

"Well, yeah, he's had a few over the years. Not any that I knew of at the present moment."

"Well," Gomes replied. "That's good to know. We're still analyzing the body and the cause of death, but it looks like he might have been hit with a blunt object or something. Did that Arthur kid know this guy?"

"Not really. I think he was helping his mom clean the office building he worked at once upon a time, but I've never seen them hanging out or anything."

"All right. Thanks, chief. We'll keep you posted, and for the love of god, keep your mouth shut when you are talking to me or anyone else. This isn't the 70s anymore, so knock it off."

The words stung, and on the way home, Lloyd was fuming. *Who did he think he was?* Yet again, he had demeaned him, and he frowned, the nerves in his mouth tingling as his blood pressure was surely shooting up. He had to do something. He had to get even and show him this was his case, not his. What to do? He would have to sleep on it...

The Honeymoon Effect was still in full force for Arthur, albeit with a twinge of anxiety. He had been debating whether to tell his new love interest about this encounter with the newest example of Bakersfield's Finest, but he had ultimately decided against it. *No sense stressing her out,* he thought. She was such a pleasant creature, and something brand new, shimmering just like peering at a museum-quality diamond that had been worn by royalty throughout the ages. He felt like he was in a daze, but it wasn't alcohol-induced at all.

He couldn't get any writing work done because all he was thinking about was this wonderful person called Marilyn. Throughout that day after their second date, he kept watching the music video to "Arthur's Theme" repeatedly, and just like Dudley Moore's character, he felt like his life was beginning anew all over again. He had been named after the character, and that cocoon had opened up, and there was a colorful butterfly. The eggs in the tree had braved the wind, ice, and the jagged brown branches, but it hatched, and he was now a colorful robin ready to spread his wings, taking flight throughout the skies.

He wasn't mad at the Bearcat any longer. Frankly, he wasn't mad at anything for those couple of days after she had gone back home. They talked for hours and hours on the phone, and he just wasn't angry. He wasn't angry until he encountered the deputy sheriff yet again...

He was on the veranda over by the town city hall. Like everything else, the whole block had seen better days, a microcosm of the general spirit of the town. He peered over at the patio that belonged to the neighboring donut shop, and that's when he spotted him. Clarence, or "Slim" was sitting there, munching on what appeared to be a glazed maple frosted offering, and he sat bolt upright in his chair when he met Art's gaze.

Slim frowned as he got up from his seat, finishing what was left of his donut in one swallow, and left that donut establishment, the prototypical bell ringing as the door shut behind him. Once Slim caught where Art was sitting, his eyes locked right on him, focusing on him like a laser, and Art knew almost immediately he was headed straight toward him. He saw the holster on his hip, and he kept peering at the new law enforcement officer's arm. It didn't move toward the gun, thank god, but it was nothing short of a miracle. Art didn't retrieve a breath for a full ten seconds until Slim was standing right in front of him, not more than six feet away.

"You know, Art," he started with an intimidating snarl. "I was in farming and ranching before I started this new gig in law enforcement. The two are pretty similar. I used to eyeball the pigs before I stunned them, getting ready to slaughter them. You gotta distract them. You gotta distract them real well, kiddo."

Art didn't say a word, but his eyes remained focused on the floor, avoiding the searing gaze of the newly-minted sheriff's deputy, and all the while his heart was pounding. In the next instant, his eyes flinched with resolve, and he knew he had to do his level-best to come up with a witty retort.

"So, I heard you go by Slim, or is it, Clarence?" Art said sardonically, rolling his eyes. The newly-minted sheriff deputy flinched, and Art knew he was raising his ire. "What is that? Is that kind of like Eminem's The Real Slim Shady, or what?"

Slim didn't skip a beat. "Well, well, well, asshole. If it isn't Johnny Carson raised from the dead! No, Arthur, or should I say, Dahmer, Jeffrey Dahmer? Just a nickname, my lovely soon-to-be felon friend...just a nickname."

Just before the deputy turned around and walked away, his hands raised up two fingers to his eyes and pointed back to Arthur, and sneered at him. "I'll catch you on the flip-side."

Roger found himself staring into the most mesmerizing eyes that he had ever seen. They were the deepest hue of blue, and they almost enveloped him like a long-lost lover, a ten-year-old lover, but still. The child was nameless, and he was just fiddling around with a stick on a nondescript park swing. Those innocent eyes stared at him, looking right through him. "What do you want to do now, Mr. Roger?" the child asked. Roger flinched, wanting to tell him of the hideous and colossal plans that he had for him. But before he uttered a sound, he woke up with a start, and he was recounting everything again; he was back in that grayish slab he called his home, back in his cell bunk, with his inmate snoring loudly.

Peering at the grotesque, foreign and alien walls, the next thing that Roger was cognizant of would be that silence. He quickly realized that he no longer heard the snoring from his now-silent cellie, and he momentarily flinched before he sprang into action. He checked his pulse. Nothing. He uttered his name. Nothing. He literally yelled his name. Nothing. The man was not breathing at all, and suddenly a breeze fluttered by, yet again an indication that he was no more. His brother-in-arms, his purveyor of this disgusting fetish that they both shared, he was dead. He knew it, but still he yelled at the top of his lungs, "Can anyone help me? Can someone please, please help me?"

He seemed to be yelling those desperate pleas for an eternity before a guard finally responded.

"What?" he snarled at Roger. "What do you need?" Roger drew a labored, tense breath. "I think my cellie is dead."

The twenty-something blond guard just glared at him. "Well, don't get your panties in a twist, nancy boy. We'll get to it as soon as we get done with morning chow."

And that was the last time that he had seen his cellie, and indeed, about the last time he had seen almost anyone. That very next week, he went up for parole, and surprise, surprise, he snowballed the liberal philosophy major-turned-butch-lesbian-parole-officer enough to demonstrate "rehabilitation" and soon enough he was out of that hell-hole called the Prison Industrial Complex. But as Roger was back in the present-day and driving in his van down the highway with the lines turned into dots, rhythmically passing under his van's motor, he knew the memories wouldn't stop. And they never had. And he was mad at the world. And he always would be until someone paid. And that's why he was on his mission to hell. Not his, mind you, but someone else's.

"He's in a better place now," Roger said in the air of the ancient van, hearing the bagpipes playing in his head. "I'm not, but he is. He's a spirit, and I'm a demon." It was just about that instant that the radio began turning in and out, like it had taken on a mind of its own, and it seemed to settle on KLOVE, that ever-present radio station that the churchies all loved.

Eerily, it was playing the Doxology, that tune that was first composed by an English cleric that would ultimately go through his own personal hell in the Tower of London. Roger couldn't help but laugh scornfully at the thought, not to mention the fact that it was being sung by someone who worked for thatJoel Osteen. It did, however, remind him of the first time that he had been on the outside in years, when he had decided it was time to take his evil demeanor to the nearest church himself....

Lloyd smirked as the glare in his cruiser started to get more intense and started to bounce off the steering wheel. He was sitting in his favorite parking lot of Bakersfield and watching the town wake up yet again, and the morning sun had broken through the clouds enough that it would have even made Cat Stevens proud. *God's creation indeed,* he thought with scorn, but it couldn't ruin his jovial mood. Besides catching up with his war buddy Slim, he finally realized there was a way to claim he had enough to take that Art kid in for questioning.

Gotta love that Slim and his aggressive stance on him, he thought. He was going to be the hero, and he was no longer going to be the disgruntled middle-aged small-town police chief nearing retirement that everyone loved to hate. He even had the stress-related receding hairline to prove it! He was going to solve this murder case and get everyone to come back to him. He was going to get his wife to come crawling back, and he was going to laugh and say, "Oh really, now you want me back? Really, well, remember that dispatcher? She's much better in the sack then you could ever be...!" and slam the door in her face. And that Slim deputy was going to help him do that. He just knew it. Boy, he's going to fit in real nicely. His last meeting with his new colleague went really well indeed...

Slim had first of all taken a drink of his coffee, which was totally black without any cream whatsoever. Then he quietly uttered those words in that coffee shop in order to avoid eavesdroppers.

"Well, Chief Lloyd, you know there are ways to get to that kid, even if you aren't quite there on the evidence..." Lloyd looked up from his drab Reader's Digest article and his expression was one of intrigue. He had an idea where he was going with this, but his only reply to his newly-minted colleague was, "Go on..."

"Well, we've got two problems here..." his voice trailed off as the waitress brought him his BLT. "First, you hate this Art kid, and I don't blame you. He's a total moron, and he's got that weird look in his eye. Secondly, we have this bastard out there at the lake killing people, and we need to get that person off the streets. People are starting to lock their doors, stare at other people, and get mistrustful. But now that Park Ranger guy is the latest victim, and that Art kid knew him." Almost as if on cue, an older farming gentleman savoring his iced tea began glaring at them.

"Okay..." the Chief said, ignoring the old farmer, with his voice dragging out and hoping that his newly-respected co-worker would cut to the chase.

Slim cleared his throat. "Well, Chief, we're close, we're really close. We just need that little nudge to get us over the finish line, if you know what I mean."

Lloyd peered down at his Reader's Digest yet again. "Really…"

"Yes, really," and Slim's voice got lower, almost to a whisper. "If you don't have any evidence, just make up some."

Lloyd smirked, and it was all he could do to keep from laughing. "Got you."

He was getting that itch again, so it was time for him to sneak out to that lake once more. He headed out his front door, the keys to his old man's vehicle jingling on his belt loop surreptitiously. The drive down to German Shepherd Lake was largely uneventful, and the reservoir looked nondescript as the slightest breeze blew a wave through the waters.

He was there for about thirty minutes and he didn't think that his hunt was going to pan out, and that's when he saw the fabric on the ground on the other side of the lake, complete with a picnic basket, a woman alone, the whole nine yards. It couldn't have been more perfect. He began intently sizing up the scene…no kids, no significant other to be her knight in shining armor…yep, just about perfect, and it was time for him to make his approach. He made his way to where she was sitting, kicking the rocks and dirt along the way mercilessly. She didn't even notice him until he was maybe about twenty yards away, and that is when she first looked up. She appeared to be studying something, and as he got closer, he realized that she was holding a magnifying glass in her hands. She looked up, and bereft of a greeting, she simply smiled and said, "Oh, didn't see you there!"

That's when he saw all of the pennies on her fabric, and it was then that he knew what the magnifying glass was for. He smiled in spite of himself, hiding the death struggle that was behind his blue eyes. "Are you a collector?" were the first words uttered out of his lips. She smiled right back, showing some of her crooked teeth that had seen better days, the sun playing off of it with a gleam, and so despite it all, he knew she must be the epitome of innocence.

"I sure am. Been looking at my pocket change since I was 12, since my grandfather passed."

Once again, he smiled, but this time even more in spite of himself. He hated this Coin Lady, and he hated everything she stood for. It was time for the next phase of his plan. "Do you like to swim?" he asked with that 1000-watt fake smirk on full display.

"Sort of. I'm mainly just enjoying the day, if you know what I mean."

No, no, he didn't know what she meant. He started looking around for a car but didn't see one except for his father's. "Well, how did you get here, honey?"

"I walked."

Oh, I see.

"You were dropped off?"

She looked down, and it wasn't because she was searching for Wheat pennies. Resignation on her face.

"Well, yeah, a trucker. He dropped me off."

Oh. Interesting….

"Yeah," she continued. "When I'm not looking at coins, I guess I'm standing at the nearest intersection caddy-corner from your friendly neighborhood truck stop…" her voice trailed off.

"Well," he said, "I don't suppose it has to be that way. I could give you a ride if you like…" Undersell. Always undersell. The sun yet again glinted off her teeth and the water at the same time, with the breeze gently rippling through yet again. He saw the brief flash on her face, a look of uncertainty, but it vanished just as quick as that sunny glint.

"Well," she replied in a New Orleans accent, encouraging him even more. "Can't say that I know you."

He stuck out his hand. "Name's Doug," he lied. "Now, I guess we know each other."

She began laughing, culminating in a middle-aged snort that belied what was left of her looks. "You're funny."

Oh, really? Well, you will see how funny I am here in just a little bit, darling.

He went ahead and cut to the chase.

"Do you want a ride or not?"

"Yeah, I guess so. I'll go ahead," she responded coyly and started packing up her stuff.

His car was overlooking the cliffs, and no one happening on the scene would be able to see anything very easily. It didn't take him very long, not very long at all. She was different than the others. She was different than the gay guy, who put up quite a fight. The bruises on his side were definitely testament to that. But no, this one seemed to get that look of recognition yet again, but it was already too late for her. He had his hands clenched around his would-be numismatist friend's throat intently and was going in for the kill. She merely gasped, and soon enough, that was that.

"Job well done, buddy," he said to no one in particular, placing the body back at her picnic location. He made it back to his father's car and didn't think much of it because he already had a girlfriend. C'est la vie, and all that sort of thing. He had some errands to run when he made it back to town, and the miles flew by, just like he was the angel and not his coin-collecting friend he had just encountered. Time to send another letter to Chief Bridges, and one of those self-adhesive envelopes would do very well for his purposes. With his adhesive gloves in tow, he wrote a lovely note to the bitter, embattled police chief, which read:

Oh, you had better steer clear of me,
    Oh, you had better watch your back
    For I'm completely bastardly

Oh, you had better be careful,
    Oh, I'm ugly and fearful,
    For I'm totally dastardly

. . .

Oh, they are going to cry,
   and they are going to scream,
   but not to worry
   I will set them free
   For that's what a little bird told me.

So chief? Do you like my little words of whit?
   Are you any closer to finding me?
   No?
   That's what I thought. I'm going to walk free.

~

It was a good thing that he was alone in that largely vacant small-town post office because Chief Lloyd screamed bloody murder and made a dent in the wall after slugging it when he read the note. He had to hold the envelope carefully after that, because the blood was pooling on his knuckles rather intently, leaving a dripping trail on the floor as he walked. Could they dust the envelope for fingerprints? Probably, but he wasn't sure what good it would do. Either way, into the evidence locker it would go. Was he any closer to catching this guy? No, and he swore under his breath. It wasn't so much that he cared about the victims, no, nothing like that. As a cynical smile escaped his lips, it was more that he wanted all the glory to himself. Why the hell should he share it with a fed? Why be treated like an underling? Angrily, he went back to his small police office and told his underlings that he was calling off for the rest of the day, to hell with all of the hot-rodding teenagers or the town wife beaters or druggies. He made it home and got into his personal vehicle and went to the neighboring town. There was just no getting around it. He needed some whiskey.

~

The crowning moment of Roger's life post-incarceration (besides getting his driver's license) was something very simple, something that even some of his 6-year-old would-be paramours would relish: he got his first library card. His church scheme hadn't panned out for him, but yet again, c'est la vie. He wondered what that aging Baby Boomer with the whitish hair and matching dentures who was tasked with greeting visitors and who had shaken his hand would think of him now if they knew. If they only knew who he truly was and how the fact that he had AC/DC's "Hells Bells" blaring from his library-issued headphones and that was the least of his sins, microscopic and a microcosm all at the same time.

The afternoon sun glinted in that library, and he briefly reflected on that ultra-friendly bearded hippie that ran the information desk and was so committed to answering everyone's questions and making sure everyone had a good time. Put him in a different setting, and boy howdy, he would have made a good bartender. Well, he had a question for him and a question that he had for himself: should I off myself? Wouldn't it be better for everyone since I am the lowest of the low?

But just as soon as he had that thought, the angels up above must have been smirking or even laughing out loud, because the auto-repeat on his brand-spanking-new YouTube account went to "Alive and Kicking" by Simple Minds. And in the quiet of that library, Roger too laughed in spite of himself, and somewhere a woman who could have been a dead-ringer for one of those old-time Catholic nuns complete with full habit and all was giving him a death stare for violating the sanctity of that cherished library, but yet again, that was a microcosm.

Getting drunk, Roger mused. That was his next order of business as a free man. Well, technically, his next order of business was to go to that drafty library bathroom for his wank without being babysat by Uncle Sam. It didn't take him long. It didn't take him long at all, and then soon enough he was eyeballing the fruits of his dalliance on the methyl flooring of that library floor, which must have been installed in the past year or so, considering that he had seen ads for it on the billboards as he drove over there in his borrowed fleabag car.

"Lasts forever!" the billboard read, but not nearly as long as that jizz that was now splayed across a few precious inches of it.

He gawked at that paradoxical white sludge, something that would normally end up in a roll of bounty or crappy toilet paper and tossed away from the freckled hands of a nervous 13-year-old boy in the grip of puberty thinking about the skirt from the upperclassmen or the centerfold that he had stolen from his drunken uncle.

Oh well, at least he had a better drunken uncle. What could he say? It was paradoxical indeed, and even though he was enjoying being out and about and meeting new people, for once he was appreciative of being alone in that largely-abandoned upstairs bathroom.

"This," he mused aloud, "is the cradle of civilization." It wasn't some fictitious Garden of Eden near the Tigris and Euphrates in Mesopotamia. This, and this alone, is what allowed people to "be fruitful and multiply." This sludge was not in the midst of favoritism. It could give rise to Catherine the Great just as much as it could give rise to Hitler. It could give rise to first responders, but it also could give rise to people like him. Men were relegated to this simple act, and everything else was secondary.

Look at the situation a hundred years ago...everyone needs extra farmhands, eh? And in his case, everyone needs their next sex toy, but he couldn't gawk at the children's wing of the library, now could he? Oh no, too obvious. Back down at the desktop computers, with his cheapjack phone (was it called Straight Talk or Straight Jacket, he wasn't sure) mocking him and laying by the mouse, he was certain that the days of nondescript, paying-you-no-mind, meh looks from onlookers were about to end, and soon the death stares would start.

Let the games begin, Roger mused. *Let the games begin after I go in a month or so and register at this county detention center to get my picture taken by some single mother with a badge and a feather up her derriere hiding her painkiller addiction and her earlier addiction to student loans from her psychology degree at a community college up state.* Metallica's Whiskey in the Jar was blaring from his headphones, and he grabbed his pawn shop jacket and thought, "my sentiments exactly." As he fired up the engine from his borrowed car, the birds were up above, not paying him any mind whatsoever.

~

"What will it be this time, Art?" the trucker barmaid turned-liquor saleswoman said to him from the county liquor store. "I guess some more, Cutty Sark," he said to the shriveled-up old biker chick. "I must be a mind-reader," she guffawed, inadvertently showing up off her missing palate. He rang him up, and as he was headed out the door, the Biker lady with enough bags under her eyes to hang blinds off of apparently must have had a moment of clarity, because she looked up from her incessant Far Side comic collection and said, "Art?"

"Yes?" he turned around.

"This really isn't you, you know that, right?" as she held up another example of the Cutty Sark merchandise.

With resignation plastered over his face, Art said, "I know," and with the space-age sound of the door shutting, he was out in the all-too-small world yet again. He trotted with his prize back home, and yet again he had the house all to himself, but it was just as cluttered as ever.

He took a sip of the booze, placing it in his "hidey-hole" downstairs, which was nothing more than an ancient oak dresser with one of the top panels missing, but it laid very nicely on its side in the rear of the drawer as a respite for later. Unfortunately for him, later was only after about thirty minutes. He didn't know why he needed to walk so much. When his mother was still well - his open-minded, progressive mother with that glitzy, reddish department store hair that got everywhere when you tried to put it on and made everyone laugh - would just laugh off his habits and simply say, "Well, he sorts things out when he walks..." and that was true.

How could he know that everyone else would think it was an eyesore, just like the spilled paint on a museum-quality Mahal rag from those brutal Muslim territories. Not the cheap, mass-produced outsourced Walmart kind, mind you, but the kind that you would have a panic attack and wipe the stain off immediately. As he poured that first drink of that burning Cutty Sark, how was he supposed to know that he was indeed the sideshow freak?

One drink ended up leading to three, and then tree to five, and then finally, five led to seven, and he sat in the recliner of that house was so many memories, and he clicked on the Samsung TV. It was Bernie Sanders again, because it was turned to that CNN station that mom constantly watched, yet another reminder of the change that he was never ready for.

He was ranting on about the "Fight for $15" or some drivel like that, something where the fast-food workers and other menial job people should get paid a living wage. *Nobel concept,* Art thought, blinking back the haze of his severe boozefest, *but hard to put into practice.* And he was a writer, and he was jealous of these fast-food workers, finding their valuables just from metal detecting on a beach while he was moving heaven and earth for even $9 per hour.

But as the haze overtook him, he found himself standing at the top of a gigantic cliff at that lake the whole town had been talking about lately, the one where all the bodies had been showing up, and as he got closer to the edge and saw the waves crashing onto the shore, there was the mildest of taps on his back. It was Slim, that newest police recruit making such a splash. He was wearing a dark trench coat that would even make Marilyn Manson pause, and he stepped back, mocking him. "You know, Art, people love a good whodunit, even if its in real life. I'm coming for you," he laughed uproariously. "I'm coming for you..." and suddenly, it was all void yet again.

Popcorn. Roger munched on it gladly, even though it would probably damage what was left of his teeth from that second-rate dentistry he had received while he was in the slammer. It settled in his stomach, protecting him from the booze and keeping it from churning up a whirl-wind in his guts. He was quickly discovering that he was more than a bit behind the times as he was watching "The Birds" by Alfred Hitchcock.

He had signed up for some kind of mail-order DVD service called Netflix, even though you could download them right on a laptop. A laptop though.... what's that? He wasn't allowed to have it yet. But he recalled watching the Birds with - who else - Uncle George, and it was one of those solid black VHS tapes that always seemed to be getting stuck in his VCR, a machine that now even pawn shops or Goodwill wouldn't consider taking.

Just like this second-rate DVD player that he had picked up at the pawn shop, but for now it was serving his purpose. The year had been 1963 when the Birds had come out, the same year that JFK's brains had splattered all over that Lincoln in Dealey Plaza. The same year that the Beatles were prepping for the magnetism of the British Invasion, and the same time that actors such as Andy Griffith and Jim Nabors were gracing everyone's television sets; those big, artistic monstrosities with a small screen and the art-deco design surrounding it.

You should have seen it in color. You should have seen it in color, indeed...but not on those old televisions! It was also the year that he came into the world, and the year that his father ran off, and the year that his drunken mother needed help raising him. Who else did she turn to but Uncle George? Egad, he wondered how many diapers that man had changed, those cloth kinds with the Velcro that would make that maddening scratching noise like fingers dragging across a chalkboard. That's the one his ma had to get because the Pampers were too expensive.

"He changed my diapers, and then when he was older, the bastard changed me!" he yelled to no one in particular, since he was a perv and was now left to his own devices. He tried the best he could to get that out of his mind and just enjoy the show. He wasn't a freak yet until he reported to his parole officer again and when he smiled his biggest forced smile at the nearest sheriff's office. He had been out a month, and he had enjoyed the anonymity, but like everything else, it was going to change soon. Commence the dirty looks, the stares, and the whispering, all here in just a few days, starting on Monday.

CHAPTER 8

"You know, this chain of evil has got to stop, you sumbitch, whoever you are, you sumbitch!" Chief Lloyd drawled in his alcoholic slur as he stared down some of his cans of Monster and Red Bull sitting on his favorite off-duty spot, that of those welcoming fence-posts. Gomes had contacted him yet again, and he told him about the newest victim, and he saw it with his own eyes, along with these odd wheat pennies littering the scene, something that fed Gomes would later insist should go into evidence.

He hadn't told Gomes about the letter yet. Whoever it was, they were smart not to toy with a CBI guy. That made eight bodies now, and neither him, nor Gomes, nor Slim, nor anybody else on staff was any closer to solving the mystery than when the body count had started, and judging from the dirty looks and stares that the townspeople were giving each other, they knew it too. He was even having people approaching him now.

"Any word, Chief?" one prototypical Southern housewife with a baby on her hip and another toddler in tow asked him. And he had to say with resignation that the answer was no. Several others had followed suit. That lake. That lake was where friendships had been made, where friendships had been lost, where relationships had been started, and where people had lost their virginity under a sea of stars, just two teenage ants on a blanket sharing and venting their passion on each other on this little flyspeck that they all called home. It was their secret to keep, usually from their parents, unless, of course, their act resulted in an expectant mother, which sometimes it certainly did.

But that quilt of stars was no longer comforting, and it was no longer lulling these teenage Romeos and Juliets to sleep after they finally wore down from their escapades. The blankets were no longer giving life, but it was a noose around someone's neck, cutting off their air and encircling their throat with the terror of a life being cut short. But for now, only the stars knew who the culprit was, and that's why he topped off another sip of his Jack Daniels in spite of himself. Under those same stars, someone was stalking that lake, and for the life of him, he couldn't tell who. Why couldn't he be the hero, just like his old man was? Why couldn't he be the hero for this town? He had to turn this over. For his own sanity, he had to turn this over. He knew that some of the drug enforcement agencies were looking for help further upstate.

He needed to knock it off and let Gomes handle this case. He was the fed, after all. He could go with Eliza to the mountains, take that drug desk job, and then coast until early retirement. He would have that early police pension and have some mini-me riding a tricycle with a white picket fence in the background in no time flat. If only it were that easy. Eliza had to work the night shift yet again, and he was always real good about keeping his job at the office. He had a full liquor cabinet in his home study, and he kept the demons at bay that way, by having a few shots on his ancient oak desk. Surely, tonight would be the same…

There was that glaring sidewalk again, and there was that ancient high school where Arthur was on the marquee in the inside lobby. Except this time, the only thing he could be sure of was the throbbing in his skull. That, and the stinging upon his chin. He reached his arm up to feel up, and it took all of the strength he could muster, the neurons firing off throughout his brain and making the pain receptor increase ten-fold.

The involuntary groan and the drool from Arthur's mouth were only capped off by the slimy red gash now perched ominously on his chin. He must have stumbled, and that was that. How he made it four blocks to the high school was another matter, but luckily it was the weekend. The street past the long sidewalk was vacant, and by a stroke of further good fortune no vehicles full of busybodies had passed by while he was there.

By some miracle, he staggered to his feet, and that was when he noticed the red solo cups at the edge of the sidewalk, about fifty yards away. There were four of them, just littering the ground, probably reeking of beer from the latest teen football tailgate party. They seared his eyes, and it was amazing that he could even see it standing from the line of demarcation on this horribly long sidewalk. It was indeed the devilish inspiration for his hangover cure, and he was ready to go with his tried-and-true epiphany: the best cure for a hangover caused by alcohol was more alcohol.

As he was headed that way, he glanced into the clearing with the rows of upper middle-class houses gracing the avenue, and that is when he saw him once more. It was Slim in his trench coat yet again, and he blinked, trying to fight off what had to be an obvious hallucination.

Slim had a smile that would have made the Joker in Batman proud. "I know you were out there, Arthur," he said in an ungodly echo that pierced the unnatural quiet, with blood red eyes giving him a deadly stare. "I know you were there. I know you were at that lake." But Arthur was still telling himself, "it's just the booze, just the booze, this is not real..." and he blinked yet again, and the apparition was gone. Drama, he thought. Too much drama. And he continued his walk to the liquor store for the second time in two days.

What was the context? Was there even a context at all? Arthur didn't think that there was, but at the same time, he knew that he was the context, simply because he was the one looking at his life through his own eyes. He should be able to live it on his own terms, even though it meant he was going to be self-destructive. The door opened with the prototypical jingling sound, and it was that same trucker barmaid manning the registers yet again. "Back so soon, Arthur?" she said without looking up from her comics, and he could still feel the resignation and disappointment in her voice. "Yep, I guess so. I'll take Jack Daniels this time. A fifth of it, please." With the transaction done, he was back out in the cold world again as the breeze assaulted his five o'clock shadow, and he got ready to make the long trek home.

It was now a windy and rainy day, and he protected the liquor in its prototypical brown paper bag just like a mother would protect her first-born son. The first two blocks of the walk home were largely uneventful, as the shadow that would be his assailants appeared to slither back into the background. His mind was drawn like a moth to the flame back to that newest example of Bakersfield's finest, Slim. He would show some disapproval to him, with fingers wagging no doubt, if he saw him at that very moment carrying the booze, just like Dan Marino protecting the football from being fumbled when he had been playing his Broncos when he was a kid.

He knew every nook and cranny of that old town, and he knew all of the hidden secrets and ways to escape. Several times during that walk home, there were allies that he could have meandered down, and he did consider it. It would be so easy to do it and take a quick little swig of his booze prize, but he didn't. For about a half-dozen times, he didn't. The last temptation was about a few blocks from his house, and the urge was overwhelming, but what if that Slim guy was hiding behind a dumpster? What if he was just itching to give him a public intoxication charge? Best for him to save it for his hidden compartment back home, since it was just a few blocks. He did the arithmetic in his head....just a few more alleyways to pass.

His heart skipped a beat each time he caught sight of that yellow gravel road where the waste management trucks would drive through every Monday, and he knew in a way it would be easier. Just chug the living tar out of that bottle, throw out what he didn't drink, and off to la-la land he would go. Out of sight, out of mind. He wouldn't have to worry about his sisters snooping through his stuff when they were (rarely) there, checking up on his old man. So simple, yet so complex.

He made it to that dull brown doorway and heavy wooden door protected by the outer storm door that he had literally walked through millions of times before throughout his childhood without incident. The house was as he had left it, and yet again no one was there except for him, his liquor treasure, and his thoughts, the incessant chirping of that ancient police scanner continuing to be an uninvited guest. He knew he should still do something about that useless scanner, but not right now. Down the planked basement stairs he went, also something he had done for literally decades, since his mid-teens.

He wasn't happy about it, and he wasn't sad about it. It just is, he knew, with "is" being a noun in that case. Oh well, at least he was carrying his ghastly coping mechanism in that brown paper sack, which he placed on the top of his closet straight away. He raised the Jack Daniels up to take the first swing, but in that instant he saw Slim stretched out on his bed, invading his space, with a shit-eating smirk on his face, almost daring him to do it. He blinked, and the apparition was gone, a vapor arising like steam from the canopy. He raised the glass yet again, but his trembling hands betrayed him, and yet again he put the bottle down. As the throbbing in his skull persisted, it would be there for later, and that's all he knew.

Retribution. Roger knew it was time to fire up old Dudley-Do-Right yet again, which was his name for his trusty DVD player, his only friend in the world other than his crotch. Dudley Do-Right's mouth opened up with a satisfying whir! And he popped in another favorite from his prior days of freedom before becoming a pariah. No, there wasn't any question he was going to watch the full movie, but he skipped to his favorite scene: The private with the hideous shark eyes called his friend "Joker" in the latrines of the battalion in the middle of the night, which was their name for the bullying drill sergeant. You could hear a pin drop as his companion nervously asked him if those were live rounds, and it didn't take long before the private shot the drill instructor and himself, because surprise! surprise! he was in a world of shit. So was Roger, and all he had was one day left. One day before he had to go register, one day before he had to go listen to a court-appointed psychologist talk about how he was society's stain on a priceless Persian rug.

His whole life was a live round. The movies allowed him to get lost in his own world, one where the whispers would stop and where someone else was the victim and taking it out on others. Movies were his narcissistic playground, and that's all there was to it.

"Thank god that damned dollar store still sells these things," he said due to the fact that he had polished off the movie in no time flat, even relishing his favorite part where the Asian female sniper was on the ground in that far-off jungle being terrorized and praying in that far-off language. The only words she knew in English were "shoot me" which was dragged out in a terrified tone, one that only matched the terror that was in her eyes, darting back and forth. But she was a sniper, Roger knew, so she was getting what was coming to her.

A microcosm of society. But alas, he now had to go and fire up that ancient van and go get another one because he couldn't afford a laptop or internet access. Thus he couldn't afford Netflix. Either way, it was better than the psychosomatic acids churning away in his stomach, thinking about how degrading tomorrow would be. The day went by way too fast, and it wasn't long before he heard a distant beeping noise emanating from the darkness, but he couldn't understand what it was.

"Sir?" he said. "Sir! Would you like to go off in the woods and play with me?" the little boy who could have been a dead-ringer for Macaulay Culkin said to him, but all the while, the distant beeping was still present. He was about to respond to the young charmer's gratuitous offer, but then he awoke in a cold sweat on a soaking wet mattress, the sunlight streaming through the blinds of his second-rate apartment. Time to start the day, and he grimaced and groaned.

At the intake office, the male receptionist seemed to be about as interested in the task as he was. "Name and date of birth, please...." he repeated in a nasal, homosexual voice.

"Cisneros, Roger," he began. "October 1, 1969." It was then that the receptionist finally looked up with raised eyebrows to boot.

"Really?" he said. "You don't look Hispanic...?"

Roger briefly glared at the man, and as far as he was concerned, he was every bit as much a police officer as the rest of them. If he hadn't been a perv, he might be interested in the guy, but all in all, it was a good thing that the guards had strip-searched him when he went in or might have shanked the dude right then and there.

"Well, I'm half," Roger finally replied without looking up. "My father was Mexican, or so I've been told."

"Okay," the detached receptionist replied and motioned to a row of chairs at the end of the room. "I've got you entered in, so have a seat right there."

Well, there is a god, Roger thought and rolled his eyes when no one was looking. That first rehab session was largely uneventful for Roger; all of the men were either looking down or very quiet unless called on. Roger peered at the chosen counselor for this violation of his rights and the contempt was probably rising like steam off his scalp. She was the typical feminist, man-hating type even under the best of circumstances; Roger had gotten adept at picking them out from the crowd even before he had been sent up the river. She introduced herself as Dr. Savage, and she had a huge scowl on her face as she arched her head with the short hairstyle this way and that and addressed him and his fellow chesters this way: "Gentlemen, you are all here due to one thing: power and control."

The men did nothing but grunt, if they made any sounds at all.

"It's time, you know," the words seemed far away to Chief Lloyd since he was still suffering the ill effects from his latest hangover. His newfound-friend started to annunciate his words just a bit louder in that crowded restaurant: "It's. Time. You. Know." Even when he was fighting off his latest drinking binge, he was still the face of law enforcement for Bakersfield and the rest of the county, so he sucked it up and leaned in closer.

"Listen, boss," Slim said adamantly. "I don't like that Gomes guy either...."

Chief Lloyd cut him off. "Really? How can you tell I don't like him?"

Slim cleared his throat. "Simple, really. Your body language when you are around him. We both served, you know that. You learn how to read people pretty damn good when you are in the Marines." Lloyd couldn't disagree with that.

"We've got to beat him to the punch, and we have a few things on that Arthur kid, but not enough," Slim continued. Both of their eyes were big as they acknowledged each other, almost like they were mind readers.

"So you're saying that we need something that 'brings it over the top', so to speak," Lloyd replied.

Slim winked direfully, which was only matched by the look of scorn from the rest of his demeanor.

"Yeah, chief," he replied. "Now you're hitting the nail on the head here."

Lloyd cleared his throat as the waitress poured him another cup of coffee, looking around to make sure they were still in semi-private quarters. The restaurant was largely empty, save for an elderly couple in the corner. Still, he leaned in even closer.

"So what do you think then, Slim? Should we bring him in for questioning and try to harass him into confessing? You know that kid's in his mid-thirties, but everyone thinks he's as dumb as a box of rocks. You know I told you that he assaulted me that one time that we caught at his ex-wife's apartment. I could definitely hang that over his head too...."

Slim looked at him with a menacing, icy stare. He had barely even touched his iced tea.

"Yeppers, sir," he said in mock derision. "The kid's not too bright, and so that's exactly what I'm saying here. We've got to make something up to haul him in for questioning, but give me a ring when you've got him cornered. I know you're pretty 'imaginative', so you can make something up..." and the two men laughed, with Slim downing his tea in one swallow.

"...and I'll get the tab this time, chief..."

Orange juice. His eyes looked straight ahead into the fridge, and that's when he noticed it. Apparently, his old man had gone to the grocery store and got some when he wasn't tending to mom at the nursing home. A couple of days had gone by, and other than noticing Slim on patrol or seeing Chief Bridges' squad car at the police station, he was being left alone. He continued to talk to Marilyn, even telling her all about his struggles with depression and the bottle, but that was still clicking on all cylinders too. He was thankful that his old buddy Richard had encouraged him to try again and stop pining for his ex-wife.

But back to the orange juice. It was Sunny D, the kind that kids half his age and younger would drink by the gallon, something they could do because the acids in their stomach hadn't started attacking them yet, or they hadn't yet been turned on to booze like he had. It was just sitting there, glaring at him, and he had some great plans for it for sure. He went ahead and poured himself a glass, but only half-full, and then it was time to take it back to his basement digs, because the Jack Daniels was still there waiting for him like an old friend. It was approaching ten, and he had obviously slept in, but just like that cynical Alan Jackson song, it was indeed five o'clock somewhere, probably on an island with palm trees, pina coladas, and beachgoers frolicking in the wind.

His father? Well, he couldn't remember when the old bastard had switched to Sunny D, because he used to drink that Tang brand instead. It wasn't one of those deals where they were in the market, and he said, "Hey, let's try this!"

With his dad's quiet demeanor, it was more something that just happened one day. Alcohol, on the other hand, was not something that had just happened one day for Arthur. When he finally realized that he too was a bastard dumb as a box of rocks, that's when he started to imbibe. That's when he raided the liquor cabinet. And this is the time that he took the glass of Jack Daniels and opened the top and began to pour the bitter substance in with the orange juice. Except that he didn't. Uncharacteristically, his hand began to shake uncontrollably before he could pour the Jack in with the juice. Momentary nerves, he thought.

For a moment there, he thought he was going to fall over, glass and all, but he steadied himself, and he was ready to pour his makeshift mixer once again. This time the orange juice was poured, cascading down into the Jack, two lovers intertwined in a passionate embrace, possibly sitting there on a picnic blanket on a seething hot evening, the kind where they would both throw rocks at the other's upstairs window. This time his hand had no problem whatsoever, and he raised his glass to his mouth, just a millisecond away now. But suddenly, his retina caught sight of the crumbling white paint of that ancient bedroom wall, and then that stupid running song from the 80's one-hit wonder A Flock of Seagulls was running through his head, the neurons firing madly, and then he was just thinking about seagulls in general, and that was just how Arthur's mind worked. He was furious, but he sat the glass down and then walked to the equally-ancient sink in that basement bathroom and poured it out. The day's still young. Time to go for a walk and go see what's left of mom, he thought bitterly. He was at least able to hold it together until he reached the main street.

"Arthur, Arthur, Arthur, you are as dumb as a box of rocks," he said as he was driving in his police cruiser and spotted him walking down the main street without a care in the world. Chief Lloyd parked his cruiser near where Arthur was getting ready to pass by, and he was still oblivious to all of it, looking just a bit unsettled over something as it was. He met the kid face to face, and he had to make a lie almost immediately, right there on the spot. "Arthur, you need to come with me, and you need to do it now!" he said in his best police officer voice that he had rehearsed over the last two decades.

Naturally, the kid looked bewildered. "What? Why?"

"There's someone else who is claiming that you have been looking in their windows, and we need to get your side of the story..."

He held up his cell phone. "Are you kidding me? Do I need to call my old man again? He's at the nursing home, and that's where I'm headed too! What the hell?"

"Just come with me, Arthur," the police chief said, and the immediate look of resignation on Arthur's face told him that he was going to comply without any issues.

CHAPTER 9

"The birds told me that I would find you here..." he said out of the blue. The grizzled middle-aged man's voice trailed off as he addressed Roger sitting on the bench overlooking the therapy building while he waited idly for his second sex offender counseling session.

"She's a real bitch, isn't she?" the guy continued, referring to the counselor that had been assigned to them last week. "No kidding, sherlock," Roger finally replied, almost inaudibly.

The guy peered at the clouds above the building. "What's that?"

Roger looked up, and he couldn't help but laugh, because one of the clouds looked like a giant phallus, just waiting for one of them to go after, although, of course, they preferred the smaller kind.

The other guy grinned. "Made you look, didn't I?"

Roger spat on the perfectly manicured grass, partly in contempt for the whole program and partly because he was just taking a momentary breather. Another guffaw escaped out of his lips.

"You sure did. You sure did!" and with that, it was about time for this mockery of a therapy session to begin, but he could tell already that he and this dude were going to be fast friends.

The man took his own turn spitting on the ground.

"Watch how I handle this counseling session, my friend. It will really make your head spin!"

Roger laughed, and the man stuck out his hand, making him smile for the first time in what seemed like ages. "Name's Dennis…."

"Roger."

"Okay, Roger, watch how I handle this session with this witch…." And away they went.

The second week of state mandated counseling for Roger and the other pervs began all too soon, and Dr. Savage looked about as happy to see him and the others as he was to see her. Unlike the first session, though, this time Roger was waiting with bated breath just to see how his newest acquaintance was going to upset the apple cart.

Dr. Savage took them through all of the standard introductions, and Roger did his part even though he was more interested in what Dennis had to say. Then, near the end of that introductory session, she finally picked on Dennis as one of the last ones to give his talk. Roger couldn't help but smirk, and he either needed some popcorn or a weapon to go after this therapist. He would show her what "Savage" really meant! Dennis began his talk.

"Thanks, Dr. Savage," he said in a voice that resembled an opening monologue and a devilish look that could have peeled paint off the wall of a 1950s farmhouse. "I think I would rather not talk about myself like the others did, though…." and Dr. Savage glared at him with a look that fit her name. "My friends, I think I would rather mention this. When I was in court, the judge said, 'how does five to ten years sound?' and the only thing I could say was 'sexy'." And with that, the whole room erupted in laughter, with Roger guffawing right along with the rest of them.

"You horse's………!" Dr. Savage bellowed, but Dennis cut her off.

"Careful there doc….don't want to get unprofessional. We have rights, you know…"

"I know," she fired back and rolled her eyes. "Your rights are a pain in the ass. There, I said it. Are you kidding me? You victimized some kids and now you're joking about it?"

"Yeppers, doc, I am. Put that in your pipe and smoke it. Oh wait,

you're a lesbian, so you'll probably pass…" the room erupted in laughter again.

This time Dr. Savage didn't say a word, just keeping her head down as the session flew by. "Well," she muttered at the end, "I guess I will see all of you next week." Everyone left the room doing their best not to snicker, and Roger literally felt like he was a cat who had caught a canary.

"Corruption is paid by the poor…." That was Arthur's thought as he was yet again at the Bakersfield police headquarters, and he was inwardly seething. Strangely, the words had some comfort to him and kept him from lashing out this time, like when he had been caught at his ex-wife's apartment. He wasn't sure how he was going to get out of this, and he wasn't sure how he was going to tell Marilyn. All he knew is that he had to take things one step at at time. He was protestant as the day is long, but even though those were words from Pope Francis, he knew they were true.

Understanding his rights. That was a good start, he knew, as he was sitting at that black plastic table waiting for that nasty police chief to get him some water. *Seems like an awful lot of trouble to go to just for accusing me of being a peeping tom,* he thought, and that was his first red flag.

Instead of the police chief, that Slim guy came out with a completely ordinary paper cup. "Here's your water, sir," he said with a rang of hollow cheeriness and an even more hollow air of respect. Art's ears immediately perked up, whether he liked it or not. *The second red flag.* Slim skirted out of the room rather quickly after that, leaving Art to his own devices. He didn't come back for what seemed like forever to Art, and part of the reason for that was because he was discussing the matter with Chief Lloyd while observing him through the two-way mirror.

Granted, Art didn't know that was going on, but leaving him alone like this? He sighed. Red flag number three right there. His gut feelings were starting to get the better of him, and he was starting to get dry heaves inching up through his lungs, slowly but surely, like the death-grip of a snowball rolling down a hill.

~

Slim met Chief Lloyd's gaze as they were watching Art literally twiddle his thumbs in the two-way mirror, and it was just like the two were kindred souls. "Are you thinking what I'm thinking?" the old marine buddy said to the embattled chief.

"Yeah," Chief Lloyd replied without skipping a beat. "We'll do the good ol' good cop, bad cop routine, and I've seen the way he flinches when he looks at you, so you'd better play that bad cop role even though you were trying to be nice. Go back in there and lead him on about the window peeking line, and then leave again, and I'll come in and spring it on him. I'll have Sakura hit the record button on the screen when I leave again and then it's time for you to go in for the kill and see if we can get a confession out of him."

The two men immediately met each other's gaze, and Chief Lloyd's eyes flickered. Slim had always been a bit obnoxious, but he was better at reading people now that he was older. There was deception in his colleague's eyes, but he wasn't sure just what it meant. He couldn't put his finger on it, but since Lloyd was a kindred spirit and could read him like a book as well, that was when he leaned over in a hushed voice that he quickly figured it out.

As if Chief Lloyd was brushing up on his mental telepathy skills, he whispered to Slim, "That's right, my friend, that Sakura is not just a total dish, but she's plenty obedient too....I'm actually going to tell her *not* to hit that record button, even though that's state law..."

Slim couldn't help but smirk. "Ahhhhh...."

Lloyd didn't skip a beat. "So, what I'm getting at here, Slim, is that you can literally do anything you want to this fool to try to get a confession out of him. It's all fair game, my friend. The sky's the limit. Knock yourself out. Put the kid in hell, and have it rain down molten sulfur on his head. You know we don't have enough to arrest him, but we sure as hell would with a confession, now wouldn't we?"

Slim was impressed by the seasoned officer's deviousness, so much so that he repeated his "Ahhhhh...." comment.

"We know he's got a new girlfriend, and we know that he's been out at that lake at least once, so that's the circumstantial stuff right there," Chief Lloyd continued, trying to give his partner in crime the writing on the wall. "Just get the little bastard to confess. Slap him around a bit if you have to. We can always say that he struggled a bit coming in here since our little bodunk town hasn't mandated body cams for us yet."

"Got it," Slim replied without looking up, and not soon after he was back in the room with Art, handing him his water and then leaving the room yet again.

"So is it time to swoop in for the kill here?" he asked his boss as they were watching Art sip his water yet again.

"Yeah, give him time for another sip, and go back in," the grizzled chief said with a void look in his eyes.

As Slim went back in, that was when Sakura came out of the office and began staring at Art in the two-way mirror as well.

"Are you getting ready to interview him, chief?" she asked. "I'll go ahead and hit the record button..."

But Chief Bridges cut her off, sticking a trembling but menacing finger in her face. "Not this time, Sakura. If you want to avoid going back to that damned waitressing job up on the hill and sucking off those truck drivers the way rumor had it, you will avoid hitting the record button!"

"But it's state law, sir!" she protested.

Chief Lloyd didn't skip a beat. "I don't care. You'll get fired if you hit that record button. This is my case, not that fed guy's, and we are going to do whatever B.S. we have to do to get this kid to confess..."

Sakura sighed with resignation, because she knew that was that, and not soon after, she watched as the two men went in to begin their harassment of Arthur.

～

"All right, sir," Slim said. "I'll go ahead and take your water now." There was just a small touch of sarcasm in the "sir", and Art's ears again picked up when he heard it. The police headquarters had a decent ventilation system for the age of the building, but suddenly he felt nothing but bone-jarring cold. The red flags just kept coming, and coming, and coming.

All the while, Chief Lloyd stood at the end of the room, not saying a word but totally glaring at him with those part Italian eyes. "Okay, Arthur," he began as Slim left the room, "now it's time that we get down to business." He sat down at the nondescript blank steel across from him. He had one of those Big Chief tablets with him on the table, and he opened it up to the first page. *They still sell those?* Arthur flinched and his thoughts were going a mile a minute.

The chief met his gaze. "You can still get them on Amazon, kiddo," he said contemptuously as if reading his mind. "Now, I'm sure you've figured out that this is a lot more than just whether you are a peeping tom or not...." and while he was saying that, Art's autistic mind couldn't help but notice a "click" sound in the background, probably the central air unit of the building turning on, but he wasn't entirely sure.

Sakura was in the break-room of the rear of the ancient police center, trying to let her sweet coffee cool down and trying to calm herself by reflecting on her days of reading Faust in the cab of some stranger's truck just about twelve years prior. She had come a long way in her life, but the words from her supervisor cut to the quick, and if only he knew.

We all have skeletons in our closets I suppose, she thought as she finally took a sip of that cream coffee. She had been taught by the best, and they told her that those lonely truck drivers would always leave an extra fifty or hundred in her tip jar if she claimed a smoke break and instead went out and did them a "favor" in their trucks. She had always had a lightweight, thin, wrinkled Vietnamese frame, so she was shocked that yes, it had indeed worked out that way.

Needless to say, she got to know all of the interiors of the different models of types of diesel trucks rather well. She got to know Faust rather well, too, and in a weird way it had helped her improve her English skills too. One of the truckers was one of those Goth, Marilyn Manson types, with piercings everywhere, and surprisingly, he didn't even ask her to do anything but take five minutes and listen to Megadeth with him.

"I'm just lonely, honey," he laughed. "I can't have sex with anyone, sweetheart. I've got crabs, I've got the clap, and I've probably even got AIDS." Nothing surprised her anymore at that waitressing job, so she just replied, "Oh," and so they held hands and listened to that heavy metal band from that worn-out cassette tape in his Peterbilt. Easiest fifty bucks she had ever made.

The song was "Symphony of Destruction" and she had it running through her head all these years later, and she had it in particular just about five minutes prior to that when she was watching Chief Lloyd berate that Art kid through the mirror, rolling up his damned Big Chief tablet like he was the head of the FBI or something. She trembled as her finger was on the button of that record setting, and she was going against the chief's orders. He could make something up and have her fired, but she didn't buy it.

She didn't think this kid was the killer. He didn't even have a car! The chief was just mad that the kid had beat him up when he was at his ex's apartment. That's all it was, she knew, and maybe this psycho with a badge on a power trip could run roughshod over him now, but she couldn't. She couldn't be this kid's pied piper. She would leave all of the pied pipers to Megadeth. So, with all of the fortitude and courage she could muster, she pressed down on that "record" button.

That tell-tale click! Sound went off, and she shuddered just for one moment out of concern that the chief was going to notice, but it passed him by. For whatever reason, that Art kid did flinch, however.

After about an hour, Chief Lloyd paused for dramatic effect. "I'll go ahead and quit beating around the bush here, kid. We think that you are the one who has been killing all of those gals at the lake."

Art flinched yet again, and it took a few seconds to register what the police chief was inferring. Still, in shocked disbelief, he uttered incredulously, "What are you trying to say?"

The chief frowned and just kept staring daggers at him. "Don't play dumb with me, kid. We all know that you are smarter than what you let on. Let me repeat…what I'm saying is that we think you are the one who has been killing those girls out there at German Shepherd Lake."

The bombshell had been dropped, and if the chief was expecting a knee-jerk reaction from him none was forthcoming. He finally said, "No, no, no…."

"You better be straight with me, boy. This isn't one of those apartment deals where you are going to get a slap on the wrist. How's that girlfriend of yours from Texas doing, eh? We saw you out there with her, so how do you know you haven't been going back there yourself?"

"No, no, no," Art repeated.

The chief continued to leer at him, because now he knew that it was time to go in for the kill.

"You know, Art, I've been in your old man's house when I was dealing with his code violations for his hoarding problems. I know that he is almost always away taking care of your mom at the nursing home, and good for him. But you and I both know that it would be totally easy for you to lift one of those keys he has to those vehicles parked at your old man's house. You could probably drive and hang out at that lake real easy, and your old man would be none the wiser."

Probable cause. Always establish probable cause, Chief Lloyd thought.

Yet again, "no, no, no" was the only thing uttered from Art's lips.

"Listen, kid," Chief Lloyd said even though Art was in his late thirties. "You and I both know that you are misunderstood. You and both know that you are smarter than people realize. You're one of those Ed Kemper types for sure…"

"No, no, no," Art shrieked in a guttural moan, stopping the chief dead in his tracks, but only for a moment. It was time for Chief Lloyd to move in for the kill and throw out another lie.

"The last hooker out there was still alive, and she was moaning and gasping your name. She kept saying, 'Art did this, Arthur did this, Arthur, Arthur, Art was his name' and then she died.'"

"I was only out there once!" Art said adamantly. "I only went out there with Marilyn, that woman who I met online. That's the only time!"

Art barely had time to get the words out, because, in the next instant, Lloyd proceeded to slap Arthur across the face. In the control room, Sakura watched the whole entire exchange, and it was about everything she could do not to run in there and start slapping her boss around as well, betraying her ruse. They had told her all about false confessions at the police academy, but she had never thought she would be seeing someone so desperate to elicit one such as Chief Lloyd. She felt like she was a Winger groupie listening to "Headed For a Heartbreak" live, but it wasn't the loss of a lover that was being agonized over, but the potential loss of freedom.

Chief Lloyd was trying to elicit a cataclysmic bombshell out of this 30-something kid, but Sakura was just watching, silently hoping that he didn't give in. It would be a costly mistake for the chief, and she knew it would be Richard Jewell all over again for Art. She knew in the very depths of her being that the bombshell was not that Art was the guilty party that had committed those murders of her fellow lot lizards, but that he was totally innocent. She let out an inaudible sigh as the respected police chief yet again slapped him across the face.

Arthur kept getting distracted and he felt outside his body, like it was a few years prior and he was still taking those online classes in Bible college, and he seriously thought this was someone else, somebody else who was being investigated for these terrible crimes. It wasn't him who was being slapped across the face by Bakersfield's finest and top brass, but somebody he was watching on Nancy Grace or Court TV. He was still in that Christian college, and he was still listening to the lesson discussing Christ being baptized, with the dove coming out and the whole nine yards, where the scripture was saying, "This is my Son, in whom I am well-pleased." Speaking of sons, his old man must be worried sick.

He had interviewed for a few preaching jobs after he graduated, ones he knew that he would never have a chance of getting in a million years. The guidance counselors had always told him that when you are nervous or scared, you should find something, somewhere, and just focus on that, so that is what he did in this scenario too. It was there, behind Chief Lloyd, that he saw the nondescript background, complete with a rarely-used bulletin board overlooking the window on one side where the assistant was still examining the two of them intently. Just on one side of that bullet board, he saw a discolored smudge, one that appeared to be a coffee stain. *That would do the trick*, he knew. Of course, he couldn't be so lucky as to do this without the nasty chief noticing, which is exactly what he did, his eyes focusing on him like a laser.

"Are you going mute on me, boy?" he sneered.

Arthur merely kept his eyes down, not even grunting or giving him the pleasure of a response at all.

"What? Cat got your tongue?" the chief continued. "Art, I swear, you don't have the sense that god gave a goose. I know you were out there, and I'll be damned if you're ever walking free again. Ever."

All of a sudden, the allergies (we'll call it that) were getting the better of Art, and just one lone solitary tear began to elapse from his eye socket and cascade down his face. Focusing on the coffee stain was no longer working. He tried to turn away, but he was too late.

"Oh!" Lloyd said in a cooing, derisive tone. "The tough boy who was out at the lake hurting all those people is crying! Can't handle it, eh? You're going to be fresh meat to those boys in prison once we prosecute you, that's for sure!" and with that, he left the room, trying to get Art to stew in his own juices.

He was grinning satisfactorily, with one of those cat-eating-the-canary grins as he and Slim watched Art in the two-way window, obviously distressed with his head in his hands.

"Now, I realize that you are still a bit new to police interrogation, but we got him right where we want him right now," he said to his partner.

Slim had the same matching grin that his more experienced co-worker had. "So, what do you do now, chief? Keep harassing him until he finally breaks, which is soon?" Chief Lloyd's eyes never left the local fool that they now had in their sights in that window. "Yes and no," he said.

"We do that, but we want to start playing on his fears. We can't move in for the kill just yet," the aging chief continued. "What do you think his fears are right now?"

"What do you mean?"

The chief remained patient, even though he thought Slim should know this as a recent police academy recruit.

"Well, you've got to look at the situation he's in. We think he's guilty, and we need to get a confession, and legally, we can lie to him, but look at where he is. Look at what he's probably worried about. He doesn't have a wife any longer, and his mom is in the nursing home, so what does he still have?"

"His old man?" Slim asked with an air of uncertainty.

"Bingo, my man. Bingo. So how about you go in there and back off a bit, playing with him the way a cat would play with his mouse prize, talking to him about his old man."

Slim kept looking at his prize in that window while Sakura quietly came in and brought them both coffees, the chief totally black and his with just a touch of Hazelnut. She appeared nervous, but he wasn't sure why. "Oh. You mean do a bit of the good cop routine before I nail his ass to the wall?"

Chief Lloyd sipped his coffee. "You got it, Slim. Go in there and get it done, my friend."

With that, Slim went back in, and he was glaring at Art with cold, shark-eyes as he nonchalantly took the chair across from him. He still had his head down, but regardless of that, Slim tried to do his best to fake a caring expression.

"How are you doing now, friend?" were the first words that were uttered by the newly-minted law enforcement officer, and Art couldn't help but look up in one full motion. He met the gaze of Slim, and the new cop looked right through him as if reading his mind.

"How's your old man doing these days, Art?"

He flinched before replying, albeit in a bit of a standoffish tone. "Fine. Taking care of mom, as always."

"You know, Art, we've been in that nursing home a few times, and I've heard him complaining a bit. Seems like people have been staring at him, giving him the side-eye. You know, one of those things that happens in small towns when people start dying mysteriously. Lots of suspicions, lots of worries about bumps in the night..."

Art cut him off.

"What is it you are trying to say?" He repeated.

"You haven't been a very good son, have you?" Slim said, expanding on the lie.

Art didn't take the bait, just staring Slim down the same as he was doing to him.

"Well, officer," he began in a strained voice because of the fresh injuries to his face. "Why don't you define what being a 'good son' means to you and we'll go from there?"

Slim blinked, and suddenly, he was the apprehensive one. He was the one being interrogated, and now he felt like he was sitting in divorce court listening to one of his ex-wives. It's a wonder he was able to get this law enforcement job after the kind of husband he had been, but he went ahead and answered the asshole's question.

"Well, a good son is one who always tells the truth. A good son is one who makes integrity the focal point of their life and always is obedient to a father's wishes. A good son is innocent, which is surely something you aren't..."

Art loudly and obnoxiously cleared his throat, throwing Slim off balance. "Tell me, Sergeant Slim, why is this town forsaking me?"

"They're not," Slim replied effortlessly. "You're forsaking yourself, and you were forsaking all of those women and girls when you were out at that lake."

Art simply glared at him icily. "I think this is enough. I want a lawyer."

"Oh!" Slim sneered. "The town idiot wants a lawyer! And how do you expect we are going to get you one at this time in this little bodunk Bakersfield? And who would take on your case with all of those bruises on your face?" and with that, Slim slugged him in the face and Art slumped out of his chair.

While Art was lying face-down on the carpet, Slim left the room and again conferred with Chief Lloyd. "He just lawyered up, sir," he told him as they watched him struggling on that floor through that window. "What do we need to do now?"

Chief Lloyd looked defeated.

"Well, put him in a holding cell and let him sleep off what you did to him. We have no choice but to let him go if he won't confess. He's definitely a person of interest, but that's all we've got right now."

"Okay," Slim said with a resigned sigh.

Sakura saw the men struggling to get Arthur back on his feet and with all of the requisite grunting and groaning of the three, she knew that this was the time for her to make her move. She clicked off the recording device, and it was conveniently downloaded to the department desktop computer. In what seemed like no time flat, she had the entire video transferred to a handy USB drive, which she immediately placed in her purse for safekeeping. *Thank god I defragmented this computer last week,* she thought.

The first thing that happened to Art after they finally placed him on that oddball plastic bluish mat in the holding cell were those shooting pains in the top of his forehead. That was the first time it happened on that day, and he had the odd thought that he was an NFL player without the girls and the glory, and he was going to be interviewed by a crime show any day now. The only inhabitants of that lake had been the birds, frolicking and playing, and he literally hadn't been out there in years other than with his new love interest. But the German Shepherd Lake now consisted of a strange apparition, an entity that had a heart of darkness and darkness covering their ghoulish face, a new inhabitant for sure. It was no longer the portrait of the loyal caretaker and his loyal pets. It was now nothing but darkness, both the lake and him.

The comfort was void, and the darkness was the only thing present, and he was in a graveyard in a moonless night. His breath came out in raspy gasps, and he was going to die in that holding cell. He was going to die an innocent man, innocent because he was odd, misunderstood, an idiot savant. And try as he might, he couldn't replace the darkness with anything of comfort. He couldn't replace it with sunlight flowing through stained glass and treating those viewing it with a cacophony of color, because all there was to see was black. The void claimed him as he finally breathed his last.

Roger was waiting with bated breath to see what hijinks his new friend would come up with this new week, but so far, he hadn't shown up. It was a cold and rainy day as he sat there shivering on the bench just outside the counseling office. He counted all of the mandated respondents as they went in, and no, he wasn't among them. With a heavy sigh and no attempt to hide his disappointment, he went ahead and filed in with the rest of them and took his seat, all the while staring at the empty one where his acquaintance would normally sit. Where was Dennis? Instead of addressing the issues that led to him offending, that was the Dominant question in his mind as Dr. Savage finally took her seat with her air of superiority yet again at the forefront.

She took a puffed-up breath before she began addressing the group. "As you will all notice, Dennis is not here this week…apparently, he failed one of his court-mandated UA's after his routine at our group last week."

The air of superiority from Dr. Savage was just nauseating to Roger, but he couldn't quite put his finger on why he felt that way.

The men were all in the same defeated, crestfallen state as always, appearing to Roger as zombies in a cheap horror flick, going through all of the degrading motions of being registered, only thinking about themselves and not those they victimized. That Dennis guy did lighten the mood, but now he was gone, and that too was something Roger couldn't understand.

It was when Dr. Savage was making her opening announcements that he briefly exchanged eye contact with her, and her pupils were surrounded by blue fire, severe fury, and mocking antagonism. And just like the prototypical light bulb going off in his head, that's when he knew. He knew that they had "cooked the books", if you will, and ruined the man's case. He could literally feel it in his bones, and he could totally picture the woman sitting in her office after working with these mindless men with nondescript, void faces, drinking her black coffee and chortling to herself. Either that, or she was discussing the matter with the man's probation officer and they were giving each other proverbial high-fives. The miles continued on his day of destiny, getting further and further away from who he was and what he once knew of himself as he dwelled on this morbid memory.

He might have been a squalid pervert, but he wasn't corrupt. He would keep his head down and go through the program like a mindless troll, but that was yet another time that his need for revenge had come to the forefront, and that was sad because he had nearly forgotten about it, even though the prosecutors had been such terrible big-shots. He would keep his head down, but it was only further proof that someone had to pay.

Art was now in the graveyard. He wasn't sure in what form he was, but he was reading a headstone, not an old decrepit one that was decades, even centuries old, but a newer one that people used to get out of one of those creepy mortuary catalogs, one that they now would simply look at online. It still had that macabre shine to it, an indication that the occupant beneath the headstone had recently died.

Out of curiosity, he stepped closer to read who the headstone belonged to, and that is when he made out those all-too-familiar letters: first, there was the curve of the "A", then, there was that unmistakable "R", following by those tree branches of the "T" as his now-ailing mother used to describe it to him when he but a small boy. There was the "H" with the two shafts pointing straight up to the heavens, then the "U", and finally the other "R" rounded it out, and that's when he knew that he was no longer of this world.

As he stood there in shock and bewilderment, the disarray of not seeing his hands grabbed hold of him like the last line from that Dear John letter so many years prior. He was in an unseemly, unearthly form, and no sooner did he realize it than the shadows began creeping out of the background, the silhouettes getting longer and larger, coming up to his countenance, and he was powerless to stop it.

They were in his face and they were staring him down mere inches away, and they were calling in a sing-song, sickening sweet refrain, saying "Arthur, Arthur...." and then suddenly, the voice got deeper. "Arthur! Arthur! Wake up! It's time for us to get you out of here!" and the faces were no longer dark and dreary, but one of authority, that of a county jail guard.

As his eyes came into focus, he glared at the guard in the same manner that an abused dog would look at their alcoholic owner. His speech was still a bit strained due to the bruises he had suffered, but he managed to get the words out as the guard was getting him up on his feet. "You don't think that I'm the one who killed all those women at the lake, do you?"

The twenty-something guard studied him for a split-second, seemingly weighing out his words.

"Well, kid," he began even though he was just fresh out of college and Art was at least a decade older than him, "that really isn't my job. You were out at that lake once or twice for sure, but I'm just a guard, my friend."

Undaunted, Art simply repeated the question yet again. "You don't think that I killed all of those women at the lake, do you? I don't even have a car..."

The guard was beginning to get annoyed, and he turned his head, presumably to disguise his eye-roll.

"Listen, kiddo. I'm just a Kansas transplant, just trying to make a dime here. That question is for your public defender. They obviously don't have enough to keep you, so let's just go ahead and get you out of here. Your old man has been calling the jail a few times, so let's get you back home to him..."

It was said just like he was special needs, and Art had to try with all of his might not to throw up a tremendous retort, but he just left it at that. He was a person of interest in a serial-killer murder case even though he didn't even own a car. *This is pathetic,* he thought, *but it is what it is.*

He was in his old beater of a car, and he was on his downtime, which was good. "Voices Carry" by the one-hit wonder 'Til Tuesday was blasting away on the radio as he kept scanning the side of the highway near that damned lake, and he wasn't sure if he should be on the prowl so soon after his last dalliance, but c'est la vie. Just a few miles out, the word "Eureka" inadvertently escaped from his lips because he saw what he was looking for: another would-be runaway, and she looked pretty long in the tooth, even with some surprising youthful beauty underneath.

Either way, she would do for the purposes of his perverse hobby. He pulled over and rolled down the window. "Where are you headed?" he asked in his most charming voice possible. "Oh," she replied with bated breath. "Out of state, probably Kansas, maybe Oklahoma."

"All right. Hop in."

"Thanks," she smiled, and that just turned him on even more. "I have a little bit to help with gas if need be..."

"That won't be necessary, trust me." Little did she know. Little did she know, indeed.

"You know," she purred. "You're not too bad-looking for an older guy..."

He smiled ever so slightly. "Thanks."

It was about ten seconds later that he turned off on that all-too-familiar dirt road, and headed to German Shepherd Lake yet again.

She did not give off the response that he was expecting, and so he had to turn his head so she didn't see his disappointment. "Ohhhhh!" she squealed in delight, somewhat resembling Fran Drescher. "Where are you taking me, cowboy?"

"You'll see," he said matter-of-factly, and she let out a big belly laugh, showing that she wasn't scared like the others had been.

"Yeah," she smiled, showing off her coffee-stained teeth, indicating to him that she was a Starbucks aficionado despite her shabby clothing. "Nice little rendezvous we got going on here, cowboy." She pronounced it randy-voos. He cleared his throat, again hiding his face because he was still on that macabre fence.

He was not one for emotion, but in another time and space he could have totally pictured himself settling down with this one. But he knew that wasn't to be either as he finally shifted the car into the park on top of the ridge at that lake.

"I can't wait to see what you have in store for me, cowboy," she purred yet again, and now it was his turn to laugh.

And laugh he did. And then they both laughed.

He got the blanket all situated, and they were two just chatting away, just like two kindred souls, and then she looked at him, saying, "So what do you want to do now?" And that's when he leaned over and began kissing her in a passionate embrace, first just regular ones and then soon enough the x-rated French kind.

They both began to take off their clothes, and for a brief instant he gazed upon hers. They were only ragged from her time on the road, but he could tell they were the type of clothes worn by a girl that could get anything that she wanted, at any time and for any price.

He looked up ahead, first down the road to make sure no one was coming (that was a negative) and that up in the sky, where the birds were yet again circling around, mating and playing, without a care in the world. They would be the only witnesses.

It wasn't long before they were both naked as the day they were born on that blanket, and she wasn't bad, with plenty to grab hold off up top and just the lightest amount of pubes on the bottom. He didn't know if she was of age, but she wasn't volunteering it and it didn't matter. She had that sly, come-hither look that most horny gals get, whether they were in the back of a car getting it all steamed up in a drive-in or looking across the room in a bar.

How many families were created that way? The good Lord, if he existed, was the only one who knew. But this time, sadly, it wouldn't be in the cards. She wanted him to enter her, but he wasn't ready yet, and the light went out of her eyes when he first closed his hands around her throat. Next, it was replaced by total shock, and then the most beautiful part to him was when she was gasping for air as he was overpowering her, ensuring that she couldn't try to fight back.

Soon enough, the arms stopped flailing, and that was when he finally entered her. *Ah, yes,* he thought. *Strangling people. Can't beat that for birth control, eh?* And he couldn't help but have his own slight chuckle escape his lips as his thrusts continued, getting more and more intense. It was time to pull out soon, but she was just so damned beautiful, an angel being taken advantage of by a devil.

Soon, he knew it was too late, and he cursed under his breath. He exploded, and jet after jet of that gooey, white sticky mess was in that girl's mid-section. He knew there was no escaping this and they would probably find out. *Two hots and a cot once the wheels of justice finally caught up to him,* he thought. He had a gun in his vehicle that would work rather well for suicide efforts, but c'est la vie. He had the cavalier mind of a morbid personality. He mused as he drove back from the lake. It was a compulsion, so no Norman Rockwell paintings for him.

"I had some Banquets ready for you when I got home, but I couldn't figure out where you went," he said with that casual, quiet look of concern that Art had grown so accustomed to.

Art tried to focus on the clutter of newspapers behind his old man instead of looking him in the eye.

"Dad, there's something I have to tell you...."

His expression only changed slightly, and that was what attracted mom to him after being married to a charmer the first time and getting beat up constantly. The strong and silent type for sure. He was yet to acknowledge the bruises on his face, but he did appear to listen more intently and take his eyes off the Price is Right at least momentarily at the other end of the room.

"You know those bodies at the lake?" Art said as Drew Carey was chit-chatting with a baby boomer grandmother in a Hawaiian skirt. "They thought I was the one who was doing all of that. I don't even drive, and they thought I was the one..."

His old man interrupted him quietly and matter-of-factly.

"So, does that have something to do with your face being messed up?"

Art just looked at the cluttered floor.

"Yes, yes, it does."

"Oh."

Arthur steeled himself with a desire to choose the next part of his words carefully, but finally, he just decided to throw it out there.

"They were trying to get me to confess to these murders out at German Shepherd, Dad," he said matter-of-factly.

That at least got a raised eyebrow out of him.

"Really?"

Art gazed at Drew Carey's smiling mug just before the program went to a commercial break.

"Yes, really. They were trying their damndest, dad. I didn't know they could do that. I didn't know that they could beat a confession out of someone after I lawyered up." It was rhetorical, though, and it was spoken out of shock. Of course, he knew they couldn't, and he knew his old man knew it as well.

He had a huge frown on his face.

"Dirty bastards," he replied, his voice raising slightly. "So I guess they think you are a person of interest now...?"

"Yeah, I guess so."

CHAPTER 10

Roger kept staring at the wall as Dr. Savage droned on and on. The names and the faces had changed constantly, the revolving door of the criminal justice system always finding more sacrificial bovines for the circling vultures. He had now been there longer than anybody, even though the medieval corrupt wheel of these probation officers had tried with all their might to send him back. He was even viewed by the other men as something of an elder statesman, but now, they would have to find someone else because this was his last sex offender therapy class ever. Was it the last time that he would ever see Dr. Savage? Probably not, he thought sardonically as a grim smile snuck across his lips, just like a soldier storming the beaches of Normandy into certain death.

"...and now that we have reached the end of another class, gentlemen, I would like to congratulate Mr. Cisneros here," Dr. Savage said, motioning toward Roger. "Because he no longer has to attend these meetings. Except for the quarterly registration requirements (Roger rolled his eyes at that), he is now a free man." And everyone did the obligatory clapping as well, with some of the men saying, "speech! speech!" sarcastically under their breath, a tinge of jealousy present.

As Roger stood up there in front of all of the other men, he literally felt like he was about to deliver a totally macabre version of the speech given by Lou Gehrig, although unbeknownst to everyone it was going to end up being yet another negative result. No, he was not going to die, but someone else just might.

"Well," he began with a fake smile that would have made Johnny Carson proud. "It's been quite a journey, but I guess like the rest of you pervs, I've learned that living on the straight and narrow is the way to go."

They clapped, and ironically Roger said it with a straight face even though it was all bull. It was all just going through the motions. Shame he was registered now, because boy, he could have run for office with all of the whit he had mustered up in that instance. But he had learned to hide behind that facade, and in that moment, he just as well could have been Richard Kuklinski for the snow-job he pulled on all of them. Yes, even in that instant, the wheels in his head were turning, just like a gruesome medieval torture rack, and he was plotting.

As he was sitting in that prehistoric van that he had purchased at the seedy "buy-here-pay-here" car dealership, he saw the social media videos of Dr. Savage even though she had set the parameters to private. They were a few years old, but there was some type of video of her at some bar and grill in Denver, one where the prices were about forty bucks for two people and that didn't even include the tip. It was one of those ritzy Cherry Creek places that Roger knew all-too-well, but only because he had been a busboy before his sick predilections had caught up with him. It wasn't because he was a customer.

Either way, Dr. Savage was at one of those tables with Coors Light, Budweiser, and all kinds of other beer mugs, salad plates, and juicy steaks, and she had a five-thousand-watt smile on her face. She was probably taking a breather after dealing with terrible clients such as him, and it made Roger's teeth clench up, and his fingers quivered so much he almost dropped the cell phone that held the social media account he wasn't even supposed to have.

"How dare you," he growled from his twisted, psychotic mind. "How dare you have a good time when I have to go to a rat-infested apartment that barely even has a good heater!" But that's when his first epiphany occurred, and he wondered if Dr. Savage still frequented that establishment, and he wondered where she went shopping, and even where she lived…

~

"It's been a while since he has ridden that weird bike of his that you were telling me about," Slim said to Chief Lloyd as they were both sitting at the supermarket parking lot. Art had just passed by, and he actually looked fairly decent, considering the beating that he took from them both. Yes, the bruises were bad, but he had an aura about him that showed them that the wind was at his sails, and that annoyed them to no end.

"What do we do about those bruises that he has, boss?" Slim continued, rolling his eyes.

Lloyd noticed a kid hot-rodding down one of the avenues and thought about taking off and lighting him up, but he decided against it because his old man was on the town council. "Well, he can't prove that we are the ones who did that to him. It's our word against his….," and here he paused for effect, "I made sure that his interrogation wasn't recorded. It's disappointing, but it is what it is. We'll keep watching him."

Just then, Chief Lloyd's personal phone rang.

The minute he heard that aggravating Lieutenant Gomes on the other line, he knew what was going on. "What?" the chief said incredulously. "You're kidding me? There's been another one? All right, me and my right-hand man Slim are on our way," and he clicked off the cell phone while Slim appeared to be nonchalantly staring out the cruiser window. He turned to him. "There's been another death out at German Shepherd…good thing that blowhard called me on my personal cell, don't want this showing up on the police scanner. Thank god they don't pick up cells anymore." With that, they both sped off down the main street toward that lake yet again.

As Lloyd parked his cruiser on the top of the knoll ad nauseum, the two men came out of his cruiser, and the first thing he noticed was that asshat Gomes motioning them over. He had already learned how to be a good actor for Becky, so he hid his disdain with his best poker face as they reached the scene. "Let me do all of the talking, including the fact that we have a suspect now, and that we interviewed him to no avail," he whispered to Slim as they approached and then he addressed Gomes. "Shame to have to see you again under such circumstances, sir. What do we have now?"

Gomes remained noncommittal at the chief's attempt to brown-nose, and his voice seemed to crackle a bit.

"Well, this one, to be honest with you, the first time I saw her, I knew she was a runaway. Probably 18, 19, been on the road for a while, but under all of that dirt and bedraggled clothing, you can tell she was from a middle-class background. Brunette, looks like she was strangled."

"Anything else you can tell us?" Slim chimed in.

Gomes just kept gazing forlornly at the remains of the teenage girl.

"No ID on her, but my people have been checking missing persons reports from several nearby states..."

Chief Lloyd decided that now was the time and exchanged a glance with Slim to let him know.

"We have a suspect that we are surveilling now, sir," he said to the state man, and this provoked a raised eyebrow from the state lieutenant.

"Really?" he replied, spitting on the drought-ridden buffalo grass just above that lake. "Well, you know," he continued, letting the last word drag out with obvious disdain. "The phone works both ways, and I have jurisdiction in this case..."

Lloyd wasn't about to let that go, and even Slim could tell. "Excuse me?" he shot back. "You have jurisdiction in this case?" with emphasis on you. "With all due respect, sir, I was born here, raised here, and I've spent most of my life here except for a stint in the Marines with Slim, as a matter of fact. Yes, you might have jurisdiction, but this is my home-town, not yours."

"I beg your pardon?" Lieutenant Gomes said without batting an eye.

"These weren't all local people, chief. We have people from all over the place, and you go and get a suspect without even telling me? Seri-ously, Lloyd, you don't even have the decency to have one of your underlings, no less, give me a five-minute phone call! Are you kidding me?"

Chief Lloyd and Slim remained silent.

"But whatever," the fed guy continued. "Since I'm out here anyway, go ahead and tell me about your suspect, but next time, tell me first before all of this malarkey..."

Lloyd didn't waste any time.

"All right, sir," he muttered, even though he was being disingenuous. "Well, it's that same guy that we were telling you about the other day. He's been telling the whole world that he was out there skipping rocks with his new girlfriend, so he has inadvertently placed himself at the scene of the crime. No, he doesn't have a car, but he could be borrowing one, so we're taking a closer look at him. So no, sir, it's not like we found another suspect. It's the same one that we had before."

Gomes was trying to be civil. "That sounds interesting. It sounds like you two have done your homework on this, at least."

Lloyd and Slim both nodded, grateful that they had at least found something that the fed guy agreed with. He still remained adamant, appearing in deep thought as he looked both of them dead-on in the eye:

"Next time, please tell me, because I might want to keep an eye on him myself before you go any further."

It was then that Lloyd decided it was best to leave out the fact they had already interviewed him. So as far as all three of these gentlemen were concerned, there was nothing more to discuss. That is until Sergeant Gomes made it back to his hotel room that night.

Sakura kept looking at that USB drive. The three men were out at that lake, so she was left to her own devices. She laughed at the pun, but it wasn't like she didn't need a bit of levity. What the police chief had said was totally true, and she knew he had the power to raise her life up or make her life come crashing down, even though the great majority of those truckers were just lonely bastards reeling from seventy-plus hours on the road eating greasy foods and never watching their mini-mes growing up.

Corruption was the name of the game in Bakersfield, U.S.A., especially at this bodunk police station. Why couldn't Chief Lloyd let the bigwigs handle it? Wasn't it good enough for his bruised ego that he was carrying on this dalliance with a much-younger police dispatcher? Her hands were trembling, but she reached into her purse and pulled out her personal cell phone, which was nothing fancy, just a late-model Samsung. She typed out the text message, saying, "Lieutenant Gomes, this is Sakura, and I work for Chief Lloyd, and I think there is something you should know about these killings out at German Shepherd. Give me a call when you get back to your hotel room," and she left her number.

She poured herself a little bit of coffee, black this time even though she was normally a Starbucks gal and went heavy on that cream. Her heart was in a rush, and that paternal instinct kicked in even though all of her kids were now college-age and doing well. She felt her forehead. No fever, just what seemed like an irregular heartbeat. She would need to have that checked out, even though the insurance at the department was cut-rate, at best. She was typing away on some unrelated matters, but out of the corner of her eye, she kept an eye on that cell phone. Would it light up? It never did, so he must have his cell phone off for now.

Gomes was getting ready to pour himself a glass of scotch from the local liquor store in the privacy of his hotel room, both of which were establishments that wouldn't last two weeks in downtown Denver. The drink was strong, but he stirred it anyway just out of habit, because he needed the buzz to take the edge off. He normally was a tee-totaler, but this case was the worst he'd seen in years. After he turned on the cell phone, it was surprising, because he was glad that the inebriation was kicking in as he read the words on that text from someone named Sakura, who claimed she worked for Chief Lloyd and Slim.

"There is something you should know." He weighed out those words, even saying them to himself with a slight slur. Who was this Sakura person? Was she a member of the force? Was she simply a police secretary? Didn't Lloyd and Slim claim to have seniority in this matter? Regardless, something about her words made him feel that he had better take what she had to say seriously.

He was going to call her back, but first things first. *God only knows what she wants, and I don't know her from apple butter,* he thought, *having never been introduced to her by that dumbass Chief Lloyd or even knowing that she had existed at all.* Still, after drinking down the last swallow of his scotch, he went ahead and jabbed her number into his cell phone. Auspiciously and predictably, she picked up right after the first ring. After the customary greetings and Lieutenant Gomes' acknowledgment of her voicemail, she got down to why she was calling. "I'm not going to beat around the bush here any longer, sir," she began, letting the words glide through the receiver and hang in the stale air of that hotel room.

The lieutenant's head began spinning, grasping at anything to try to think about the possibilities of what her call could be about.

He was short of breath, but he managed to keep his composure. He had a five o'clock shadow because he was too busy to get a thorough shave because of trying to find this monster out at that German Shepherd. People could go whole careers without investigating serial killers. Even still, in the midst of that nondescript surreal hotel room, the words, "Go on...." escaped from his lips.

"Well," she began, slightly hesitating and he could tell she was having a difficult time with whatever news she had. "It has come to my attention that you have been told by my superior that they are trying to get a confession on the murders out there at German Shepherd. He's a local guy. A lot of people think he's not too bright and all, but there are a few things about the confession that do not sit well with me, even though I'm about the most junior police officer on the staff, sir..."

He knew that it was her attempt at both diplomacy and self-deprecation, but he continued with just a thundering tone, "A confession? They attempted to get a confession? They never told me about a confession from the guy! Keep going!"

"The first thing that happened was that Chief Lloyd was pressuring me not to record the interview, even though it was our department's policy to do so," she said, followed by a huge release of relieved breath for finally getting it out. "He threatened me with termination, sir, if I went ahead and hit that record button."

Suddenly, there was a release of endorphins in Lieutenant Gomes' middle-aged head, and he was no longer feeling anxious. Instead, he was now becoming irritated. "Oh really?" he responded.

"Yes," Sakura replied. "But there's more."

That phrase hung in the air, and even though Gomes now had a fully-composed demeanor, he didn't say a word. He simply nodded his head, even though that was kind of stupid, considering he was on his cell and he was alone.

"They didn't treat this 'person of interest' very well, sir," Sakura continued, with some sarcastic inflection in the middle part.

"Go on," Gomes replied, trying to keep his cool and not throw his drink from Subway that he was using as a chaser for his scotch against the wall.

"Well, sir, both Chief Lloyd and his assistant verbally and physically abused him in an effort to get him to confess..."

The lieutenant couldn't hold in his disdain. "Are you kidding me?" he repeated.

Sakura had her head in her hands. "No, no sir, I'm not. I wish I was. But the boy lawyered up. He might be a person of interest, but he asked for a lawyer and we had to release him."

Gomes was seething. "Is there any evidence for your allegations?"

Sakura took a deep breath. "Oh, there's plenty, sir. He had all kinds of bruises when we had to release him. I'm guessing the chief would play it off as him resisting, but that just isn't the case."

"My word...." and Lieutenant Gomes' voice trailed off. The air in that dusty local hotel room seemed almost tangible now.

"I downloaded the video on a USB drive, sir," Sakura said matter-of-factly.

"Damn," was Gomes' only reply, quickly followed with "bring it to me as quickly as possible."

"Okay, sir. You'll have it in your hands within the hour."

And with that, the call on his cell phone ended, and Gomes had to sit down on the edge of the bed.

~

Even from roughly a hundred yards away, Roger could tell that Dr. Savage was a woman of refined taste. He noticed as the middle-aged gentleman in gray slacks and a polo shirt opened her car door and then hurried to the passenger side of the Lexus. *She has made good money counseling pervs like me*, Roger mused. No doubt about that. There was also no doubt that even though she was only in her late thirties, she had probably gotten her share of catcalls when she was younger. Hell, she probably still got them, if anyone was being honest. No one could claim that chivalry was dead, especially from those on the right side of the law. But no bother. She might be getting chivalry from this guy, but she wouldn't be getting any chivalry from him sometime in the near future.

It was nothing more than a nondescript bar on a nondescript day in the Cherry Creek neighborhood of Denver, and sure enough, it was the same one from her social media profile. He'd had to save for this little jaunt; his crappy fast food job didn't pay nearly enough for the privilege of even being in this bar, much less ordering from it as regularly as he had been that day. It was a wonder he had been able to get a job at all, considering his status.

But he didn't have time to think about that right now. It was a slow period in that bar, and Dr. Savage was the only one in there except for two twenty-something lesbian lovebirds laughing and giggling in the corner. He used that to his advantage, as he was constantly grabbing his top-notch binoculars that he had used the five-finger discount to snatch out of Doc's Sporting Goods.

His target? Dr. Savage and the large barroom picture windows the owners had probably installed to influence the atmosphere and to take advantage of natural sunlight also gave him the perfect vantage point to watch her and see what she was up to, as he had tailed her in his beater of a van to that restaurant without being noticed. He then settled on this upscale bar a few blocks away and peered upon that Lexus in between drinks while the bartender and the lesbian patrons weren't looking in his direction.

The binoculars were the high-powered kind, and due to Roger's inner numbness, even when he was stealing, he desired the very best. Taking merchandise, taking lives, he mused. All the same to him. But even from his vantage point, Roger could see Dr. Savage and her love interest chatting away in her Lexus, their heads bobbing and gyrating in their lively pre-coital discussion. They were normal, sickeningly normal, and they were about the start the car and leave, so it was time for Roger to make his move as well.

He quickly paid his tab and strolled back out into the open air, getting into his van that slowly turned over and then finally came to life. He had to at least know what this guy's vehicle looked like.

Chief Lloyd was on patrol yet again, and oblivious to everything except for the traffic and the local scenery. He was once more surveying the town druggies, and he had already made the rounds by Art and his dad's place twice already. He heard the mockingbirds playing up high in the trees, and even in that neighborhood, it was just a sleepy morning in that sleepy town as usual. They had been hiding out for a few days, and Art's old man's car hadn't even budged. He evidently was letting the nurse aides take care of his wife this time, he thought. Good thing she's out of it, because she would be just beside herself if she knew we all but think her son is a monster.

He didn't want to be too conspicuous, though, so he quickly made the turn on the avenue, well on his way to the main street. He also pressed and held the side button of his cell phone in order to turn it on, a bit of a double standard considering that he had pulled over Bakersfield civilians for the same mundane activity.

It was one of those older models, and it was taking its sweet time catching up, but as he held it up to the steering wheel so he could get a good look at it without taking his eyes off the road, he saw several phone calls that looked to be nothing more than spam, and several text messages that appeared to be the same, but he pulled off on the side of the street just to make sure. He scrolled though the texts with the methodical precision of the burned-out police chief that he was, and he began deleting them just like normal until he came to the last one, which predictably caught his eye. She had been working the night shift while he had been asleep, and she likely was now asleep herself before she went back to work at the sheriff's office at four that afternoon, but it was that welcoming text of Eliza that made him spring to life, made him feel motivated, even though it was still about the most mundane thing ever.

"Lloyd, I'm probably at my house asleep now, but I'm thinking about coming over later and putting a nice pot roast on for you when you get home. It'll be in the slow cooker and all you have to do is get yourself a plate! Love you and stay safe! Eliza."

Even though the hitchhikers and runaways were dropping like flies at that damned lake, a smile almost involuntarily creased across his unshaven lips, yet again, she had outdone herself. About the only time, Becky contacted him was to iron out the details of who was supposed to get what, and the whole thing made his blood pressure boil. Still, he did the math in his head: he reckoned there was about another four months before it was all final, and he ought to marry this gal off the day after just as a final snub. That made him smile again. He remembered when he and Becky were still kind of in love and they were trying for their third child with Belinda Carlisle getting weak in the background, and they produced a girl, one that had been hanging around her mother too much and she hadn't talked to him in years and was in college last he checked.

But either way, duty called, and he knew that he was daydreaming just a bit too much in that trusty police cruiser of his, so he put it back in drive once more. No time for pity-parties. This time he thought he would cruise down the main street, and it wasn't long before he saw something that yet again perked up his interest. Surprise, surprise, Art was making a liar out of him! There he was, just walking down the main street like always, strolling past those decrepit, abandoned buildings in this town that were far past their former glory, and it was just like he wasn't a person of interest in literally the worst case the county had had in over a hundred years. It was time for him to pull over and see what he was up to.

~

Morning came on that big old ball called planet Earth unabated just like it always did. Strange as it seemed, Art no longer had the house to himself any longer, because his old man had literally not even budged from his favorite brown chair, watching the boob tube from dawn until almost dusk. That impersonal sunlight began streaming through the windows and the drapes that mom had picked out at Sears just about two decades prior, and he was still there in that cramped, dusty, crowded living room, sawing logs.

The walls were closing in for Art, and he kept figuratively hitting the panic button, but he knew it was time, even with these personal problems. He hadn't seen mom in ages, but everything in that old house was a reminder. It was time to venture out and go see her, even with these curious bruises on his face that he could not possibly explain away to the busybodies that worked at that hospital.

So that's what he did, leaving the house as quietly as possible as the first morning breeze infiltrated his nostrils. The old man wasn't the easiest person to read, because the only thing that ever emanated from his expression most of the time was a solemn gaze, one that would make a meditating monk in some far-off country proud. Thus, he was killing two birds with one stone, giving his pop some space and going to see his mother.

As he made the turn down that ancient main street, being a murder suspect was actually about the last thing on his mind. He knew that his mother's dementia was getting worse, just like pieces of a clay statue or knick-knack falling off little by little. He had given her that German Shepherd statue, and it was now sitting in her room with Aunt Lizzie right where the two of them could see it, even though Lizzie would have to squint to even be able to see an outline of it. Just like his mother, the statue, too, had seen better days. Several parts of it were missing, including the tail and one of the feet, but still, it was a testament to the gentle soul that his mother was and just how much she loved animals. When she hadn't been spending hours talking on the phone, she could be found simply gazing out the window at one of those dollar-store variety bird feeders, watching those little hummingbirds playing without a care in the world.

He was still daydreaming when he saw the tell-tale police cruiser, one of those late-model SUVs that everyone was proud to use their tax dollars on and not some idiot like him. He saw it approaching, and he knew it was Chief Lloyd, and somehow, he knew he was going to stop. He wondered if this was it, and if he was going to become the protagonist in one of those stories of false accusations, just like the West Memphis 3 in that backward town in Arkansas a few decades prior. Sure enough, the cruiser did stop, and it was indeed Chief Lloyd who got out.

He approached Arthur with cold, dark, menacing eyes, mocking him and doing it almost telepathically. "I know what you are doing," these eyes seemed to be saying in those surreal few seconds. "I know you were out there. I am waiting. I am just waiting for you to goof up and make a misstep."

He got face to face with Art, with moves that would have made LBJ proud. "Well, well, well, Artie, Artie, Artie, what do we have here?" Art just gulped.

"You look awfully confident, out and about just a few days after our encounter...just what, pray to tell, are you doing out so early this morning? We aren't going to find another victim out at that lake again, are we?"

Other than some slight flinching, Art didn't back away. Again, it took some courage, but he responded. "Where I'm going isn't your business. Like I said, I'm not talking to you unless I have a lawyer present. Unless you have a warrant, that is."

"Warrant, warrant, warrant," Chief Lloyd said with derision. "What a funny word that is. How about I go back to the squad car real quick and just take a look and see? Don't be running off now, boy..."

He opened the doors, motioning to the inside, with a mock hand over his eyebrows, and then came back to where Arthur was. "Nope, no warrant, but it's coming."

Not a second after that, though, he stepped back because his cell phone began ringing. It wasn't a spam call, either. It was Gomes, so he backed off from Art for a brief moment. "Chief Lloyd, I want you to come back to the station pronto," Gomes said, and Lloyd only uttered, "Okay."

"Well, I have to go back to the station, hotshot," he said to Arthur, and then he motioned with his two fingers at his eyes and pointed them back at him. "But rest assured, we're watching."

The police chief walked through the doors of the police precinct superciliously, with the swagger of a man that finally thought that he had the world by the tail. As high as his head was, when his eyes met Lieutenant Gomes and Sakura, the first thing he noticed was that they were seated in that small interview room with their backs to him, and his countenance changed to a flinching fear as he finally noticed what they were watching. He saw the video where he was interviewing Arthur, and he knew. He was being double-crossed. Gomes turned around, and Sakura didn't even leave her post. The lieutenant motioned toward the third chair in the room and with the air of authority that even a state officer could have, simply said, "Have a seat, chief," with the last word being inflected with an unmistakable contempt.

It was an instant later that the chief noticed that he and Sakura were watching the part where Slim was totally berating Arthur for wanting a lawyer and calling him the town idiot. Sakura was now facing him, but she didn't say a word, just glaring at him icily. Chief Lloyd knew then that she had disobeyed his order, and his blood pressure made him quiver. Still, he tried to do his best just to play it off.

"Oh," he said in about the most confident tone possible. "I see that you are watching the interview we did of our suspect, lieutenant."

Lieutenant Gomes was doing his level best not to roll his eyes, and Chief Lloyd could tell. He was in hostile territory, and the hair on the back of his neck was starting to stand up.

Gomes did not acknowledge Lloyd's characterization of Arthur as a suspect, instead going straight to the point. More sarcasm.

"Well, chief," he said, letting his response hang in the air for a few moments. "Just what is the meaning of this? Seriously, chief? Are you kidding me? We have been here since five this morning, and we have reviewed this tape over and over again. Just who do you think you are? It's all well and good that you two brag that you've got a suspect, but you can't just violate his rights! Why in the hell did you two beat him up after he asked for an attorney?"

It was Lloyd's turn to get angry.

"Oh really, Mr. Gomes!" he said, intentionally using the mister as a slight and his voice was getting heated. "You think that you can just waltz in here and take this thing totally over just because you're a state guy? This is my jurisdiction, you mother-"

But he couldn't finish his sentence because Gomes pounded the blank table that had the tv monitor on it.

"Really, chief? Like I said a few days ago, there were all kinds of victims from just about everywhere out at that lake. This isn't MIPs or traffic tickets, buddy. This is people's lives at stake here and not just in your locale..."

Chief Lloyd's blood pressure was exploding, and that was when the hideous knee-jerk reaction came.

"Buddy! Buddy?" he screamed in mock derision at the top of his lungs. Gomes briefly glanced down, and it was just like Chief Lloyd was getting his disapproval from his decorated war veteran father yet again, and so that was when he took his opportunity.

With stunningly fast reflexes for a man pushing sixty and nearing retirement from law enforcement, he took a swing at Lieutenant Gomes that would have made Mike Tyson, Rocky, and Muhammad Ali all rolled into one proud. Gomes pupils raised up just for a brief split-second, long enough for him to duck the infuriated police chief's glancing blow, and just as quickly, Chief Lloyd felt that all-too-familiar electrical shock of someone being tasered, that too something that he had gone through during one of his many training sessions.

Chief Lloyd found himself sprawled out on the floor, and the lieutenant was staring daggers disapprovingly at him. He was in terrible pain from the tasers, and almost robotically, Sakura reached out her hand so he could get up. After he had dusted himself off as best he could, Lieutenant Gomes finally spoke. "Seriously, Chief? Hand me your badge and your gun. I'm placing you on leave."

Lloyd turned his face away from the fed guy, but mainly just because he didn't want the man to see that he was grimacing, not in pain, but in anger. He had guarded respect for the man, but now the indignation was boiling over. Obviously, the man was quicker than he was and he had lost a step or two, so he had no choice but to comply. Gomes proceeded to turn to Sakura. "Go ahead and take him to the hospital to get those taser bolts removed, but what is the system password?"

"Bakersfield11, sir."

Gomes didn't look up. "Okay, thanks. I'm going to review some of the evidence you guys have on this case, and then when you get back, if you would kindly start typing a note about Chief Lloyd here being placed on leave, I would sure appreciate it."

"Yes, sir."

"And one more thing, Sakura…where's Slim?"

"We never were able to get a hold of him, sir. It's supposed to be his day off, but he probably needs to be aware of the steps you've taken."

"Well, we need to find him."

"Got it, sir. You bet."

"Now get your soon-to-be ex-boss to the hospital," he finished, and Lloyd could do nothing but shake his head because the words stung even worse than that taser.

Predictably, the nurse practitioners were staring at the chief quizzically, wondering just how he had managed to get those taser prongs stuck in his chest. Throughout the whole entire ordeal, both the chief and his assistant remained quiet, and soon enough, they found themselves standing in that recognizable parking lot at the police station. *Lloyd's* police station.

"I'm sorry, Lloyd," Sakura was saying, and it stung all the more that she wasn't using the word chief behind it. "As much as I'd like to, obviously, I probably shouldn't let you go in there. He could have done a lot worse than taser you, sir. He could have had you arrested."

"I know," he said calmly and matter-of-factly, belying the storm of fury and boiling rage he felt inside.

And with that, Sakura watched as Lloyd got into his personal car, backed up and left. Solemnly, she went back into the police station, and Gomes, who apparently was her new supervisor for now, was typing away furiously on what used to be the chief's desktop. "Notes," he said without looking up. "I'm taking notes, Sakura. Time to get to work on that letter to the rest of the department." Sakura took a seat across the seat. "Got it, Lieutenant."

The words just flew by, and she soon found herself hitting the "send-all" button on the department e-mail.

"I'm done, sir," she told him without leaving her seat. He was still typing just like a mad-man. "Fair enough, go ahead and try to give Sergeant Slim a call. Like I said, we need to find him. I need a word with him, obviously."

Sakura returned the sentiment. "Obviously."

She tried calling Sergeant Slim's phone several times that morning and even into the early afternoon, but to no avail.

Yet again, the rays from Sakura's cell phone zoomed out into the stratosphere, well past the birds and the helicopters circling ahead in the sky, and it dived back into the other cell phone ringing like crazy in the console of Slim's off-duty vehicle, a late-model Jeep Wrangler. The waves of the lake were tranquil with a slight breeze that was only briefly interrupted by those helicopter motors, and the water just might be hiding darker secrets, but for now, the only thing he saw was a lone bearded figure walking his dog. Mr. White Beard, Slim was calling him, because he certainly resembled a younger Kenny Rogers. "Nice day, isn't it?" the man said in passing as he tried to corral his overzealous dachshund. "Yeah, yeah, it is," Slim replied and then proceeded to show the man his badge. "I work for the police here, sir. Do you know what's going on at this lake?"

Mr. White Beard finally got his dog under control. "No, can't say that I do, but I did notice the helicopters..."

Slim quickly responded as the man's voice trailed off, but he wasn't ready to show his hand just yet. "Where are you from, sir?"

"Ah," the man laughed. "I'm an Okie, the Central part, over by Arcadia, just outside of Oklahoma City."

Slim knew it was time, and the man had an air of innocence about him anyway. "Oh," he replied. "Well, we've been investigating about a half-dozen homicides here, sir. Have you seen anything while you've been out today?"

As if on cue, the man flinched, and his dog started whining, probably ready for some movement yet again. "Really? I didn't know, and no, I hadn't seen anything. I'm just a part-time professor enjoying my day off and getting a change of scenery."

A quick glance from Slim around the lake revealed that the man was alone, as he only saw one car other than his own and no one else walking the path around the lake off in the distance either.

Nothing to see here, and he would have to wait until the helicopters stopped circling to get a better look at everything. "Okay, well have a nice day, sir."

The man started walking again. "Yep. You too, and good luck. I've always supported the men in Blue, the whole nine yards..."

It was time for him to go back to his Jeep, and it was only then that he noticed his cell ringing off the wall. "Sergeant Slim, where the hell are you?" an irate Sakura answered. "German Shepherd," he replied. She was nonplussed. "By yourself? What the hell? Get back over here! We've had to put Chief Lloyd on leave and Gomes wants to have a word with you now!" and then it was his turn to flinch. "All right," he replied. "I'm on my way."

CHAPTER 11

"I need to ask you some questions about how you and your suspect and you and the chief conducted yourself during said interview," Lieutenant Gomes began, even though he was still feeling a slight buzz from his scotch drink about five hours or so earlier. Thank God I didn't get too carried away on that, he thought.

The good news was that Slim's face didn't register any emotions whatsoever. "For starters," Gomes continued, "what kind of questions did you two ask him?"

"Well, just the standard stuff, lieutenant," Slim replied, suppressing a cough.

The lieutenant didn't skip a beat, figuring that Slim was just vying for extra time. "Such as...?"

"Well, you know..." Slim stammered slightly.

Gomes didn't let up. "No, sergeant, I *don't* know. By all means, enlighten me."

Slim was still stuttering. "W-well, the first thing we did was ask him about the lake and how we k-knew that he had been out there..."

Gomes briefly relaxed. "Okay, that's better, go on."

"...and then we kind of intimidated him a bit, compared him to Ed Kemper and different people, and we implied that even though he didn't have a car, he could have borrowed one because his dad's got all kinds and he's never there..."

"He's never there? Why not?"

"Well, he's taking care of the kid's mother in the nursing home, so he's got plenty of time by himself, and this guy's got all kinds of cars around that property. The kid's got a license, sir, so it wouldn't be a total stretch for him to take one of those cars...that's kind of what I was getting at there."

So far so good, Gomes thought, but he wasn't ready to give this Slim guy a free pass just yet.

"Well, Slim, did you get into the kid's personality any? You know, analyzing it? Feeling him out?"

"What do you mean?"

Lieutenant Gomes was beginning to get agitated now. "My god, kid," he said derisively, "just what are they teaching you all at that police academy nowadays?"

"I beg your pardon, lieutenant?" Gomes shot back scornfully. "Being a cop has been a lifelong dream of mine ever since I got out of the Marines in the late 70's..."

"Well, dream or not, did you touch on the kid's personality any?"

"What does that have to do with anything?"

Gomes was trying his level best to be patient. "Everything, especially when it comes to investigating a serial killer, sergeant. That's what I meant by my snarky comment a few moments ago..."

Slim knew the lieutenant was trying to be civil, but it was a challenge for him. As for himself, he was considering coming at the higher-up fed guy with his pocket knife. The cold sweat of anger was taking over. But for now, he merely listened as Gomes began a quasi-college lecture, something that was old hat for him.

"You see Slim. There are a lot of personality flaws that a serial killer might possess. Of course, it's just the beginning, but usually, when we are investigating a serial killer, we want to see evidence of a little thing called the Macdonald Triad."

"Yes," Slim uttered. "The Macdonald triad. Go on."

It took everything in Gomes' power not to roll his eyes. He knew he was dealing with people in the minor leagues when talking to this rookie. But he continued nonetheless.

"First, we have fire-setting, which is something that occurs at an early age..." and Slim nodded his head, demonstrating his familiarity with the concept. "Then," Gomes continued, "we have the cruelty to animals." Slim yet again nodded. "Finally, for many serial killers, we have a childhood full of either sexual abuse, enuresis better known as bed-wetting, or a combination of both." Slim nodded a final time, and Gomes caught his gaze, finally noticing that something about this man, his supposed colleague, something about him was off. He couldn't quite put his finger on it, but at that instant, he was getting a persistent chill down his spine.

Business is business, he thought, so in that moment, he tried his best to brush it off. But his eyes...his eyes. He tried to avoid looking at them as he asked the next question...

"So, Sergeant Slim, did you ask him about any of these characteristics? Did you ask him if he was mean to animals when he was younger, had sexual abuse, or if he had ever set any fires?"

Slim seemed dismissive, and for some reason it didn't aggravate Lieutenant Gomes like it normally would have, but made his hair stand on end. "No, lieutenant," he finally replied. "I can't say that we did..."

"Well, Sergeant, did you even ask him what make of car of his father's that he might have been using if he had been going out there? Seriously, this is elementary stuff here..."

For some reason, Slim was silently tapping the table. "No, Gomes, I can't say we did."

"That's too bad, sergeant, because we could have seen if some of the tire tracks matched, you know, things like that." As he finished those words, he happened to glance in his direction, and this man, who was supposed to be one of them, was licking his lips, and not in an automatic sort of way, but deliberately. As a state investigator, he had interviewed hundreds, if not thousands, of subjects to demonstrate his expertise in criminal interrogation. He had the house in the suburbs, the RV, and the large 401K to prove it. But in this instant, he was the one squirming, even though his demeanor was still cold as steel, and he was hiding it well. Still, Slim's behavior was strange, and now the respected fed was second-guessing himself. Was he enjoying himself? He looked like he was eating it up, totally glaring at him, proceeded by an ungodly smirk.

"You know, lieutenant," he began, "let's just call a spade a spade here…nobody *really* knows what was going on at that lake, my friend. You and me and my boss Lloyd that you are now trying to fire, we can pick up all the clues in the world, but we're not any closer, my friend, we're not any closer…"

He kept up his rambling, but Gomes' ears perked up with each and every word, every little bit of his spiel.

"Here's the thing, lieutenant. There is indeed someone-or something-who knows what is going on at that lake. Those birds, my friend. Those birds. They know it all, and they see everything, they see it all, they see everything, lieutenant."

He kind of let the lieutenant part of the speech drag out, and then he met Gomes' gaze once again. It was a split-second flash, and it was something about the way that Slim looked at him, but suddenly, a macabre light bulb turned on in the seasoned state investigator's face, just like he was looking at the stain on a priceless French painting in a heavily-guarded museum. Things were marred now, and he now knew, within the very fiber of his being, that he wasn't dealing with a fellow cop any longer. He was dealing with someone else entirely, and he was bereft. His normal poise had abandoned him. In his years of investigations, he had seen it all and done it all. He was very familiar with the stench of human decomposition. He also knew when people were not telling the truth, and on rare occasions, he would get a powerful feeling that things were horribly wrong, and this was one of those rare times. He didn't want to show his hand, not just yet, so he kept his poker face on.

"Are you talking about the birds of the animal kingdom, sergeant?" he said as calmly as possible. "Because it's not those birds I'm worried about. God only knows it took me forever to get helicopters out there, Slim. It's those kinds of birds we need."

"Yes, that's true. Wasn't it those helicopters that caught that Artie Shawcross a couple of years back?"

It was said with fascination, and even though Gomes' heart skipped a beat, he cleared his throat so that his body reaction would not betray his emotions.

"Yeah, that guy in upstate New York..."

"Funny how we were investigating another Arthur until you came around, lieutenant..."

"Yeah, real funny, and I'm beginning to think some odd things about this, Slim, some really odd things." And as Gomes said that he felt like he was the one backed into a corner.

Slim was laying on the sarcasm real thick. "Such as?"

The state lieutenant remained evasive. "You know, really, Slim, I think that it's best if we put you on leave just like your partner."

The reply from Slim was unexpected and very soft-spoken. "Why?" he uttered, and that threw Gomes off too.

He felt like a namby-pamby even though he had seen it all and done it all by now, but the adrenaline was coursing through his veins and there was no turning back now. "I-I just don't feel comfortable with either of the two of you working on this investigation. That's all. Get your things and get the hell out of here, Slim. I'm serious. Now!"

In mock submission, the other man went ahead and began gathering up his things, all the while presenting a look that was almost other-worldly to Gomes. Had he opened up the pandora's box?

There was no reply from Slim at all while he methodically went about the room, getting ready to leave. No "okay", no "I guess", no passive-aggressive words whatsoever. Nothing but deafening silence. Finally he spoke as he was standing in the doorway.

"You don't realize what you've just done, do you, Lieutenant Gomes?" The fed guy wanted to retort that he was taking the investigation back, but try as he might the words simply wouldn't come out.

Arthur felt the bruises on his eyelids, but he was thanking his lucky stars nonetheless. As he started out to go see his mother at the nursing home, it was yet again another day filled with nothing more than maddening silence. The typical traffic was everywhere, both from the vehicles driven by people running errands and from the feet of people doing the same. He was eventually going to make it to that nursing home yet again, and this time dad would be there tending to mom like the unassuming but great guy that he was. Life was going on, and that was a good thing. He knew that. People were paying him no mind whatsoever in that little small town that had been named after settlers from California over a hundred years prior. But there was still something gnawing at him as he hurried down the sidewalk. He began rubbing at his temple, just inches away from the evidence of the beating that he had taken. Despite enjoying the average day in that average small town, he kept vigilant, peering at the activity just as if he was looking at some ominous storm clouds. Where were those two town bullies masquerading as police officers? It seemed as if they had disappeared off the face of the earth, and he couldn't make heads or tails of it. He passed one avenue, then another, and then another, and there was nothing that would indicate the ordeal he had been through. Even the sun was out, glaring at everyone doing their errands.

The first big bout of adversity for him was passing the police station, which stood there as a testament to his fortitude, but it was also there alone, glaring at him disapprovingly, ominously, and arrogantly. No one was coming in or out, though, so why should he pay it any mind, either? He passed right on by, not even giving it another moment's thought. But several blocks down the street, he saw yet another obstacle, one that would be more difficult to overcome. It was the liquor store, and he gave it a second, third, fourth, and even a fifth look. He saw that late-model Volkswagen Jetta parked in the employee portion of the liquor store parking lot, one that the heavy-set woman that worked there was very proud of. He not only knew the car was hers, but he also knew that buying the spirits was tempting, just like the feminine charm of an extramarital lover. How many times had he sobered up in the can? How many times had he partied with his now ex-wife's friends? Over and over again. But at the same time, he wanted to believe. He was trying to believe, that what that butch, lesbian biker woman had said the other day was true. No, the alcohol wasn't him, and he was trying with all of his might to believe that.

He very easily and nondescriptly could go in there, deluding himself that he had a virginal hand, buy a pint of bourbon, go behind the bushes and drink it down without even giving it a second thought. He grinned, momentarily thinking that he would do just that, even going on to the hospital as planned and fooling everyone, from the CEO in the front office, right down to the nurse's aides and even his parents and his aunt in their room. His eyes darted from the ancient liquor store building grimly, however, because he realized the opposite was true as well. He could very easily go in there, buy the pint of bourbon, finish it off behind the bushes and go on to the hospital and be a total stumbling and cursing jerk to everyone within earshot and within his view, getting kicked out of the hospital for life and possibly earning himself another meeting with Chief Bridges and Slim. That's why he couldn't go through with it, and that's why his would-be dalliance with the liquor store was only a momentary synapse within the recesses of his cranium. He continued on to the hospital, showing up sober and clean as a whistle.

Things looked as ordinary as they always were. Dad was there, but other than a wave, he was vigorously feeding mom, who was doing nothing more than just taking the bite and staring off into space. Aunt Liz was sitting next to them, and she was yet again straining, this time staring with her magnifying glass at a somewhat frayed and out-of-date National Geographic. Even though she was pushing one hundred, she had always been a creature of habit, so she squinted up at him, saying, "Oh hi, Art, been a while..."

He tried his best not to smirk sarcastically as his dad momentarily met his gaze, each of the two men sharing that elephant in the room. "Yeah, I've been a bit distracted, Liz." The old gal was also full of surprises, and so she asked, "Who's this Steve Irwin guy?" out of the blue, probably in reference to what she was reading. Dad couldn't help but chuckle silently, also typical for him.

"Oh, him? He's a guy who had his own nature show a few years back, but he was killed by a stingray."

"Oh," she replied. Funny how it wasn't always the big things that people should be worried about, but the mundane things, Arthur mused. Funny how it seemed like whatever higher power people subscribed to could just snap their fingers and just like that, someone could be just dust to the wind, pure and simple.

Time to cut the small-talk. "How's mom?"

"Same old, same old, she hasn't said much, nothing to write home about, right?" and she called out to Art's old man. "Right," he replied without looking away from his task of spoon-feeding her a bit from the fruit tray.

A split-second later, Aunt Liz looked back at Arthur, and those cloudy eyes might have been blinded by glaucoma since her 80s, but he knew that she was an old soul and had been one ever since she had been a child riding around in a horseless carriage with her ma and pa. She could only make out shapes, but that was enough for her.

"Something's bothering you, isn't it, Artie?" she said, and my god, she had always been so good at reading people. Art and his old man exchanged glances, then they both nodded slightly in silent agreement. "I just have a lot on my mind, Auntie Liz," Arthur said matter-of-factly. It was the truth, but the seemingly telepathic understanding between the two men was that he should not divulge it any further.

She laughed, showing off a crooked, toothless smile that was almost a century old, and it immediately put both father and son at ease. "Oh, Artie! Whatever it is, I know it will work out....you know, your dad and I have been trying our best to watch over your mother. And you know that God and Mary and the angels are watching over you too!"

Arthur appreciated the pep-talk from this woman who had literally been born when Teddy Roosevelt was thinking about running again for President, and he and the old man yet again exchanged glances. If you only knew, Arthur thought, and his dad seemed to echo the sentiment, but now was not the time to admit to anything, even with the butterflies from his heart, so he played it off.

"Thanks, Liz, I appreciate that. I really do. It's not an easy deal, but I appreciate that positive attitude of yours. Good to see you two are looking after her so well..."

To his credit, his old man was keeping a positive attitude. "See you back at the house, Art."

"All right, dad," he replied quietly as he headed out the door, possibly out to his own doom in that cold, cruel world where the only thing keeping him from an executioner's needle was his book smarts.

~

Roger had it memorized by now. He knew her facade all-too-well, and he knew she was a fake. He was safely tucked away in Dr. Savage's closet now, having snuck in when she was away and careless enough to leave it unlocked. He had her middle-aged love interest and the sound of his voice memorized by now as well, and it wasn't long before he heard the front door open and the two were laughing and chatting, just like they were some kind of newlywed married couple.

He heard a faucet turning on, and he momentarily thought that she was going to cook him some dinner. No dice, though, because the laughing and carrying on traveled down the hall of that behemoth apartment, finally arriving at the bedroom that had the closet that Roger was hiding in. He couldn't help but finger the Glock in the formidable darkness of that closet, and they continued to chat and move about the room. She took off her jacket, and he heard her drape it over a chair. It wouldn't have mattered either way, he mused, because this Glock would make easy work of both of them, especially considering how many rounds could come exploding out of the magazine. No matter, they both came close to the other side of that closet, but then they scurried like teenagers to the other side of that immense room.

"How were you able to afford such a splendid apartment?" he heard the guy say, and if the context had been different, he would have sworn the gay wasn't straight in the least. She did her best to laugh off his question good-naturedly, still oblivious to the hatred that was behind her closet.

"Oh," she finally replied coyly, "I have my ways..."

"Really?" the guy popped off, half laughing. "Do tell." And yet again, Roger couldn't help but think he was literally in the closet himself.

"Well, daddy, you know. He had a thing for the younger women, meeting my mother and rescuing her from that communist Russian hell-hole, you know, and it helps that he's loaded..."

Ah, Roger about said aloud, almost giving away his hiding space. That would definitely explain a lot, and the rage about overwhelmed him. They were about to make love, but he wanted them to make love to his magazine instead.

"I guess you could call me one of those trust fund babies," she concluded. "Oh, god in the heavens, no!" her companion squealed, and Roger about burst out, gun-a-blazing, just listening to him. "You mean to tell me you didn't get all of this fancy stuff on your good looks alone?"

She laughed. "In a way, I guess I did. Good thing I take after my mother, I suppose...all I had to do was snap my fingers and the old man would cater to my every whim!"

Luckily for them, that was the end of the playful conversation, because Roger couldn't take anymore. They started locking lips, and he heard the rustle of belts, pants, and shirts coming off, and he knew it wouldn't be long now. He knew they were moving to the bed, and Dr. Savage was soon begging her companion not to stop. After what seemed like an eternity, he heard the both of them standing up, and he thought that was the end of that. His hand grasped the closet door, poised to make his move. No, just more movement, more grunts and groans, and suddenly she was talking dirty to her companion in their last release.

"Oh, you like doing me there, don't you?" she said in mock disapproval. "You like it there better than the front, don't you, bad boy?" and he just moaned his approval.

Soon enough, they both screamed, collapsing on top of each other on that poor bed once again. He thought they were going to fall asleep, but it wasn't long before he heard them getting their things and clothes back in place like the upstanding citizens that they were. "So..." he heard the guy say, "this time next week?"

"Yeah," she said matter-of-factly. "Let's shoot for that. It's been fun."

They both left the room, softly closing the door behind them, and he heard them laughing and cavorting on the outside of the hideously expensive apartment. He had a sneaking suspicion that this man would be in her life for much longer than just one night, that he was going to be a large part of his wonderful therapist's life for many years. He smirked though, because now it was just a waiting game, and he fingered the gun on his side once more, just like it was his own phallic organ getting ready to get him off as well.

Such a large apartment, he mused, but those windows were so thin because he heard the guy's sedan starting, and he knew that he was getting ready to leave. Sure enough, the car pulled away, and he could picture Dr. Savage walking back up the granite steps until Voila! she was opening the door to her apartment yet again. It was now or never, he knew, and he was ready to make his move just as his heart skipped a beat, making him seem frozen in time.

But soon enough, he snapped out of it as he heard her obliviously walking down the hallway. As she was in the bedroom yet again, she didn't seem to notice that her closet door was ever-so-slightly ajar, and that the retinas from his greedy eyes were watching every move she made, every breath, every slight dalliance. Little did she know, that she was about to have a dalliance with death. Right now though, his ice-cold pupils were simply taking in every modest movement that emanated from her body, which had always looked good for her age anyway. She stripped out of her clothes yet again, and she was down to her bra and panties, and that's when he was ready to strike. He reached for the wooden portion of the closet door, and in just a split-second more he was going to open the door, his gun blazing, riddling her with bullets and ripping her apart.

Except it was that very moment that something caught her eye, and she herself flinched as she noticed the door. She stared him down, not even fully realizing that someone was behind the door, and he heard two words that he would come to dread that night: "Who's there?"

And suddenly, all of the self-doubt and self-hatred came flooding out of him, and it took everything in his power not to do something stupid and reply, "No one!" at the top of his lungs. Suddenly, he wasn't a middle-aged man who was about to commit a felonious capital offense, but he was yet again that terrified little boy who was all alone on his uncle's boat. Suddenly, there was no more darkness from that closet, but nothing but sunlight emanating all around him off of that wretched water. Suddenly, he was the one being violated, and not the violator.

But as he was about to do that unthinkable deed and play God storming out of that closet, she took another look in that crack in the door, and this she stood taller, and she seemed even more confident and professional than she had been in those counseling circles. The tone was unthinkable and repellant to Roger: "Who's. There!"

His hands trembled, and it was an involuntary reflex, but he knew he had met his match. He kept his silence, and everything quieted down soon enough. He lost track of all time in that closet, finally leaving as she fell asleep in that darkened room as her traditionally reddish alarm clock was flashing three a.m.

Chief Lloyd had found a new best friend, but it was one that was of his own doing and was going to ultimately stab him in the back. At that very moment, Eliza was looking him dead in the eye.

"Why so glum, chum?" she asked him with a hint of intentional sarcasm in her voice. For his part, Lloyd didn't even look up from his exorbitant cocktail of Jim Beam and Coke.

"Well," he replied, "I uh-, kind of jumped the gun, you know, and this kid probably isn't the one. He probably isn't the serial killer out at that lake. Me and that new recruit, that ex-farmer, that guy who I used to know from the service that went by Slim and used to be a farmer? We both roughed up that Arthur kid *after* he lawyered up and that Gomes bastard was so ticked off over it that he put me on leave over violating the kid's rights."

"Lloyd, Lloyd, Lloyd," Eliza purred in a manner that was meant to be as disarming as possible. "As I've told you before, my father and stepfather were both cops, so it's not like I haven't been around the block a time or two."

"I know, I know, I just really wanted to solve this case without this guy," he growled quietly.

"Yeah, well, you still got me, as long as he doesn't make a run at your pension, which I doubt. Here in a couple of years, we'll be on a beach in California and you'll have another mini-me running around..." and the chief couldn't help but laugh.

But she wasn't done yet. "And that Arthur kid? Well, he's a mess, and even if he didn't do those killings at the lake, I'm sure he'll be turning tricks in the pen at that time anyways."

"True, Liza, probably true," he said, and he suddenly raised his eyebrows in an epiphany. "You know what? Even though I'm still on leave, there's nothing that says I still can't keep an eye on the kid..."

Now it was Eliza's turn to laugh. "That's my boy. That's my future cop husband right there. I was out at that lake once anyways, and there's nothing that says that you can't drive out there as a private citizen..."

Lloyd smirked. "No, there really isn't. There isn't any reason at all."

With that, she walked into the bathroom, humming to herself, and she soon emerged a few minutes later in her jogging shorts. "I'll talk to you here in a bit, Lloyd. I'm going out for a little run here..."

If only that damned Becky would just hurry up with the proceedings, he thought bitterly as he was now sitting alone. He fingered his badge on the side of his pants. Thirty years, he scowled. Thirty years down the drain because of that retarded kid and that high-and-mighty fed guy. Thirty. Years. He continued to think that, letting it sink in.

He was running the risk of losing Eliza, and he knew that. But he couldn't help it. The demons were getting the better of him, because he was not ever going to be married to anybody. He had been married to his job, but now, he not only was going through a marital divorce but a career divorce as well. So he was digging through his wallet to find the key to the liquor cabinet, come hell or high water. He found the key, unlocked the liquor cabinet, and poured himself another strong glass of scotch.

Arthur was still terrified of his own shadow, and he thought it was going to be just like that Ghost movie where the demons with sinking faces and ungodly moans were going to come out any minute and completely vaporize him into oblivion.

He was in the garage now, and that space had that all-too-familiar musty smell that was usually present in the homes of older senior citizens. The place was familiar to him because it stirred up a whole host of childhood memories as he gazed upon the vintage Mustang. It had been considered a classic car for the better part of twenty years, and in its heyday, it had been in several small-town parades. Now, it was just sitting there collecting dust, and it was in a room that had nothing more than cobwebs and dust anyway. The Mustang had a dark side to it, though, because he knew what was in the trunk of the classic car, and he knew that the keys were present on that trunk, just sitting there minding their own business, but also just waiting for someone to occasionally open it up. It had his rare coin collection in it, which was yet again another symbol of his half-hearted attempt to chase down some type of status and avoid being so weird.

He kept second-guessing himself, so without further adieu, he made his way to the trunk of the Mustang, turning the key and opening up that trunk to reveal the glory of all that had been concealed. Viola! It was a Beretta M9, and it was one of the possessions that his old man had salvaged from his prior vehicle buying trips in his work as a used car salesman, back when it had been better days for all of them. His dad didn't even have a license to own it, but there had been several times when he had been younger that he stuck it out to the firing range outside of town, so he knew it worked just fine.

He also knew that it was loaded with a fresh magazine, and all it would take was one discharge, and he would no longer be the town pariah. Indeed, he would no longer be the Earth pariah, either. Maybe an otherworldly one, but oh well. He fingered the gun as he held it in his hand, and there was no doubt that it was the epitome of craftsmanship. He knew every curve on the gun even better than some girlfriends that he'd held in the past. Now, just like the cunnilingus he had engaged in with those girls stemming back to high school, he held that lovely little beast up to his mouth, placing the chamber right there on the interior. Just one second, he thought. Just one second, and it would all be over.

His fingers continued to tremble and he wasn't certain that he could go through with it. It was so simple, yet so difficult at the same time. With his other hand, he fingered some of the pocket change in his trousers, and he settled upon a compromise: a coin flip. Heads, he would go ahead, and tails, he would put the gun back. In almost one fell one-handed swoop, he tossed the quarter in the air, caught it, and placed it in the freezer, which was about as ancient as the Mustang itself. He held his breath, briefly closing his eyes before looking at the quarter. Tails. Damn. It was tails. He put the gun back, closing the trunk, even though everyone hated him.

It was just a simple coin flip. He knew that. It didn't matter whether he abided by it or not, but the shadows in that house were playing with his head now, and something otherworldly was yet again after him, urging him, pleading with him, telling him that he shouldn't do it. He knew he would get his day in court one way or the other. He knew that the evidence just wasn't there. Above all else, he knew he was innocent, even though the rumors and glares kept getting overwhelming yet again. He could play Radiohead's "Creep" all by himself to try to get these thoughts to stay in his head, so that's exactly what he did.

In the darkness of that snobby, college-educated, high-rise Denver neighborhood, Roger stumbled upon another brainstorm for how he could get even, how he could show the world that he was the victim instead. The synapses of his middle-aged brain kept firing away even though the world was asleep. The good news was that the life of his counselor was going to be spared, and she could go on to torment as many other men like him that she wanted. The bad news was that someone else's life was going to be sacrificed.

He felt the slightest breeze fondling through his locks, and for a moment, he thought it was some earthbound force that was trapped, struggling to reach another plane. He blinked, and the sensation was gone, but he had to think that some entity was smiling widely, dripping with fluids, in its approval down upon him. The old-time television home movies kept flashing through his mind, the ones where the technological marvels of the 8mm were on full display and where Dad took the only car-usually a paneled station wagon to his industrial job and the mother stayed at the house, changed diapers, and kept the dishes down until he came home. Ah, those ones were difficult to produce, and they are now even collector's items for some, he thought sardonically. With cell phones, making movies was old hat by now, and goodness knows he had made a few, albeit unbeknownst to the subjects, and he couldn't help but laugh even in the icy overnight air.

His idea was so simple that it was profound, and he knew that even if it didn't work out as planned, it would still have the same destructive results. He would have to plan for Johnny Law to intervene, and he wasn't sure exactly how to do that, but as he kept walking in that icy night-time Denver air, he came upon an all-night convenience store that happened to have some booths reserved for the old-timers to sit on for a few hours and gossip. He ordered one of those pre-packaged sandwiches and got a stale coffee from the machine from the inattentive clerk, and he knew at the very least it would give him time to think. As he sipped that coffee and munched on that cold sandwich, it quickly came to him: guns. That's what he needed.

Strong, solid, powerful guns. The kind of guns that Kurtwood Smith from RoboCop would have a total field day over. The kind of guns that would give him the redemption that he needed even if his plans went totally awry. Guns that had the kind of explosive power that would allow him to go out in a blaze of glory if that's what the situation warranted.

All he knew was that he would need to have some kind of backup plan, and that's what these guns would be for. His thoughts drifted back to those home movies, and he thought about that little kid he used to be before Uncle George had sunk his clutches into him, and how like everyone else, he would go everywhere on that prepubescent bike. The general rule in those little towns before the dawn of video games, social media, and the internet was that you were expected home once those streetlights came on for the night. Within the mist of those foggy evenings, as they all headed home, there were always streets that their young minds were hesitant to steer their bike towards. They usually

consisted of nondescript yards with green lawns and all of the other trap-
pings of suburban life, but in at least one case, there was always some
man standing at one of those doorways.

Maybe he was a little bit unshaven, maybe he had a glass of one of
those bad drinks in his hand, and maybe he was staring just a little bit too
long at the youngsters and their bicycle crew. Ah yes, Roger mused.
*These were the people that our parents tried to warn us about. They tried
to warn us about that stranger danger, but all the while, they forgot to
warn us about people like Uncle George.* Oh well, no matter, it was his
turn to be a stranger. The plan was coming into focus, along with the
reason why he would need the firearms. He was going to pick an unassuming day, and he was going to drive to a small town, far away from
Denver, and he was going to stake out one of their little parks. He knew
that even in today's world, there would be plenty of streetlight kids, and
even with some parents there, he could simply hold them at gunpoint and
nab the kid. And if the kid was alone? All the better for his plan. All the
better for his act of revenge and his reign of terror. The kid would go off
in his van, and he would possibly be kicking and screaming, but he
would never be seen again. That is, never to be seen by his parents.
Roger would see the kid plenty, both in real life and on those missing
posters, and he smiled sardonically at that.

He also smiled in mock approval of himself, because this was such a
better plan than his initial idea of raping and murdering his therapist.
This was loads better, and with that thought, it was a good thing he was
alone, because he began laughing hysterically.

"Well, you both are free to go on your merry way," the judge said, raising
his gavel as he turned his head to both a hungover Chief Lloyd and his
now ex-wife Becky. He sighed, mainly because it was finally over, and
he briefly leered at her with a smug look. Her face was noncommittal,
devoid of emotion as she walked out of the courtroom. It was a nice
change for both of them after years of growing apart, and he now could
propose to Eliza, and that's exactly what he did later that afternoon at a

high-price restaurant right there in Colorado Springs. She said yes, and they began planning their engagement. Although it had literally been at least three decades since Chief Lloyd had been planning one of his own weddings, he immediately realized just how different the two of them actually were.

Unlike Mr. Bridges, the soon-to-be next Mrs. Bridges had never experienced a wedding where she was the bride. Thus, she wanted all kinds of different things that any would-be bride would be thrilled to have just so they could make their day complete. She wanted brides-maids, groomsmen, even a ring bearer and a flower girl. You name it, she wanted it.

On the other hand, the ancient and bitter ex-police chief would have been content just to go to Vegas and find a decent-looking wedding chapel on the strip. Sign, sealed, and delivered, it's time for a new life. But he kept his mouth shut, because even back in Bakersfield, he and his prospective bride were meeting every day to iron out the details and plan it out as much as they could. It was giving Lloyd a headache, and that wasn't good, especially considering that he was just sitting in front of the boob tube while he was on leave. He should be happy. He knew that. Other men his age were giddy about buying their first RV, but he was not only going to get a camper, but also a hefty police pension and a younger bride to boot.

He was crestfallen, and the reason for his discord was because in his heart of hearts, he knew all the years of earning that police pension didn't matter. It. Didn't. Matter. Eliza had to take a break from all of the wedding planning because she was busy at work, and that was all the encouragement Lloyd needed to go back to his makeshift firing range. Except this time, it was going to be his own beer that he used. And so it was, and so the drunker that he got, the worse his shot actually became. It began with the usual ranting and raving, and that was when he kept knocking those Coors Light cans off one by one. After he had knocked back a dozen beers that is when the only thing knocking those cans off was the slight breeze glancing against those fenceposts. He was cursing and swearing when he heard the call come in on his cell phone and picked it up. He was hoping that it was Eliza needing something, but no such luck. His heart raced with dread as he realized that it was Lieutenant Gomes.

"Yeah," he answered with as much false bravado as he could muster. "Lloyd," Gomes began, and the embattled chief couldn't help but notice that he had left out the "chief" part, "I need you at the station pronto! We have some things we need to discuss."

He briefly glanced at his private vehicle, which was yet another reminder that he was the same as a private citizen. He knew that he had a pretty strong buzz from the beer and that he was borderline intoxicated. Still, he ambled to the car in his tipsy state, all the while knowing that should he get stopped, he no longer had the leeway of being the chief of police any longer. He would be treated just like any other private citizen. Luckily for him and for his fellow motorists, he arrived back in Bakersfield uneventfully, making it back to that all-too-familiar police headquarters, parking the car in a nearby retail store so it would at least look like he had been walking. He knew that this meeting was ominous to say the least. He walked through that door just like he had millions of times before, and the receptionist greeted him with somewhat of a fake smile, saying, "Hello, Lloyd, they're waiting for you in the back." Yet again, no "chief" had been uttered before his first name. Not good. Not good at all.

It was in the conference where he and his department would hold weekly meetings, and he saw the lieutenant seated on one side and Sakura on the other. "Have a seat, Lloyd," Gomes said gravely, without any type of warm tone whatsoever. "Chief Lloyd..." and he blinked at this because there it was! Maybe it wouldn't be so bad after all! "...we've had an internal review of your interview with that Arthur kid and other incidents of misbehavior, and I have decided that not only should you be removed from this case, but you should be relieved of duty entirely." Lloyd knew now that it had just been wishful thinking, and it was all a blur as he turned in anything at all related to his now-former life as a small-town police chief. His badge, his gun, his department-issued cell phone - all of it was turned in. His whole life was reduced to this in just ten minutes flat, and the only positive he could glean from the situation was that somehow, someway, Gomes hadn't smelled the strong odor of the beer on his breath. "Should I go find that Art kid now and tell him that we have eliminated him as a suspect?" he heard Sakura say, and his ears couldn't help but perk up. "Yeah," Gomes replied. "The DNA evidence we got today didn't match. It's also time to find that Slim guy and tell him he's out too."

Well, good god, Lloyd thought. Those were revelations. Artie the retard has been eliminated as a suspect and my buddy Slim is going to be fired too? He had half a mind to storm back in there and start yelling bloody murder, but he didn't want the public intoxication charge.

~

"Thoughts are funny things, I suppose," Arthur said to himself as the birds were yet again playing again in the trees. "What I think, that is what I become," he continued, paraphrasing Gandhi, and he knew he had to take his mind off of it all.

He didn't know how it was going to happen. He just knew that it had to happen one way or the other. The oblivious birds up above him started darting to and fro, not because he was walking, but in response to the train siren that was ringing out in the distance. It wasn't really Art's cup of tea either, even though he briefly stopped his stroll and looked off in the distance of where the train tracks would be. It wasn't long before a sudden realization struck him, and it was one where he was no longer a mile or so from that train, oh no. Instead, he was Corey Feldman in Stand By Me, and he was staring the damned thing down, uttering the words "train..." with every alternating breath.

Issues. Corey Feldman's character had issues. Don't we all? Arthur thought. Didn't the character that I was named after in that other movie, Arthur's Theme, have issues too?

That person in Stand By Me wasn't the worst by a long-shot, though. He had some kind of major depressive disorder, something that caused him to disassociate from reality, something that gave him a serious death-wish, something that prompted him to act the same way that one of his high-school chums had acted like one night after he had received a Dear John letter from his girlfriend even though he had just joined the Navy and arguably should have had his whole life in front of him. But those train sirens were absolutely fascinating, and they sounded off at all hours of the day, with a haunting melody all their own, and if the only thing he had to worry about was a Dear John letter, he would be in much better shape now.

It made him angry that a kid who was perfectly normal and who had had everything handed to him felt the need to kill himself with a train. He knew that it should have been him. How dare he be different! How dare he not be above reproach! How dare he have to look at the disapproving glances from the townspeople and go through this hideous stigma! But no matter, he had to snap out of it because he was going to go vent to Mom and Lizzie. His mother wouldn't register what he was saying, but Lizzie's century-old eyes would register the same shock that he had, even though she would likely give him the benefit of the doubt like she always did.

The intersection to the nursing home was in view, and he was getting ready to start heading down that way, but suddenly he spotted a big black suburban driving past him and parking just in front of him. A man in a suit came out, and for a minute, Arthur thought he was going to head to one of the coffee shops or the restaurant on that street, but he seemed like he was headed straight toward him, and his eyes were straight away tensing up. Now what?

"Sir?" the man said after he had stopped about six feet away from him and stuck his hand out. "Are you Arthur?" the man asked and Art nodded in response. "Lieutenant Gomes."

Arthur recoiled ever so slightly, and Gomes picked up on it almost instantly. "I know, I know, Arthur," he said, attempting to reassure him. "I'm not bringing you in for another interview, and I know you don't know me from apple butter, kiddo, but I just wanted to tell you that you've been officially eliminated as a suspect for those murders that have gone on at your lake..."

The next thing this seasoned law enforcement officer knew, Arthur was sobbing on his chest, and his steely resolve melted, his lips quivering in befuddlement. "We had some DNA evidence, kid, and it doesn't match you..."

After Art peeled away from him and gained his resolve, the only thing that he could say to the fed guy on that sidewalk was, "Really?"

"Yes, really," the big-shot law enforcement aficionado replied. "We don't have anything on you, sir. Let me repeat: you are no longer a suspect."

"Well, Mr. Gomes," Arthur said as the wind started picking up, "I about solved the problem for you anyway...maybe it's a good thing I didn't. I've got two words for you: Smith and Wesson."

"What are you trying to say here, Arthur? Do I need to take you in to be evaluated?"

Art was now being a little bit too cavalier for his new-found acquaintance, and he knew it. "No, I'm all right now, but for a minute there I thought I was going to end up like those boys in Arkansas that were on that HBO show..."

"Ah yes, the West Memphis Three."

"Yeah, that's what I'm talking about, sir."

Lieutenant Gomes stuck out his hand one more time. "Well, like I said, Arthur, you're free to go. You're no longer a suspect." Arthur sighed in relief, thanking him profusely, and at least for this round, his dance with the grim reaper was over, if only in this realm.

As Roger began thinking about the second phase of his diabolical plan, he was ironically humming that Nancy Sinatra tune from the sixties about her boots. She was the child of a star and a star herself, he thought as he was peering at the impressive array of illegal firearms in that graffiti-ridden garage in that back alleyway. He knew that it might have been easier for him just to go to a gun show and find some local redneck that was unloading some of his firearms, but with his luck he would be recognized at one of them, especially considering his arrest made the local news just a few years ago.

He kept eyeing one example in particular and it wasn't long before one of the black guys that was running this underground show came over and unceremoniously slapped him on the back.

"Pretty nice one, isn't it?" he said. "That one's a straw purchase, and it's a Glock 19. It's truly a thing of beauty, isn't it, wonderbread?" and he laughed in a way that could only be described as off-putting to Roger, and so he was glaring at him.

"My last name is Cisneros," Roger muttered. "I'm half-Mexican." Even with that, the would-be black gun trafficker didn't know when to stop.

"Really?" the guy laughed again. "You sure don't look like it."

"So I've been told," Roger grunted. "Let's get back to the guns, shall we?"

The black guy backed off. "Right, fair enough. You're a man on a mission, seems like."

"You could say that." If you only knew. If you only knew indeed.

Even though the guy was rubbing him the wrong way, Roger did end up leaving that corner garage with that Glock 19, along with a Smith and Wesson and three other fine examples too. He had to have some type of Plan B, even if the shady guy selling them was driving him nuts. If anything, even if he didn't ruin some small-town family's life, he could ruin a pig's life, eh? and it was his turn to laugh.

"I hate you!" he screamed in a low guttural moan that would have made any death-core metal artist proud. There was no getting around it, though. He had been caught red-handed, and he was no longer the colleague of Lieutenant Gomes, but instead the one that was being arrested by him. The man might have been middle-aged, but he had a fantastic grip as it was clasped around Slim's neck in an effort to get him to stop resisting. It had been just dumb luck that the lieutenant had decided to drive out to the lake before heading back to Denver for a while. But once he arrived, he stumbled upon a strange sight indeed. There was Slim, the man that was supposed to be his colleague, and he was lying next to an obviously deceased young twenty-something, and he was not attempting to help her in any way, shape or form. Instead, he was touching himself. As luck would have it, Lieutenant Gomes sneaked upon him and startled him, with the two men engaging in a tussle in his attempts to cuff him.

The sounds that were coming from this man's throat were not those of a peace officer, but instead that of a serial killer, and Gomes knew it for sure now. He knew that those vials of DNA he and his crew had diligently collected would lead to this man and his morbid fascination with killing. Above all else, he knew that confronting that Arthur boy and having him officially eliminated as a suspect had been the right thing as he finally overpowered Slim and got the cuffs on him.

"So! It was you all along!" Gomes shouted in vindication. "No wonder you and Chief Bridges were trying so hard to get a confession out of that Arthur kid!" In response, Slim just tried to spit on him, missing badly in the process and watching his spittle land in the murky lake water below.

"Clarence 'Slim' Johnson," Gomes continued, "you are under arrest for the murders at German Shepherd Lake. You have the right to remain silent. Anything you say can and will be used against you. You have the right to an attorney. If you cannot afford one, one will be appointed for you.."

Lloyd was glaring at the flat-screen television and mocking Joyce Meyer in his drunken stupor when Eliza showed back up again. He quickly switched it off, but Eliza was just as quick to respond. "Don't shut that off! I like listening to her!"

"Well, excuse me!" Lloyd fired back to the future Mrs. Bridges with no effort whatsoever to hide his slur.

She had her hands on her hips, and suddenly he thought he was looking at a younger version of Becky.

"How long are you going to hold on to this?" she asked in a dispirited tone.

He remained defiant. "As long as I want to, babe."

She did not answer, instead going into the adjoining bedroom where he could hear her changing out of her dispatcher clothing into something more comfortable. After she reappeared in sweats, she said with a touch of sarcasm, "I'm going out for an evening jog. Have fun, Lloyd."

He was ignoring her and he didn't even look up, but she wasn't quite done yet. She began lecturing him as she stood in the doorway.

"Just remember, Lloyd, we'll be off on that beach somewhere in just a few years. You'll be going through all of the same stuff that a man half your age is going through what with raising a young child and you'll have everything back that you lost..." and then she motioned toward his alcoholic drink. "Or, you can have that and die alone and unsung in some hospital bed...your choice."

The words struck a chord with him for all of five minutes after she left, with that all-too-familiar scent of hers spurring him on. But then, just as quickly as it came, the urge to walk the straight and narrow was gone like a shooting star in the evening sky.

He wanted some echoes of the good old days before he got totally snickered, so he yet again began fingering those military dog tags, first his own, and then his old man's as well. He felt the lettering, lovingly going over each part of the "Lloyd" and then going up to the "Bridges" and then painstakingly feeling the numbers. He then felt for the tiny "C" for his long-departed "Catholic" religion. Then, he felt his dad's, and they were exactly the same because there was no "Sr." that had been added on those tiny tags. He fingered those dog tags just like he was feeling up the middle of a Cambodian hooker, and it guided him through each and every shot of that strong liquor. Each shot he hurled back was like he was a man on a mission, and it didn't take long after that. Not long at all...

Suddenly, he was looking at his hand, and it lacked the normal body hair that he was accustomed to. Indeed, it looked like a much-younger version of his hand, and that is when he noticed the floor. It was that hardwood that his old man had been so proud of when he was growing up. It had been a do-it-yourself job; he was always a serious man, but he would still host neighborhood backyard barbecues in that humongous yard and brag about it and showed it off. Indeed, that was about the closest he came to cutting up with people. But then, Lloyd looked up, seeing the oak wall background that had been the family den. Suddenly, his old man came into view, and he too looked much younger, with a fuller head of hair and a fuller face and arms that rippled with middle-aged muscles. He stared daggers at Lloyd at that very moment, and then he slowly shook his head. Lloyd couldn't help but notice the large shadows bouncing off his head on the den area in an unnatural and ungodly display, and somehow, someway, they became larger and larger, to the point where they were covering the entire room, making it not quite light but not quite dark either.

His drill sergeant father proceeded to put his head down and then, just as an apparition, he walked through the sliding glass door to that backyard in that home that was an idyllic picture of the 70s, rivaling only the Brady Bunch. Lloyd's life began to flash before his eyes, and he saw his courtship with Becky, where they would lay on the hood of his old hot rod, peering at the stars, watching the mosquitos dance with the whippoorwills while the crickets chirped and they were just talking non-stop. Then he saw when his first two kids were born and the happiness the two had shared as he cut those umbilical cords. But then, he saw then angry words, the crying, and the cursing from both of them, and he saw the affair he was now having as an older man with Eliza, and then, he came to. Or rather, he unraveled.

He grimaced, and the tears were welling up in his eyes, and he was in a different backyard, the one he shared with Eliza, but he was hearing the ancestors of those same crickets from when he was a younger man. He continued to be small, both in stature compared to those stars, and in achievement compared to his old man. He should have relieved Sakura of duty for the day. He knew that now. He could have beat a confession out of that kid, even if the capillaries in Art's eyelids had been ready to burst and make a terrible gash. He could have gotten his man. Not now though. Not ever. And he had a throbbing headache in that surreal darkness of the fenced-in patio to boot.

CHAPTER 12

"Marilyn," Arthur began, his voice quivering over the cellphone. "There's something you should know."

"What is it?" she replied in that voice of hers that was always somewhat anxious but tended to expect the worst.

"They were investigating me..."

"Investigating you? Whatever for...?"

"Well, do you remember that German Shepherd Lake that we went out to on our first date? Well, there were some people showing up dead there, and they thought I was a suspect, but I've now been eliminated..."

There was a brief silence on the other end of the line, and Art crossed himself even though he was Protestant as the day was long, preparing for the worst.

"Oh my god!" her voice raised ever-so-slightly, apparently in shock.

He knew he had to try to sell her on this next point because he didn't want to lose another woman. "D-DNA!" Arthur stammered. "It was DNA, Marilyn. They said that the DNA didn't match me..."

Her reaction was a bit more pensive this time.

"Well, I am going to have think about this, Artie...this is a lot to take in..." and he was crestfallen, but she continued anyway.

"But you know that I loved my first husband, and I thought the world of him, but well, he did have his issues, believe it or not, Artie. He wasn't pure as the driven snow either. He kind of got too carried away with the weed, for one thing..."

"Oh."

"...and he was always arguing with people, you know, and it kind of embarrassed me, but he was a good man, and so are you.." and with that, Art briefed an almost-audible sigh of relief.

"And we'll probably be able to continue to date, but I do need some time here, I do need to give this some thought..."

Arthur was nonplussed and surprisingly strong. "Take all the time you need, Marilyn."

It was going to be tough though, and he knew it. From that day forward, he was going to be waiting on her with baited breath.

Even though he continued to have distractions thrown his way in the coming weeks, Roger remained focused on his grisly objective. It was his fantasy life that spurred him on, thinking about some of the things he was going to do to the child he kidnapped. He had thought about trying to kidnap the black child in the adjoining apartment, but that would be too obvious, so instead he retreated back into his thoughts. He checked out a Stephen King book called "It" and he yet again became enthralled with the story of that clown, and how it was a terror to every little kid that it came across. He pensively reflected on how that creature damaged everyone's psyche, just like that cold great depression apartment damaged his. It was not just the only place he could afford, but the only place he could live at all.

As he became one with Mr. King and made his way through that master of suspense's work, he began seeing clowns while he was tossing and turning during the night. The dreams quickly threw him into a dingy and dirty crevice not soon after he turned off the light, and it would begin with just scratching, even though he couldn't tell if it was dreaming or just him hearing those damned rats. It would only escalate from there, and he was soon peering at the sharp jagged edges of a clown's smile, as well as their frizzy black hair and their bright red eyes.

Red. There was red everywhere, and it wasn't just on the clown's makeup, but from the stiletto knife that it was carrying, the blood oozing out maddeningly slow, in one little droplet at a time. The contortions of the clown's unnatural and unseemly grin were ever on display, and the eyes looked through Roger, and he knew it too. As if in acknowledgment of that fact, the clown let out a laugh that filled the realm with a tremendous echo, and then the features slowly changed, the skin being peeled back like the layers of an onion, until it was no longer a clown, but instead his wicked Uncle George. "Remember, boy?" he said in a hideous toothless grin. "What happens here stays on the boat..." with that last word once again reverberating as if in an echo chamber. "Go to hell, Uncle George!" he screamed, not in the deep adult voice he was accustomed to, but the pre-adolescent one where he was being tortured. "Go to hell, Uncle George, go to hell Uncle George, go to hell Uncle George..." and he awoke in a cold sweat.

After collecting his thoughts and coming out of that sleep-induced stupor in that cramped bedroom, his next thought was extra weapons. He needed to have more weapons. Knives. He needed knives so that he could intimidate the kid. The shinier, the better, and even a butcher knife would do. Still, he knew he shouldn't be reinventing the wheel here, and he probably shouldn't go to a mom-and-pop store when buying them and leaving a paper trail. Didn't his grandfather give him some knives one time? He could have sworn that they were in a safety deposit somewhere in a better part of Denver, but it had been forever since he had been there. Either way, it had him rifling through his aging dressing drawer, looking for the safety deposit key, desperately looking for them like the madman that he was. It took just a little bit of perseverance, but he was able to uncover the key he was looking for, and all the while, it had been buried under a mountain of other unused and forgotten keys, some to vehicles, some to padlocks, and still some old apartment keys that he had never turned back in. He flashed a grisly smile at himself in the mirror and reached over in all of his arthritic glory and patted himself on the back.

It was time for phase two of his unseemly plan, and all that took was just a quick trip to the Home Depot to get some more weaponry and he was ready to hit the road. Since he couldn't kill Uncle George, he might as well kill someone else.

Lloyd was back in the pasture again, and for the time being, he had lucked out. He had not only hit on some stray beer cans at his favorite firing range site without having to do some dumpster diving, but when Eliza had come in the other night and realized that he had been drinking and had even passed out, she hadn't said a word before going to bed. He still despised that Arthur kid even though it turned out that he was innocent. He was just too weird, Lloyd reasoned. Even if he had been officially eliminated as the killer, he had to be guilty of something, but no matter. The target planted on those beer cans this time was not going to be him this time, but Lieutenant Gomes. He wished them all the best at trying to solve the case, but it should have been his case to solve, he thought defiantly. There wasn't even a breeze for his firing range hobby, so at least he had that blessing. He knew it was just one more shot, and he would run out of beer cans, but he didn't have the foresight to take his own with him because he didn't need Eliza going through his car and seeing the ones that he was merely saving for his private pastime and making him the talk of the town.

He wasn't ready to leave that refuge where he engaged in his unusual pastime after that last beer can was gone. He began scanning the sky carefully, looking for birds that he could pick off with his firearm. He didn't want to go after the eye-appealing ones such as the robins or kingfishers. Instead, he was after the outcasts, the unattractive birds like the crow or maybe an ordinary raven. There were a few that fit the bill on that ordinary summer day, and he gleefully was their judge, jury, and executioner. It was idyllic, and it was calm, and it belied the turmoil he was facing in his personal life. But then he felt that all-too-familiar feeling against the aged skin in the pocket of his khakis, and he knew who it was on the phone before he even reached in to grab it and answer it.

"Yeah," he said, after seeing it was Eliza and answering the cell. She probably was going to berate him for his binge the other day. "Lloyd," she began sharply, "I don't know where you are at, but you need to get back here now!" The former police chief peered at the rifle laying on the ground just by where the grass stopped and the dirt road began, and part of him wanted to hang up and keep firing at the birds.

"If this is about yesterday, I-I..." he stammered, trying to find the right words for his defense.

"No, Lloyd, this isn't about that. I'm disappointed in you, of course, but no, it's not that. Just get back here. There's something you should know."

As he drove away in his personal vehicle, the look in the reaview mirror would have shown a man with neither a smile nor a frown on his face, but only a grave look, the look of someone who couldn't help but think that this was going to be another Lieutenant Gomes bombshell all over again. Luckily, the drive back to Bakersfield proceeded without incident, and Eliza was sitting at the kitchen table when he made it back to the house. "What is it?"

Eliza kept looking at the refrigerator, which had plenty of evidence that they were a cohabitating couple, and one that was considering marriage, and Lloyd was preparing for the worst.

"They've made an arrest for those people killed out at German Shepherd."

"Oh," he replied, relieved in more ways than one. "Who was it? Somebody local? A drifter?"

She finally met his gaze.

"That's what I wanted to talk to you about. It was Slim."

Lloyd cleared his throat even though he didn't need to. A few seconds later, the surreal moment sank in.

"My god.... really? My newest hire? The one I met in the Marines about forty-odd years ago? We caught a guy and it was him?" he rambled in disbelief.

"Well, Lloyd, you mean they did...you're not a part of Bakersfield's finest any longer..."

"I know, I know, Liza, don't rub it in."

Their eyes didn't meet in that kitchen, partly because he realized that she was not going to mince words.

"You know, Lloyd, we've built a life here even though for a lot of that time, I was just the other woman. But you know, I have half a mind to pack up my things and get the hell out of here." Yeah, she was angry.

"What's stopping you?"

"Answer me this, Lloyd...did he at any time act weird around you when you guys were investigating out at that lake? Did he say anything or do anything that raised red flags? How was he any different than that Arthur kid?"

"No, I can't say he did..."

"...and the only thing you had against that Arthur kid was that he had once been out at that lake skipping rocks with his new girlfriend and he had been bragging about it?"

"True."

"...and you thought it was okay to violate his civil rights and try to beat a confession out of him when he tried to ask for an attorney? And now you are wondering why the fed guy got you fired?"

Now it was Lloyd's turn to get defensive.

He lightly tapped the brim of his coffee mug, belying his immense frustration. "Just what are you getting at here, Eliza?"

"Don't you think that you should write a letter of apology to that kid?"

Lloyd couldn't help but laugh incredulously. "Me? Write a letter to that 35-year-old moron? Are you kidding me?"

Eliza glared at the wall in an effort to maintain her composure. "Nope. No, I'm not. My father and stepfather were very flawed men, but what you did takes the cake. You and that colleague-turned-serial-killer tried to frame somebody totally innocent just because he looked a bit different. You'd better think about apologizing to him, or I might just have to look elsewhere for a man in uniform that has a bit of personal decency."

He just sat there, at a loss for words, and she silently went into the other room and put on her jogging shoes, and was out the door in no time flat.

~

The old Mexican fast food restaurant stood ominously against the afternoon sky, yet again an echo of better times that had passed everyone by, especially Arthur. That restaurant had been his mother's brainstorm; his dad complied by slowly moving that red brick building from fifty miles up north in a 12-hour project that had occurred about thirty years prior. Even though he was more prone to listen to RATT and other examples of 80's rock, he still had fond memories of hearing Randy Travis, the Desert Rose Band, George Strait, the Judds, and many other country mainstays on that radio in that dimly-lit back room. It was where his old man had diligently kept the books and the remnants of the women employees' cigarette breaks could be seen right there in the middle of it all. To say that it was a popular fast food restaurant and one of the local high school hangouts would have been a serious under-statement.

The building itself was now vacant, and the cracks in the brick showed that the foundation was sagging, just like mom's mind was sagging too. It was depressing to see her that way, but he yet again had to do it, so he left that building to its own devices and headed back to that dreary nursing home yet again. Thank god that Aunt Liz was still sharp, and thank god that the long walk proceeded without incident for Arthur, with not even one stare from anyone, even from those driving by on the main street.

Liz yet again had her handy magnifying glass when he arrived, and as usual, mom was just staring off into space. Her eyes were still deterio-rating, evidenced by the fact that it was a National Geographic she was looking at this time and not one of her trusty large-print Reader's Digest periodicals.

She looked up her sense of hearing as good as ever. "Artie, is that you?" she asked.

"Yeppers," Arthur answered. "How's mom?" It was said even though he could already make an educated guess.

"Seems the same as last time. Not much change. She's muttering something else though..."

This pricked up Arthur's ears yet again. "Oh?" he responded. "What is she saying this time?"

Even though she was visually impaired, Aunt Elizabeth still made a point to have good social etiquette, so she looked in his direction, and he caught of a glimpse of the watery eyes of a borderline centenarian. "This time, she is saying 'mockingbird, mockingbird, mockingbird' over and over again..." She motioned toward where his dementia-ridden mother was sitting. "Here, try talking with her..." and she went back to her National Geographic.

Arthur got just a foot away from mom's face. "Mom, what is it that you are trying to say?"

As if on cue, his mother blinked, murmuring, "mockingbird, mockingbird, mockingbird" yet again. It was about that same instant that Art happened to glance out one of those large picture windows that the nursing home was so proud of, and he saw the hummingbirds darting to and fro, playing in the wind and with each other. The light bulb went off for him. He turned toward Aunt Liz.

"That's what it is," he said to her. "She evidently was looking out that window and saw some of these hummingbirds that are out there, and she must be mistaking them for mockingbirds or something.."

Aunt Liz had now gone back to her picture magazine. "Oh," she responded quietly, barely acknowledging Arthur's epiphany. They said their goodbyes, and he hugged his mother and soon enough, he was on his way back to the house, reflecting on her "mockingbird" mantra.

Mockingbird? Just what does that mean? He pondered as the wind picked up in that dust-bowl era town, just as it always did. He peered at the loose papers from the overflowing trash bin at the nearby local accounting office, even spotting a few of them just listlessly blowing around in the wind. The paper reminded him of words, and the written word reminded him of the classics, and the world of books, and all of those teachers who were normally in a foul mood, glaring at him with their disapproving demeanor. But even they had no choice but to admit that "yeah, Artie is a holy terror, but he'll calm down if you get his nose in a book."

All the while, he couldn't help but think that whatever higher power that was up there in the sky - call it God, Vishnu, Buddha, the Force, or whatever - was probably peeking down at him and lip-synching that same song that was going through his head, about how he was their "Favorite Mistake", just like Sheryl Crow in all of her 90s glory.

He was drawn to that enigma, that noun called mockingbird that mom had been muttering, and still he wrestled with just what it meant. Most of the walk home was devoted to that unusual, minor event in his life, and perhaps it was nothing but yet another person - albeit someone who watched him intently throughout his life, seeing his first steps and watching him become who was today -who was now suffering tremendously because of the agonies of dementia and mental decline. Either way though, that unusual noun for a type of bird reminded him of something else entirely, and that was Boo Radley. Ah yes, he was the character in To Kill a Mockingbird that everyone despised, that everyone looked down upon. He was the subject of small-town gossip and idle chit-chat in the fields and farms and picnic tables, and he was more similar to Arthur than what he cared to admit. How many years had he spent living out that role? How many years had he believed that because he had a special education individualized education plan that he would not go as far as everyone else? How many years had he limited himself because he was poor with his hands?

As if he needed proof, he even thought of the time that he had been putting the cord up to the vacuum at one of his mother's nighttime janitorial jobs and his old man had said, "I can do this so much faster that it's pitiful." He believed that. He internalized that. This inability was just as much a part of him as his ear, but it was that same ear that had heard not long after he had developed that love of reading in grade school the words from various people in his life, "oh wow, you can write too if you just apply yourself!"

Almost immediately, he began putting pencil to paper and making up tales of knights in shining armor and princes and princesses became as natural to him as breathing. When the teachers weren't dismayed at his daily behavior, they were totally shocked at the idea that this kid - this same kid - could articulate his thoughts on that elementary school stationary so well. As he grew older, aging out of the elementary school and moving on to the middle school across the street where the long side-walk greeted him every morning, he became less and less interested in his writing abilities.

There's no money in it, he reasoned at the time. Now, he was in his mid-thirties, and fast approaching middle-age with his every waking morning, and the clock just kept ticking away. He had not one, not two, but three failed professions under his belt, and the poor motor skills weren't helping his job prospects. He was distracted for the moment though, watching the wind blowing the trees and seeing the remnants of a nest in one of them, and it was time for him to create yet again, just like some higher power was always creating. It was time for him to write, so he went back to his old man's house, where he was yet again alone with his thoughts, and after he opened up Word, he typed out the first of many creations, a poem:

Monsters
Monsters are not some
mythical creature
shown proudly
In that small-town double feature.
Monsters are not
in some Stephen King book
hiding behind
every terrible cranny and nook.
Monsters cannot be
mythical, a creation
from our imagination
our limited station.
Sadly, Monsters are
from us
intolerance, bigotry, and strife
from the end
of our gun or our knife.
Do unto others
regardless of creed, station, or race
away with these monsters

we all have to share this space.

Lloyd had some serious writer's block, and it didn't help that he still despised who he was addressing the letter to. He kept eyeing his waste paper basket in the far corner of the room, which was already half-full of the remnants of his and Eliza's everyday life. Unused coupons, receipts from Domino's Pizza in a neighboring town, and promotional tickets for Eliza's next oil change were all intertwined with those wadded-up pieces of paper coming from Lloyd's desk. He had a pen that was completely full of ink from a pack that Eliza had purchased at the dollar store just a few weeks ago, so he couldn't use that as an excuse.

The letters kept starting off just like he was talking and stammering, and just as if he viewed himself as the disabled one instead of the one that he was writing to. Just before he clinched his fist and destroyed it in a tight ball, the latest piece of printer paper had read, "Dear Arthur, I would like to-," and that was that. He couldn't think of any other words to say. He had been a certified peace officer for thirty years. He had diligently built up his career from simply being the "gopher" for the police chief and nothing more than a glorified hall monitor at the high school to being the police chief himself. Either way, all of it was gone now.

He felt his heart race and he knew it was time to take a break from this pointless exercise and take a dose of his high-blood pressure medication. He had done far worse in his life than writing out a letter to someone. Yes, he had preferred to type it out, but Eliza had thought that wouldn't be contrite enough. And why was it an issue in the first place? he pondered as he swallowed the pill and washed it down with a sip of that Evian bottled water they had bought during one of their trips to Sam's further upstate. Wasn't the whole entire cradle of Western Civilization built on letters and those damned archaeologists finding them? Wasn't the great majority of the New Testament comprised of letters that the writers had composed under terribly stressful extenuating circumstances? If they could do it, how come he couldn't write a simple apology? He was going to have to leave the room for now. The air in that room was too stale anyway.

~

He was on his way again, and now back in the present and away from his grisly recollections of memory lane. He was motoring that van in abject silence, and he had a deer-in-the-headlights look as he thought again about his recent encounter with the panhandler. "I'm not on the right path?" he screamed in his primal state. "Really? I'm on the wrong path?" And he couldn't help but weave his van a little bit and shake his fist at the ceiling, thoroughly convinced that some higher power was laughing at him. Well, they would laugh no longer. He was going to shake some family's faith in a deity when their kid didn't come home, if not on this trip, then another one.

With that, he redirected his thoughts to more enthralling emotions, thinking about what souvenirs he might take once he had become a boogeyman in the flesh to this would-be young victim. Would it be the kid's shirt? If it was a girl, would it be their little cute pink handbag? Hell, maybe he could just take the whole entire little bike with him? "Hmmmm...." he smirked. "Possibilities, possibilities..."

He wasn't done yet though, because his thoughts drifted somewhere else, but at the same time it was closely related. He wondered what kind of underwear the child that he captured would have. Would he have Toy Story underpants with Woody in full view? Would she have pink panties even though she hadn't hit puberty yet? It got him going again, and he didn't need a Viagra pill even though he had a fresh supply in the glove box.

Almost immediately, his attention was drawn to the sign on the side of the highway, and it told him everything that he needed to know, which was "Bakersfield 50" as that was the town he had selected for his crime of the century. He knew that he should be elated, but he felt nothing, just like he would feel nothing when the cops would finally track him down. He thought maybe a little bit of music would increase the endorphins in that depraved mind of his, so he turned on the radio. He had to laugh at the irony though, because it wasn't thirty seconds later that he was singing along to AC/DC's "Highway to Hell."

~

Lloyd briefly glared at the fridge and all of the magnets before he opened the door to get out some of that day-old homemade potato salad. "I can't do it, Eliza. I just can't do it." She paused for a second, and then finally looked up from her cellphone. "That's too bad," she replied in an attempt to come off as demure. "You put that kid through total hell, and now the whole town thinks something is off about him even though they got a different suspect that was Slim no less, and you can't even apologize. Yeah, that's too bad."

"Maybe I ought to keep trying," Lloyd replied in a sarcastic, nonchalant tone.

Eliza didn't take the bait. "Yeah," she replied flatly. "Maybe you should."

~

"That will be $11.50, Mr. Cisneros," and Roger just about cringed at the clerk's attempts to be polite. He already knew that Bakersfield was going to be the town he would target, as the old-timers were gathering for their coffee and the mid-morning sun was perched high in the sky. Well, well, well, he needed some refreshment himself and he also needed some fuel for that gas-guzzling van of his in case he needed to beat a hasty retreat, either from the kids or as a sick voluntary babysitter. But either way, he didn't need people remembering his name around here, that was for sure. He was no longer going to be that little boy in the boat. Someone else was going to fill that role, and it would be their turn to cry in terror.

As he strolled out of that convenience store, he smirked, thinking about the handguns in his glove box. He might as well go out in a blaze of glory, either through blowing a police officer away who was checking him out or laughing his perverted head off when he was watching tv and listening to some stupid redneck couple's emotional plea to "bring their child home" while the kid was on the bed in the background handcuffed to the bed and with duct tape where his eyes were supposed to be. He had researched the park thoroughly on Google Street View and now that almost everyone in that Mayberry-Esque town was done with lunch, it was time for him to go to it and lie in wait for as long as it took if need be.

As he turned on the ignition in that crowded small-town parking lot, the engine turned over slowly, and for a moment, he thought that was going to ruin his plans right then and there, but he was elated when the ancient van yet again sputtered to life. It wouldn't be long now.

It was time for Arthur to piece together his writing talent yet again, so the day after he wrote his first poem that is exactly what he did when he had the house all to himself. He knew that even in mom's subpar state, it was what she wanted. Even though his first love would always be those creative outlets and the hours he spent writing poetry, he knew there was more money in writing articles about plumbing and other blue-collar pursuits, so as he sat down to write that day that was his focus.

It was a site he had discovered a few years prior called Writers Incorporated, and the pay wasn't too bad. He found a piece to work on about plumbing projects on houses in Maine, and he began focusing on it about lunch time on that ordinary Labor Day. It was pretty mundane, and even though his mom would have told him it was honest work if she had been well, it still was pretty boring to him, like watching the paint dry. Even though he was tapping the table that the keyboard was on because his ADHD was acting up, he had to take a break and compose a poem, and one completely dark and out of the blue at that:

There is only you,
there is only me,
that's what the little birds tell me.
The earth is barren,
the earth is free,
it's the final day of reckoning.

Nobody can hear you scream,
we can't really be free,
and that's what the little birds tell me.

He smiled for what seemed to be the first time in ages. It was meant to be some type of gloomy, post-apocalyptic poem for a science work and it wouldn't have been something that either Marilyn or his first wife would have appreciated, but it did motivate him to go back to the plumbing pieces for another half-hour. Soon enough though, it was time for him to take a break from all of it because the sun was perched high in that mid-day sky and shining on him through the sliding glass door. He had always enjoyed walking, ever since he was a kid, so he headed out for the first time that day. The park was just as idyllic and peaceful as it had always been. He saw the apartments where Richard lived just across the street and he saw the elementary school where he had been a student many years prior on the other side. There was someone walking their dog and there was a late-model GMC van parked on the side with the elementary school on it. He made his lap around the park and made it back to his mom and dad's house around two or so. Life was good.

Chief Lloyd knew that he needed just a tad bit of inspiration, so he figured that visiting his favorite restaurant while Eliza was at work would do the trick.

It wasn't long before he saw his favorite waitress, another twenty-something who he had considered hitting on before he had decided to settle down with Eliza. She swayed her hips over to where he was sitting. "Why so glum, chief?" she asked. Lloyd was busy surreptitiously staring at her impressive figure, and for a few brief moments, it did do the trick. "Well, it's kind of a long story, but I'm no longer chief anymore. I went after the wrong suspect on that nasty going-on out at German Shepherd and screwed up the interview, and the fed guy let me go..."

"Ohhh," she cooed in response. "I'm sorry to hear that..."

"It gets worse," he continued. "Turns out the guy that really did it was one of my new hires, a guy I met way back in the 70s when I was in the Marines..."

She let out a friendly gasp that would have given any schoolgirl a run for their money. "No way!"

"Yes, way," Lloyd responded, not meeting her gaze but for a moment thinking he should have considered this one a lot more closely before going after Eliza because she literally would have been at his beck and call and not as independent.

Unfortunately, it was time for this waitress to get on with it and get his food order going, so she asked him, "Well, Lloyd, I'm sorry that it didn't work out for your work, but you also need to work out what you would like to eat. Would you like the usual?"

Lloyd didn't pause this time, not even for a second.

"Yeah, I'm pretty hungry, so this time I'll have a 12-ounce ribeye along with a generous helping of a Bloody Mary to go with it for me to drink. And no, don't worry, I will walk home if I get too carried away." It was an obvious lie again, but she didn't catch on. She merely answered, "Got it, chief, and sorry to hear about your bad week. I'll get this going for you."

"Thanks so much," Lloyd responded in an effort to be polite.

"How's Eliza doing these days?" she asked, as if on cue.

He was taken aback, but again he kept his poker face. Still, he just as well came out with it.

"She's good. She wants me to write a letter of apology to the person who turned out to be falsely accused." He didn't think that he should let on just who the suspect was, though.

The waitress proceeded to put her hands on her hips, and, as if reading his mind, asked, "It wasn't that Arthur kid was it?"

The now-former police chief shot her a quizzical look.

"It's all over town, Chief Bridges," she continued without skipping a beat. "The whole town is talking about this."

Lloyd could have died. "Just get me the steak..."

"Coming up here in about twenty minutes, sir, and I'll have your Bloody Mary here in about two..."

"Thanks."

Soon enough the drink was finally placed before him, and he enjoyed it in slow, deliberate sips. He did want to get a good buzz on, but he wanted to enjoy it as well. It didn't take long before the accompanying giddiness and bravado came too, especially after the Bloody Mary had finally started to hit him just right. Just about then, the steak was also placed before him.

That ribeye steak went down his gullet and settled in the abyss of his stomach, mixing with the overtly powerful remnants of that Bloody Mary. He wasn't one for taking things home when he ate out, and it wasn't going to happen this time either. That red meat and the Bloody Mary created the perfect concoction for him to swallow not just the food and drink, but also his pride on one of those rare occasions in his life. As he staggered out of that restaurant, he was now ready to write that apology letter. He still wasn't ready to do it without his personal vehicle, though. It did cross his mind that he should obey, because he WAS the law until the town council completely terminated him. Alas, he knew that it was only a matter of time, so he fired up the engine of his personal vehicle anyway, and even though he had a pretty strong borderline buzz, he made it home anyway. As he glanced at that familiar front porch and that perfectly manicured lawn paid for by his law enforcement salary and that abode that he and Becky had shared and now he and Eliza shared, he knew it was time to write that letter at last. But he had to do one last thing. He had to take a walk to that nearby park just to clear his head and make sure that he said the right words to that kid, even though he just might have ruined his career and his chances of having a better 401K for Eliza.

Simply put, he had to get the bitterness out of him, if only briefly, and that is why he strolled out of his home office and out the door on that lovely afternoon. It was not two seconds after that, in the middle of the trees swaying and a robin darted across his vision, that he spotted it. He knew all of the local vehicles in town because of his work as the town law enforcement, and when he saw that late-model van sitting at the end of the park and across from the school, he already knew that it probably wasn't local.

Could it have been from one of the Emory County towns that dotted the landscape across from Bakersfield? Possibly, but he wasn't sure. He sat at the park bench, nothing more than a private citizen now. His hands trembled as he looked at that late-model van and thought about how he had lost his temper when he was interviewing Arthur and how that had led to his current predicament. Screw the person in the van. It was probably just somebody that was sleeping and couldn't afford a hotel room. All he knew was he still needed more of that liquid courage to write that apology letter to Arthur, so instead of the easy jaunt back to his house, he headed back to the liquor store instead. "What will it be, chief?" the heavyset barmaid woman asked him. He barely managed to grunt out "Grey Goose" and the size, but she handed it to him. "How's Eliza doing?" she asked in an attempt to make small-talk. *Why does everyone keep asking me that today?* He thought. "Fine, she's fine," he muttered without looking up, leaving out that musical doorway just about as quickly as he came in, but now with a brown bag to show for it. Luckily for him, the walk home proved to be uneventful, and he was yet again back in his home office and still with the house all to himself. The van was still there when he was back and fishing for his keys on his front porch, but he had plenty of other things to worry about.

CHAPTER 13

Roger was bored and he wanted to make something happen, especially with his array of weapons, but all he did was stare straight ahead and past the steering wheel of his ancient van. Other than seeing a man caddy-corning from the park with a brown bag go into his house and some guy walking around the park earlier, there was absolutely nothing going on in the town he had picked out. No matter, though. Even if it was just a dry-run, he knew he would get it right somewhere or die trying. His eyelids were becoming heavy and he kept encountering some thick otherworldly smoke in that van, but he was suddenly jerked awake by a loud knocking on his passenger door. He looked over to see a pair of prepubescent hands silhouetted against the scratched and stained glass, and he wistfully reached over to roll down the window.

"Sir, can you help me out?" a voice said timidly, and he quickly determined that it was coming from a boy of about nine or so with a mop of brown hair, one of his personal favorites. "My bike is busted…could I get a ride, or have you look at it?"

"Sure," he finally replied with gritted teeth that would have given the Joker in Batman a run for his money and ambled out of the van as quickly as he could, looking around to make sure he and the boy were alone.

He walked over to the bike, giving it a longer-than-needed look to buy himself some time, and then finally said, "your problem is right there, kid," as he motioned toward the chain of the bike. He slowly put it back on, but all the while, he was thinking about a ploy. "Hey kid," he finally said, "Before you go, you want to come to my van? I've got some video games..."

"Oh, okay," the boy replied, and Roger's heart just about skipped a beat with elation as they walked back to his van. "Close your eyes, boy," Roger said. "I'll give you a surprise..." as the boy stood back and Roger was rifling through the van, not looking for video games but for his antique knife.

As he clutched it, it was time, and he had all of the opportunity he needed as the boy was still standing there with his eyes closed. In one fell swoop, Roger pushed the dagger on top of the skin of the boy's back and clasped his hand over his mouth. Oh, the things he was going to do to this kid when he got on the open road!

"Just be quiet, kid, and you won't get hurt..." but both he and the boy knew he was lying through his teeth.

Suddenly, Roger awoke with a start, and little droplets of that cold sweat on his forehead were cascading down his forehead and down to the upholstery on the seats and the console. He looked around, and there was still no one in sight. It had either been a fugue state or some type of dream, but nothing had come to fruition yet. Nothing at all. He pounded the steering wheel and swore under his breath and then went back to being quiet and watching, always watching.

Chief Bridges was at an impasse, and what better way to handle it than to take a swig of that Grey Goose right out of the bottle? So that's what he did as he was sitting in front of his Chromebook, getting ready to place his trembling fingers on those home row keys and start typing his note to Arthur.

"Dear Arthur," he began, half-way wondering if that's really what the kid went by. Was it Art? Artie? He wondered, and it was just a microcosm of the second thoughts he was already having. He fingered his Marine dog tags, yet again alternating his and his old man's, and it was something that he had always done as a way to relieve stress in his high-stress occupation. He fingered his badge, which he knew was now nothing more than a paper weight. What the hell had he been thinking, trying to force a confession out of this kid? Why didn't he realize just how weird this new recruit and old war buddy of his had actually been? So many questions and not enough answers, so instead of fingering the dog tags, he took another tremendous gulp of that Grey Goose, and he had to laugh bitterly as he briefly glanced at that flying bird emblem. He could be as carefree as possible if he was just one of those birds, he mused. He could be just flying around, mating, and looking here, there, and everywhere for food, whether it be diving down in the open sea or just pecking at some loser like Arthur's lawn. He wouldn't have a care in the world, and he definitely would not have to swallow his pride and write a letter to someone who ruined a 30-year police career just because he had a momentary temper fit.

~

"Basement...I'm putting up drywall in the basement," Arthur sang, improvising the lyrics from the tune of that "Car Wash" song by that 70's one-hit wonder Rose Royce. It was a boring writing piece, and he had to stifle a yawn as he was typing away. Still, someone was paying ten dollars for this work, so he would go ahead and tough it out. He got it done soon enough, and it was time to take a break. Time to call Marilyn once more because they had now patched things up yet again, thank god. She answered on the second ring, which was fast for her. "Hello?" she answered in that common, unassuming voice of hers.

"Hi Marilyn," he responded, and she replied with, "oh hi, Art...how is it going?"

"I guess they arrested someone for that deal at the lake..." and his voice trailed off.

There was a brief pause, which made him uneasy, but then she responded. "Yeah, that was pretty heavy, but as long as you aren't the culprit, I guess we can keep on talking..." and he breathed a sigh of relief. He had gotten to know her fairly well, and he made an educated guess that she was going to try to change the conversation. He turned out to be right.

"Interesting that you have the name Arthur," she said softly. "What does it mean? Were you named after King Arthur or something like that?"

"Well, no, not really," Art replied. "I wondered the same thing when I was a kid, so I asked mom, you know...she said I had been named after the Arthur character in that 80's movie 'Arthur'."

"Oh wow," she chirped. "That's interesting. That's why we'd better keep talking, I suppose."

Arthur kept peering at the empty screen while he held the cell phone in his other hand. "Yeah, that's probably why we should."

"I have to get back to my paper now," she said not long after that.

Arthur nodded his head even though she was hundreds of miles away. "Me too, Marilyn. Me too. Talk to you soon."

"It's been fun, Artie. Talk to you later. Neat little story." And they parted way too soon and Arthur was back to his dull blue-collar writing pieces again. No one cares about drywall, he mused. Except for those that have to work with drywall, he thought, and about had to stifle a chuckle. He knew his skills were limited, and he knew it was hard being the savant that he was, but if he wanted to have that white-picket fence and a house with a garage, he was going to have to not only work on his talent, but learn to go faster. He had to pat himself on the back, because even though the drywall was boring as hell, he got it done in thirty minutes flat. Time to reward myself, he thought. Time to go out on another stroll.

~

"Someone is going to be screaming soon," he said through his wicked clenched teeth in the confines of his GMC van. "Actually, two people, to be precise, but both of them are going to be plunged into sheer terror, I'll see to that. This is the day," he himself screamed with vindication. "This is the day! This is the day that I get even. This is the day I've waited for ever since those pigs arrested me! I haven't been to mass since I was a kid, but this is the day that both the Madonna and Child boy cry in sheer misery!" he said with morbid satisfaction and then glanced at the glove box of his old van again.

Those guns. Those guns again, just sitting there, buried in that glove box. They were so rigid, and they were the only thing that turned him on other than little kids. They were the only thing that got him going, except for that Viagra, of course. Just then, he happened to glance just a bit past that ancient glove box, and he saw a bearded guy at the far end of the park, walking his dog. It looked to be a Siberian husky, no question an elegant, beautiful breed. But it wasn't even remotely as beautiful to Roger as what was on the other side of the man, a kid that looked to be about four or so, and was just jabbering away to the larger version of himself. *If only,* Roger's devious mind thought. *If only that child was by himself...*but just as quickly as his lusting came, it vanished, and the intrusive and unwanted thoughts came yet again.

Suddenly, the ranting of Bill Graham came into sharper focus in his mind, even though he was now the age of one hundred. "You are destroyed for lack of knowledge!" he said in that thunderous voice of his. It cut him to the quick, down into the marrow, the pores, and down into that maddeningly consistent heartbeat of his, down into the blood vessels and even the blood cells. Suddenly, the thoughts of his former cellie came into sharper focus. Was this all there was? It had to be, because he was representing the world and the pits of despair. Then, he blinked, and ever-so-briefly, that young child with the brown hair that was a hundred yards away was now in the cab of the van with him, but again, it disappeared in a flash, and he was back where he was supposed to be, next to his purebred dog and what he presumed was his old man. He sighed because the child was too close. Not to him, but he was too close to safety. He had his dad on one side of him, and he had that dog on the other side. He knew full well how territorial those Siberian huskies could get, and he watched helplessly as the boy, his dad, and the dog all walked back into one of the apartments that was overlooking this nondescript park. He knew that the incisors would draw blood on his skin and the only way he would get the dog off would be through getting into handcuffs, and off in the back of a law enforcement car he would go. Sadly, he knew that, so he continued to wait.

~

"You know that everybody fucking hates him, right?" That was Eliza's first comment after she came back for her lunch break from her shift as the sheriff dispatcher this time.

The slurring of his words was even more prevalent now. "I know, I know," he responded without even attempting to hide his sarcasm. Eliza peered at him and he knew almost immediately that she wasn't done yet.

"...But like I've said many times about my father and stepfather, you made a vow to serve and protect, and this isn't the 1920's anymore, buddy. You might have been law enforcement, but you couldn't just run around giving people hell just because they are different. People have rights now."

The soon-to-be former police chief might have been intoxicated as he took yet another swig of the half-empty fifth of grey goose, but as he stared dejectedly at the floor, he knew she was right. "I know," he muttered with a slur and more than a hint of resignation. "I'm going to try to type this out, even if it kills me..."

"Try, try, try," she cooed. "Do it for me. He's going to screw up soon enough. I doubt he's killed anybody, but he's going to mess it all up soon enough. Everybody knows he's a little bit off..." and with that, she patted him on the back and headed out the door and back to her shift, leaving him to his own devices. He took yet another swig of that Grey Goose, and it made him wonder just what hideous apparitions were lurking in the shadows while he was at that keyboard, ready to spring out of the woodwork and terrorize him.

He knew what it was like to be the scapegoat. He knew what it was like to have an overachieving father who expected only the best and to be looked down upon by the blue-collar kids as nothing more than an "army brat." That's why he hadn't made a career out of the military like his old man and instead charted his own course in law enforcement, working his way up from being just a volunteer beat cop and deputy to the head honcho until his temper fit made it all come crashing down. *So sue me,* he thought, *but how often do small-town cops like me get to investigate serial killers? I could have sworn I had my man. How was I to know "my man" was the one I was sharing coffee and doughnuts every morning with, my co-worker?* But since he knew all of these things, how come he couldn't write this letter? How come he was having the worst of all writer's block?

This kid was just some country bumpkin though, and he would never reach his status. He would never reach his prestige. Except for this last blemish, his career had been a shining city on a hill. He had been the last vestige for so many people, and he had looked upon by many as their sole protector. He knew how to escalate and de-escalate all in one breath. He knew, just by looking at someone, when they were too intoxicated to be driving. He had those field sobriety tests down to an art. He knew the law by heart, and that is why he should have known that he couldn't violate the law during this interview.

It was all coulda, woulda, shoulda now, and that is why he paused to drain another shot of his Grey Goose. His head was swimming now, and he stared at eye level with the only two words that he had been able to accomplish in this letter. The "Dear Arthur" seemed to be bleeding together, and it was no longer just fonts on a page, but a ghastly apparition that was coming to haunt him. His eyes came into focus ever-so-briefly, long enough for him to get his fingers on those home row keys just like he was back in typing class years and years ago and start adding to this letter.

"As a police officer, it was (and that past tense word really stung) always my responsibility to serve and protect, and I..." and he couldn't type any longer. The dizziness took over, and suddenly he had a tremendous weight on his skull, and his forehead came down on the surface with a resounding thud! And just like that time that his now-estranged son kept playing that Gin Blossoms song over and over again, he was finding out some things about himself that he really didn't like.

~

Arthur was giving his typing muscles a break and enjoying nature all at the same time. He wasn't sure that he wanted to take up bird-watching, but he couldn't help but recall a Methodist preacher that did it that used to call Bakersfield home for a few years, and there was no doubt that it was an interesting pastime.

As he walked down that long sidewalk by the high school, he kept scanning the clouds to see if he could catch a neat variety of birds migrating, and there were a few times where he could have sworn that he had seen a white-tailed ptarmigan, even though they weren't normally in that area. They mostly frequented the more mountainous areas of Colorado, and he remembered when he was still in education and motoring down the million-dollar highway and seeing a few playing in that endless sky broken only by the peaks. It was truly odd to see that one streaking across this sky instead, because Bakersfield never had any mountains, except for one nearby hill that everyone seemed to refer to as a mountain instead. He couldn't help but wonder if that lovely example of God's palette had lost its way, and if it was going to be lost in the snow-drenched hills a few months from now, risking a wintry demise. It could be that the bird was just migrating, he reasoned. It was probably worthy of a poem or a painting one way or the other, but he put it out of his mind as he continued making his jaunt yet again toward that familiar park.

His brief hike around the park was largely uneventful, and he spotted the guy driving around in the Forrest Gump-like snapper lawnmower, a guy he had known since childhood, waving at him, and he smiled and waved back. Besides looking at the birds, he had always enjoyed the smell of a freshly mowed lawn. After he reached the other side of that park, he paused just briefly as he spotted that unfamiliar van yet again. He did glance at the van, even staring at that relic of Detroit engineering, even though he knew that had always been a problem for him. He chuckled at the guy, probably just an out-of-towner who was tired and worn out from the road and burned out on his cheesy old van. He had to hurry home because he had a piece for a person injury lawyer's blog that was waiting for him to churn out, hot off the press.

~

As the whir of the lawn mower buzzed by his van and the strange man was yet again walking the sidewalks of the park, Roger was retreating into his compelling fantasy world yet again. The titillating imagery had him drenched in a cold sweat as he glanced over at one of the mundane park benches, imagining a boy right in his target age of eight sitting there with a teddy bear. But the most gruesome aspect of this mental picture would have to be the fact that the boy was scared out of his mind, and the teddy bear had been beheaded. He was no longer the boogeyman hearing the powers that be scream "off with his head!" but he was the one who was doing the beheading. He wasn't just a Romeo and Juliet offender like his old fellow inmate Pee Wee had been either. He was going full throttle, and that meant a new image was coming to his mind straight away.

In the corner of his mind, this depiction was now making him salivate, and it was one of a nondescript motel room with the typical floral bedspread, and he was lying on it watching the television. He saw the characters on the screen, seemingly placed there for his hateful and sadistic amusement, the first one being a police officer reading off some vital statistics.

"He is eight years old, he has strawberry blonde hair, he likes Pokemon, and he is still fond of his teddy bear. He was last seen at..." and he stopped paying attention at this point, looking over at his unwilling companion right next to him in the bed and laughing uproariously. All the boy could do was muffle a scream because he had duct tape all over his body. But almost instantaneously, Roger's attention was diverted once more to that archetypal TV screen, and the prototypical suburban housewife was out there for all the world to see. She was fit as a fiddle even though she probably ate the chocolates that her committed husband brought back to her while watching her favorite soap opera. Now, she was living one, and a morbid nightmare of one to boot. The look of sheer desperation and horror in her was evidence right from the start, and Roger ate it up like a cub scout at a fast food joint. "Please bring him home," she was saying. "Please bring my boy home..."

He laughed again, but more softly this time. "No such luck, ma'am," he muttered with a sarcastic contempt through gritted teeth as the boy glared at him with those same pleading eyes. "We're all lost, including him. It's my time. It's my turn."

But he blinked, and in a flash, he was back in his van again, and it was all just a facade, a microcosm of a life, a morbid allegory and nothing more. Still, his grim determination dragged on. The dark apparitions were surrounding him in an ungodly crescendo, and they were whispering in his ear with "Roger....Roger....Roger...the birds are telling me that we are going to work this out for you. You will prevail. You will make people cry..."

The migraine was now crushing his skull again, and he knew that as long as Lieutenant Gomes didn't mess with his pension, he would be all right, but boy, what Chief Lloyd would have given at that moment to not only have clarity of thought, but to be back at his makeshift firing range taking out his fury. The words. He kept peering at them, and it was only one paragraph that he had completed. That's all it was. He had been in hostage situations. He had been at the scene of countless accidents. He had been a public servant for as long as he could remember, but this was too much. He was going to figuratively throw up his hands as a painful groan emitted from his nostrils. He was a glutton for punishment and he knew it. He wasn't Charlie Manson trying out for the Monkees, he was just ex-chief Lloyd Bridges, and he was trying to show one last bit of leadership and write this damned letter.

He went ahead and read off the beginnings of that letter out loud to himself yet again. "As a police officer, it was always my responsibility to serve and protect, and I..." He was agonizing, and he knew it. What could he add to it? "...made some serious mistakes when I was investigating you for those murders out at German Shepherd Lake."

He shook his head. *No, no, I'm not really sure I care for that*, he thought. He glared at the Grey Goose, looking at the perimeter of the clear bottle where it was evident that there was still a third of the intoxicating liquor that was just waiting to be imbibed. He sighed, and with the expulsion of his breath, he knew that if he had been on the other side of the law that he would have probably been making an arrest for public intoxication. He mused bitterly. *Should he go out and clear his head?* he thought. Should he stretch his legs? He nodded his head even though he was alone. Yeah, probably get these creative juices flowing. *Writing was never my best subject anyway.* He had always let the flunkies back at the station write all of his correspondence for him, and there had been many over the years simply because they usually left for greener pastures. But either way, he stepped away from his computer screen and quickly began thinking about where to go. The grocery store? He shook his head. The town square? No, that was a thumbs down too. The park? That was a big no vote too. He knew full well just from years of patrolling that everyone and literally their dog loved that park, so that was too obvious. He couldn't show his face - his shallow, intoxicated pallor - to these people that he had been tasked to serve and protect. Not to mention the fact that those bathrooms were so basic that they didn't even have mirrors.

What about just getting some air by just going down his block a little way? Yeah, that would work, he reasoned. *Sometimes the simplest solutions are the best ones.* It was truly too bad that Becky had taken the dog when she left and that he and Eliza had never gotten around to getting another one, but oh well. It was a calm day with just the smallest breeze trickling across his five o'clock shadow, and none of those clannish busybodies on his block paid him any mind whatsoever. He was thankful for that, so much so that when he got back to the house, he decided to pour out the rest of the Grey Goose, as beautiful as that intoxicating bird might have been.

~

"Kind of boring," he muttered and stifled a yawn. It was one of those personal injury websites and it was going to be a piece for those who had been the unfortunate victims of motorcycle accidents, and Arthur knew all too well that he had no choice but to plunge headlong into it sooner rather than later. That's why he went ahead and clicked on the "Write" button to get started. Luckily, he had a 24-hour deadline, and that was good because he had some other writing business that he wanted to take care of first. As he opened up a new document on his word processing interface, he had Marilyn on his mind, and so he typed out these words:

She walks in beauty
    she is a paragon of elegance
    she has so much grace
    she has never been afraid
    to run life's race.

She is such a free spirit
    she looks at life
    and thinks there is no need to fear it.

She is so beautiful
    she is such a natural
    in everything
    believing in a prayer
    on a heavenly wing.

There is no one better
    there is no else
    that will make your heart melt
    Only Heaven can tell
    how she does it so well.

He just sat there, looking at that creation he had made there on the computer screen, and he was just itching to send it to her. He was an artist, and that is what artists did; they shared their work one way or the other. Even though his hands were quivering with anticipation as his fingers grazed the speed dial next to her name, he decided that one time calling her today was probably enough. They were back on speaking terms, thank god, but she still needed her space, so he left it at that.

He was antsy, and that was a common theme for him ever since his childhood, but he found it in him to sit long enough to write that personal injury blog. He completed it with an air of satisfaction about thirty minutes later, and he again had to get some air, and it was again time to reward himself. Yeah, he was a terrible creature of habit, but time for another walk to that park. It was an all-too-familiar jaunt that ended in another sight that was becoming familiar and not in a good way. The van. It was still sitting in the same spot, and he glimpsed at it as he made his rounds across the concrete of that ancient park. The van was silent, and it even looked abandoned, just sitting there. He strolled right past it, even thinking that he should knock on the door to see if someone was in trouble. But what was it mom had always told him? *Don't be a busybody,* he recalled her saying. *Let sleeping dogs lie.* So that's what he did, and he still had work to do anyway. He was getting ready to become a husband again. He could just feel it in his bones, and so he had to start applying to some of the better writing jobs, and no longer settle for the work found on Writers Incorporated. He devoted himself to submitting his resume to the different job listings on a site called Writing and Blogging Jobs. The focus was the key, and not any exterior issue.

"Well, well, well, what do we have here?" Roger mused, not at a potential unattended child, but at the strange man that was yet again walking around the park for the third time. He knew this goofball wouldn't be able to see him because of the tint on the windows on his van, but that was the way he preferred it. It was also a good way to hide a kid if he could prevail in that goal. Whoever this guy way, he was definitely a creature of habit. He was walking the perimeter of that park, and he made it to where his van was, and for some godforsaken reason, the man just stopped, staring dead-on at his van. Was he on to him? He was weird for sure, but was he some type of undercover police officer?

Whoever the kid was, he was damned near middle-aged, but maybe he should be the target? He sighed. It wouldn't be the same, but the Lawnmower Guy was gone, so it wouldn't be that hard. These guns are locked and loaded, and all it would take is just one shot. *People would hear it, but if I hurry up and drag his body to the van, I might get off without any witnesses,* he thought. He coldly grabbed one of the guns from the console while the idiot was standing there, his hand gripping the archaic power button for the passenger window of his van. He could just roll it down. "What are you looking at?" he would growl, and the next thing that fool would hear would be a gunshot, headed straight for him just like he was JFK in that morbid motorcade. Obviously, he was not as smart as JFK, but still...it wouldn't be that hard. But the split-second before he began to finger the small lever to roll that window down, the strange man started walking away again.

"Your lucky day, buddy. Your lucky day for sure," he growled. "Someone else won't be so lucky if they just decide to go to the park on their bike or what have you..." and he cackled once more.

"What happens in the van, stays in the van, right Uncle George?" he continued tauntingly to whatever realm of the afterlife that his ghoulish uncle might have been haunting. And then he had another ungodly cackle as he started addressing his mother, wherever she was. Heck, maybe they both were right there in the back of the van, their ghostly apparitions just watching his every move. "What do you think, Ma? I guess violence runs in the family, doesn't it?" And there just was nothing more for him to say. Even though it crossed his mind to fire up that van and get out of there, he couldn't bring himself to do it, so he continued to lie in wait.

Lloyd's vision was still blurry, but he was looking at a picture of the Ten Commandments and thinking that he should have gone to the town square to look at their example instead of just walking around his block. Anything to kill time, anything to take him away from this ridiculous and humiliating task of writing an apology letter to someone he never cared for, even on a good day. Glaring at that photo of those Ten Commandments brought to mind another jarring mental picture, one of his mother and those rare silent tears that would glisten, tiny pinpricks at the top of her face. She knew the rigors of being a military spouse, just like Becky had known the stressors of being a law enforcement spouse.

But it wasn't that, and it wasn't the booze floating around and making his head dizzy. It was those dog tags. That's what it was. For god's sake, he had been shot at, even though Vietnam had already been over with. He glanced off in the distance, and he saw that imposing giant that was his father, and he had a wrinkled, graying face, so he must have been in his mid-seventies, but his tremendous frown was blocking everything else even though he wanted to take a hammer to his computer because of his writer's block. He wanted to hide behind that badge. Especially now, since he was yet again getting his father's disapproval. You had to be tough to be in the Marines, and that was the family business. You had to be tough to be in law enforcement, so being tough was a family tradition. It was just words on a page, and just as soon as he was ready to put his drunken fingers on the home row keys to finish his letter of apology to that kid, he let out an intoxicated primal scream. Before he knew it, his laptop keyboard was indeed in pieces.

To Arthur's astonishment, the poetry was helping him focus on other things. He was working on another piece for a personal injury lawyer, and he had Motley Crue's Dr. Feelgood blasting on his headphones as he typed, taking a break every now and then to air guitar. The sunlight kept flooding in the room, apparently not ready to give up on the day just yet. As far as he knew, he didn't have any Egyptian descendants (at least not that Ancestry.com had told him), but he couldn't help but laugh as he was getting those keywords for this Philly-based lawyer just right and perfecting his craft. "Those who fail to learn from history are doomed to repeat it...." Art was once more talking to himself as Nikki Sixx was telling how Jimmy was the king of the barrio streets. "No one does sun worship anymore," he rambled through his headphones as he continued to tap away on his lawyer's promotional sentence.

He was clicking on all cylinders as long as he had a tune with a nice beat in the background, and it was all endorphins, just like it was for those ancient Egyptians as they saw the sun greeting them every morning and etched those designs on dusty stone for archaeologists to unearth thousands of years later. The tune changed fairly often, and so did his task of writing jobs. The lawyer piece was soon finished, and he switched to another plumbing piece, this time in upstate New York. By the time he looked up again from his trusty screen and keyboard, the sun was about to wear down and go to bed, and the last vestiges of brightness were shining off the sliding glass and everything within its reach.

CHAPTER 14

The kid with the beheaded teddy bear was back. So was Uncle George. So was Pee Wee. And so was the baby-faced prosecutor that had handled Roger's case. They were in the back of his van, shaking their head at him disapprovingly. He, too, shook his head, this time in fury. He couldn't even handle a child abduction right, and he knew it. It was time to get out of there. This time was just a dry run. There was plenty of time to find another spot, and so his trembling hands grabbed for his keys in the ignition, but once he glanced again, all of his company in his cavernous back area was gone. His resolve came back, and he still needed to lie in wait.

~

"Go to the park. Go to the park!" That was Lloyd's mental telepathy as he looked at the aftereffects of his temper tantrum on the jagged pieces of his now-inoperable keyboard. Where were the thoughts coming from? Even though his joints were now in disgraceful retirement along with the rest of him, his legs were still good and the exercise would only help him. The thoughts continued unabated, and he was unaware of their genesis. His father coming back from the grave and overcoming his migraine? He was normally a man of the law, and no one except his superiors told him what to do, but in this case, maybe he should. The park would be good. He could see the community that he had served faithfully even though it had all ended on a bad note. He would go. All he had to do was rest his eyes for a moment...

More Cutty Sark or Jim Beam? Alcohol had been Arthur's excuse for everything, and it crossed his mind to go see that charming older lady at the liquor store yet again. Nah, he'd better stop. He would take one last trip to the park and bathe in the last, best hope of that sun just like Nefertiti had done as that star had glimmered off the Nile millennia ago.

"What about a home invasion, Uncle George?" Roger sneered as he glanced at that apartment door off in the distance. The guy with the kid and the dog were probably in there, but what about the dog? What if it attacked him as he breached the door? He would probably have to first aim his gun at the sound of the dog barking so he could get off a good shot at it, then he could save the last few bullets for that man before taking his progeny alive. Nothing else had panned out that day, so it was time to do just that. It was time for this sleepy town to wake up with a vengeance. He gripped his pistol and his fingers were on the key in the ignition. He would drive around to where the apartments where so he didn't stick out like a sore thumb. The van's motor turned over, but he stopped it before the spark plugs brought it to life as he just happened to glance in the rear-view mirror. That guy again. Damn it to hell. That guy was walking again for the umpteenth time. Well, that was a change in plan for sure. Instead of the ignition, he was going to open his driver's side door instead.

"The very definition of insanity is doing the same things over and over again and expecting different results," Arthur said to the air. Booze wouldn't work. It would never work for the rest of his life. It would be a total irony to go to the park again after what he had just said, but it was innocent, harmless fun, so that's what he did. He was going to take one last trip to the park that day. The first couple of blocks on that last jaunt for Arthur flew by, simply because he was buoyed by the benefit of a clear conscience. As the clearing for the park came into view, that was the first time he pondered the odd events of that day. *Surely that man in the van has gone on now*, he thought as he continued walking. But as he walked to the clearing just past that second high school parking lot, he saw something that made him pause dead in his tracks. The strange man was still parked there, and it was just like Arthur was in the woods and had seen a mama black bear in the distance. Just like being in those woods, he would have to turn around, not in intense fear to see a cub, but simply to wonder what he should do.

He had to reason with himself to start walking again, because that's what he always did. That, and overreacting. *Just a guy down on his luck and sleeping,* he thought again. *That's all it is. That's it. Nothing to see here.* When he got home, he would calm his nerves by putting on Metallica's Enter Sandman again and becoming one with the momentum of their guitar prowess. He did his normal pass through that age-old park, and as he approached the van, he heard what he thought was the engine turning over and could have sworn he saw the driver's side door vibrating just a tiny bit, getting ready to swing open, perhaps?

The door had jammed, and that was when Roger noticed that the lock mechanism at the top was still engaged. The man was still there, and he was getting closer, and as if in response to this turn of events, he wheeled around and began walking the other way. He was grateful for that, and even though Roger was a total pervert, he couldn't just shoot someone in the back.

"it's too impersonal anyway," he muttered scornfully. "Wouldn't it be so much more fun to simply place these filthy, near-homeless hands around someone's throat and just watch the life go out of their eyes?"

~

Walk the other way, walk the other way, Arthur kept telling himself after encountering that van. So he just calmly turned around even though his heart was racing. He reached the intersection where the child care center and the preschool was just before a person would reach the high school, and his chest slumped down, finally able to breathe easier. *The guy will be on his way soon. Just homeless. He's just homeless or down on his luck,* he repeated. He reached the intersection where the child care center and the preschool was just before a person would reach the high school, and his chest slumped down, finally able to breathe easier. In a few moments, he was at the concrete again, that long sidewalk the length of his old high school football field just a few yards away on the other side of the campus.

It was a nondescript walk, one that he had done a million times before, both as an adult and as a teenager struggling with that awkward transition into the adult world. The concrete of that sidewalk appeared to be different, something like the foreign surface of a barren, frozen planet. He suddenly wasn't the low-class town idiot, but he was an associate of Neil Armstrong or one of those Russian cosmonauts. The surface of that sidewalk was, in a word, new. *Brand new.*

The pathway had been marked by solid wooden posts about every ten yards, and he counted them during that dusk evening, running through them in his mind. One, then two, now three, and here we are at four. But just as suddenly as he started counting, he stopped, almost as if he heard an otherworldly voice.

Arthur, I want you to call the police on that van. Plain and simple, and a gentle command at that, and more like an admonition. He shook his head, and that was the one thing that the counselors had always told him. He was stubborn. He didn't want to bother some transient gentleman, so he continued on his way, taking a few more steps and approaching the fifth post on what would be the fifty-yard line if he had been on the football field, the one that he had never been on other than as a fan because of his poor motor skills. He had things to do, but some part of him stopped again. Some invisible linebacker that would have given Billy Bob from Varsity Blues a run for his money got in his way.

Arthur! Call. the. police. on. that. van!!!

It was no longer just an admonition. It was now another word, and that was adamant, and it was proven by the accompanying dry heaves that were present in Arthur's lungs. Trembling, his hands reached into his pockets, pulling out his cell phone. *Still, probably nothing, but I'll let the police sort it out,* he thought, and he dialed the number to the sheriff's department.

'Emory County Sheriff..." the gal on the other end chirped obliviously.

"Yeah," he answered, "This is Arthur..." There was no need to give out his last name, because everybody in Bakersfield knew who he was, for good or bad. She tried to cut him off.

"Hey Arthur,' she responded. "What's going on? Do we need to send someone...?"

"No," he replied resolutely. "Not this time. I was calling because there is a suspicious vehicle out at the main park. It's an 80's model GMC van, and he's been sitting there literally the whole entire afternoon."

There was a brief silence on the other end of the line as she tried to process that information.

"Oh," she finally said and then almost went back to her professional voice. "Okay, we will send someone to the park so that they can investigate your concerns."

"Okay, thanks," he again said resolutely and went ahead and hung up the phone. Better safe than sorry.

~

"Well," Roger said to himself in a morbid motivational tone. "This obviously didn't work out. It's okay. This was just a dry run. There are plenty of other towns dotted along the Colorado prairie where I can do this again. It only takes once..." As he was reaching to turn the key in his ignition, that was when he saw the police cruiser rounding the corner.

His eyes flinched slightly, but he put on as straight a face as possible as the police officer approached his van. It was a standard question-and-answer deal; the cop asked him for his license and insurance, the whole nine yards, and then asked him what he was doing and where he was headed. He came up with the best lie he could think of.

"Yeah, officer, well, I'm actually starting to drive cross-country, going to my aunt's funeral in Michigan, but just trying to take my time, you know?" the officer didn't even glance at him.

"Okay, buddy, just hold tight, and I'll get you squared away here..." and he walked back to his cruiser.

The police scanner that Arthur had such a love-hate relationship with was crackling to life yet again, and the Emory County Sheriff's Office was going through the standard procedure. "Your plates are clear, sir," the dispatcher said through that scanner.

"All right," he responded. "Do me a favor and run this license for me..." and he went through the numbers, and soon enough, her reply came back.

"Sir, your respondent's license comes back as belonging to a registered sex offender..." and Arthur shot bolt upright in his chair, spilling his tea, with the rest of the words being a blur to him. Like flicking on a light switch, his blood pressure kicked up a few notches, his heart racing as he walked up and down that cluttered hallway where he had learned to walk just over three decades prior.

The surreal light floated through those dusty blinds, and he tried to scream, but all that was coming out was otherworldly gasps. "Oh my god," he rasped repeatedly. "Oh my god, oh my god, oh my god..." as the gravity of the situation came to full fruition and the stark realization of what had just happened overwhelmed him.

It was a foreboding realization, cold and clammy, and suddenly he was thinking of that bird-watching hobby he had thought about taking up. But he wasn't thinking about one of those doves that had erupted with wholesome goodness out of Christ when he had been baptized. Instead, he was thinking of one of those dark and impersonal ravens that had haunted Edgar Allen Poe's dreams or a vulture eying a starving child like in that Nobel Prize-winning photo. The feeling was just as grotesque as those birds, and multiplying just as rapidly. *That man was trying to abduct a child.* He let the realization sink in as the room spun. *Water.* He needed some water. His old man had always been frugal, and he'd never been one to buy that bottled water, but even tap water would do. Getting water straight from the sink was always kind of a hit-and-miss proposition, but he felt the water going down his esophagus and settling in his stomach, purifying him just like holy water as it went.

Even with the water, the panic was still overwhelming him. It suddenly sank in just what he had done. He knew he would be a better man because of what had happened, but he also knew he would lose part of his innocence as well. He looked all around him in his mind, the flashes of his childhood, early adulthood, and his thirties, that same small town that was in him, and he knew that this was a fork in the road, a defining moment, and that was probably why he couldn't breathe.

It was only, "Oh my God" repeatedly, coming out in little gasps, and he almost thought he was going to have to call the emergency services number yet again to get help for himself this time. It was the same air that he always breathed in that house, the same house where he had spent his whole formative years, where he had had all of these milestones and where the evidence of the height chart still existed, but now the air seemed different, even palpable and tangible. Spinning. His head was spinning, and he was thinking about all of those odd random things that his unique mind always darted to, just like the odd movements of one of those uncanny but beautiful butterflies in the random fall wind. *What was that Unsolved Mysteries episode he had watched when he was ten? The one where the choir in Nebraska had all been kept away, and then they showed up, and the church exploded just as they got there?* It was something uncanny, something *otherworldly,* just like right there, in the here and now.

And then it dawned on him. He couldn't cut it as an educator. He couldn't cut it as someone in the ministry. He couldn't even cut it as a husband the first time around. But he could cut it here. Just like those Bible characters he had studied, he was the right person, at the right time, to do this. He had a purpose on this little ball we called Earth.

"Okay, I'm heading back to the station now," he heard the voice on that small-town police scanner say. "I gave respondent a warning and told him to be on his way. Told respondent that he is not allowed to be at this park and the next time, I will clear this situation by arrest. Baker 2 en route back to the station."

Arthur flinched. He didn't agree with the decision. Marilyn was already getting after him about being an encyclopedia, but didn't the state of Colorado have a law where people like this guy weren't allowed to be at parks? No matter, he did his part. He put on some Hall and Oates and got back to work, even though he knew that the carefree days of the 80's might still elude him from time to time. He knew the road was still going to be challenging. He knew there would be bumps here and there and that he was still going to be labeled, but now, well...something felt different now, like finding a long-lost lock that had opened up a door of possibilities. Everything felt new and alive, just like he was the Andy character in the Shawshank Redemption with his arms outstretched in the rain. He was going to remember this day for the rest of his life. He might be a prodigal, but he didn't have to be ashamed of who he was any longer.

~

Roger also flinched as the police officer came back and told him, "sir, please step out of the vehicle."

He met the man who was tasked with serving and protecting face-to-face, and he saw the clearing in the distance over the man's shoulder glaring back at him just like an invitation. He glanced at his van, most notably that glove box again, and he could probably beat the guy to it if he tried...

"You need to be upfront with me, sir," the police officer said in that serious, professional tone they always seemed to have. "Just what are you doing at this park? You are coming back as a registered sexual offender."

"H-housing," Roger stammered, trying to perfect the lie. "I can't find housing because of who I am..."

"I guess I will buy that," the officer replied, even though he was giving the guy a death stare. "You *do* need to move on from here. Apart from clearing out the drunks on Saturday night and a few spats here and there, we don't have that many problems, and we want to keep it that way. Time for you to get some help, too, while you're at it."

Was he being let go? Roger couldn't believe his luck later as he was sitting at a rest stop just off the highway. But the birds and God, if he existed, had seen it all. They knew what he was trying to do. He was a freak, and he was not normal, and he never would be, but there would be no dry runs, not now, not ever. He would never have a family. He would always have his mug pasted on every community's website wherever he called home. He knew that. But the anger and rage had to stop.

He had to take the sneers head-on. He had to take being viewed as a second-class citizen head-on. He had to take his mother head-on. He had to take Uncle George head-on. People have a right to protect their families and keep them safe. Perhaps it was time for him to change his ways. He reflected on that whole ride home and even when he was unpacking as nightfall had replaced the sunset. He was going back to his lonely life and his decrepit, dusty old apartment, and he knew then that it was too late. He kept glaring at his firearms lying on his pathetic excuse for a kitchen table, just like he was an 80's toddler eyeballing a shiny department store toy. "Well, Uncle George and Ma," he said to himself. "I guess I'll see you two in hell very soon..."

In another sleepy community not too far away in the big scheme of the Milky Way Galaxy, the birds were playing and making nests above yet another small park. Down below, a man was sitting on a bench, watching a dog chasing a frisbee that had been thrown by a first-grader. The kid was laughing, and so was the man. He saw the woman near the boy, grinning a thousand watts, and so he approached them and picked up the frisbee...

"Hey Karen!" he called out. "Looks like these two are getting pretty good with these frisbees." He had never cared for the dog slobber, but at least his boy was happy. He wasn't Karen's favorite person anymore, but they tried to get along for his sake.

"Yeah," she replied without turning around. "He's getting pretty good at fetching, isn't that right, Charlie?"

"Yes ma'am," the boy clad in his baseball cap and Metallica t-shirt and jeans replied. The man in his khaki shorts and plain white t-shirt smiled. That was his boy. He and Karen had tried and tried and tried to make it work, but it hadn't. But at least they had a smart, articulate and beautiful child come out of it.

He meandered closer to Karen even though he knew better than to put his hand on her shoulder.

"Hey, Karen..."

"Yes?" and she finally turned around to meet his gaze.

"Karen, I've been meaning to tell you...I know things didn't work out with us, but at least we've got a great kid out of the deal, right?"

She blinked back a small tear that she could blame on allergies if he noticed. Their two miscarriages prior to their boy hadn't helped their marriage, that was for sure. "Yeah, we sure did. We sure did. Let's make sure he has the best life possible. Let's try to be civil for his sake."

He nodded his head. Yep, keeping him safe and happy was the name of the game, for his kid and billions of others all across the world.

AUTHOR'S NOTE

To say that writing a book like this was a difficult undertaking would be an understatement. Arthur is loosely based on me and some of my own personal experiences. However, he is also a composite of everyone on this little ball we call Earth who has been dealt a bad hand. No, in real life, I was never investigated for a series of homicides at the local lake, but like most everything else in the book, that is allegorical. The event that the book is based on is one of those watershed moments where everyone remembers where they were when it occurred, much like when that second plane hit the South Tower during 9/11 or when Walter Cronkite announced to a shocked nation that President Kennedy had passed away. There was a lot of religious symbolism in this book from all of the characters, and that, too, was allegorical. As a graduate of a bible college, one thing that you quickly realize when you study religious texts is that they are rife with less-than-perfect heroes. In the Bible, you have Moses, you have Gideon, you have David, and you even have prostitutes such as Rahab and Mary Magdalene. The Good Lord seems to have a way of using cracked vessels to fulfill his purpose.

Such was the case with Labor Day 2015. I was newly divorced, but I was getting ready to get remarried and start a new life. I was working on my writing, and that is literally something I have been doing my whole entire life. Ever since I was six years old, people have told me that I could write. I was doing it then, I was doing it during that instance, and I am doing it right now. Unfortunately, as someone with high-functioning autism, I am very easily misunderstood, so it's easy to become one of those "unlikely heroes" like in the Bible.

One of the things that I have always enjoyed doing in my free time is the simple act of walking. Indeed, some would say that I like it just a little bit too much. On the day that the event that this book is based on occurred, that's what I was doing: walking. Namely, I was taking frequent breaks in between some of my online writing jobs. Basically, I would finish an article, and then I would walk to my local park and back. The first time I did this, it must have been around twelve or so, just a little bit after lunchtime. I couldn't help but notice an old GMC model parked on the side of the park over by the elementary school. I paid it no mind, and I ultimately took several more breaks that day, repeating my routine of going to the park and back. I didn't really get nervous about the van until the last time I saw him, which was about a quarter until seven. As I was walking from the park back to my father's house for the last time that day, something told me to call the police on that van, and I did. Much like the details in the story, I heard on my old man's police scanner that he was a registered sex offender from a Denver suburb.

Am I asking for a medal? No, not really. I just did what anybody else in my shoes would (or should) have done. It has now been almost seven years since that Labor Day weekend when I noticed that strange van at my local park. I am now married and as I am typing this, I am listening to my wife rearrange things in our kitchen. There are still fumes from the wood stain on our floor. Has my life become perfect since then? No, it hasn't. But there's not a day that goes by that I don't think about the trajectory that various lives could have taken had I not listened to that "still small voice" and called the police on that van. I believe that I could very well have prevented a child abduction that day. Thus, it doesn't matter whatever "higher power" or "higher force" that you believe in. I still have to believe that the forces of good will ultimately prevail. Call it God, call it Jehovah, call it Buddha, call it Allah, or simply call it intuition if you are atheist or agnostic, but something watches over us and promotes our best selves each and every day.

Vaden Chandler
August 2022
Amarillo, Texas, USA

ACKNOWLEDGMENTS

What you see here is a book that is largely allegorical, somewhat in the vein of C. S. Lewis and his Chronicles of Narnia or John Grisham's "The Testament." Yes, I realize I am putting myself in some rather lofty company there, but the reason I chose these two is because there are indeed a lot of spiritual principles in this work. First of all, we have the battle of the good and evil present not just in work, but also in the main characters and their personal battles. There is a scriptural parallel to this; I've always found it fascinating the personal stories of some of the Bible heroes of both the New and the Old Testament. Thus, the first acknowledgment that I have to make would be to this higher power or force that compelled me to call the police on that van at my local park so many years ago. Whether you call it Jesus, God, Buddha, Allah, your higher energy, or even just your subconscious, if you are atheist or agnostic, someone or something directed me to make that call after the fourth time, I saw that van at the park that day. The van hadn't budged an inch, and come to find out the driver was a registered sex offender from the Denver area.

As I write this, it is almost four in the morning, and sleep is escaping me, simply due to the fact that I am just overwhelmed at the plethora of educators that have encouraged me from as early as kindergarten. I am not going to call them out and embarrass them, but they know who they are. Special education teachers, speech therapists, occupational therapists, regular classroom teachers and even some substitutes noticed something far beyond just some little kid who couldn't sit still, and I am eternally grateful for that. I also have a lot of personal friends that I have kept in touch with throughout the years, and who accepted me just as I was. Troy and Josh, I appreciate you guys a great deal.

I would be remiss if I didn't think of my mother right now, who was literally one of the most encouraging and positive individuals I had ever known. She knew that with my autistic tendencies and other issues, I was going to have some obstacles; either way, I have to believe that if she hadn't been afflicted by dementia during that Labor Day of 2015, she would have been thrilled to death that I stopped a registered offender that was at our small-town park. My two older siblings deserve some of that credit as well.

Finally, as always, I could absolutely count on the love of my life, Cheryl, for her constructive criticism on this and other areas of my life. They say that behind every good man there is an even better woman, and that is definitely true in my case.

Made in the USA
Columbia, SC
23 June 2023

18755789R00148